HOPE BLOOMS

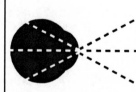

This Large Print Book carries the
Seal of Approval of N.A.V.H.

HOPE BLOOMS

JAMIE POPE

THORNDIKE PRESS

A part of Gale, Cengage Learning

GALE
CENGAGE Learning·

Farmington Hills, Mich • San Francisco • New York • Waterville, Maine
Meriden, Conn • Mason, Ohio • Chicago

GALE
CENGAGE Learning

LIBRARY OF CONGRESS CATALOGING-IN-PUBLICATION DATA

Names: Pope, Jamie (Romance writer), author.
Title: Hope blooms / by Jamie Pope.
Description: Large print edition. | Waterville, Maine : Thorndike Press, 2017. |
   Series: Thorndike Press large print African-American
Identifiers: LCCN 2017012460| ISBN 9781432840372 (hardcover) | ISBN 1432840371
   (hardcover)
Subjects: LCSH: African Americans—Fiction. | Large type books. | GSAFD: Love
   stories.
Classification: LCC PS3616.O65424 H67 2017 | DDC 813/.6—dc23
LC record available at https://lccn.loc.gov/2017012460

Published in 2017 by arrangement with Dafina Books, an imprint of
Kensington Publishers Corp.

To Phyllis:
Thank you for allowing me to crash the party and come to your beautiful home. I could have never written this book without that trip.

CHAPTER 1

"Bring me my damn daughter!"

She shuddered. Her mouth went dry — that uneasy, indescribable feeling hitting the pit of Cassandra Miller's stomach. She knew that angry voice. She could hear the slightly slurred syllables of his words, even though she was down the hallway. She knew this day would come. She tried to deny it to herself. To put it out of her mind, but she knew this day was coming.

"Right fucking now!" There was a crash. Glass breaking. A bang. It was coming from the front office at the entrance of the school. Immediately her mind went to Mrs. Mortera, the school secretary, who was weeks away from retirement. And the principal who had just seen her firstborn graduate from college. She touched her own belly as her mind spun with so many thoughts she had trouble keeping them straight.

Her room was close. Just the third door

down from the entrance.

There were seventeen kids in her class. She could put them in the closet. Some could squeeze into the bathroom.

Get up! Get going!

Her brain was shouting at her to take action, but she sat there almost paralyzed. She was waiting on the announcement: "Farnsworth Elementary is in lockdown."

A lockdown.

She was supposed to lock down. To stay put. To follow the procedure she had practiced four times that year with her kids.

But the call for lockdown wasn't going to come.

It was too late already.

She couldn't just let them sit there and wait.

She looked at her aide, Mrs. Simmons, and then to her class. They were babies. Her children. Her babies. The kids she loved for seven hours a day. Kindergartners. She had been a teacher for almost ten years now. She had taught in this school, in this classroom, ever since she graduated from college. She was educated here as a child. This had always been her safe place.

Her youngest students were just four years old. They were looking up at her in question. They had heard. They knew that something was about to go wrong in their little worlds.

She couldn't let that happen.

He was coming to this room. He was coming to get Kayla. The little blonde with the missing teeth and beautiful, lopsided smile. Cassandra's eyes found hers. The little girl was frozen, paralyzed. It was more than fear on her face. It was her father. Her father who terrorized her family. Her father who almost killed her mother. He wasn't supposed to be there. He wasn't supposed to see her. The courts had ordered him to stay away.

There was another crash, another scream. Another bang. She jumped, knowing what that sound was. Knowing that the clock had long ago started ticking. "Boys and girls." She crossed her classroom to the large sliding glass window. The protocol going right out of her head. She was supposed to lock her door. Shut her blinds. Hide the kids. But she knew that wasn't good enough. She knew he would get in. A simple door wouldn't stop him.

"We're going to do something different." She tried to keep her voice calm. She tried to keep the trembling that was overtaking her body at bay. "We are going to go out the window and across the stream, and we are not going to stop until we get to the fire station."

For once, nobody questioned her. Maybe they sensed it. Maybe they knew. Maybe it was divine intervention that caused them to rise and line up at the window. Mrs. Simmons helped without question, but she was shaking as they lifted the kids up and placed them outside. Cassandra left her for a moment to get her purse.

Another bang. The voice was louder. Screaming. She couldn't make out the words this time. But she didn't know if it was because they were incoherent or because the blood was rushing too loudly in her ears.

"Sir, please. Come with me." It was Terrance's voice in the hallway. She would know the sound of her husband's voice anywhere. He was the school's psychologist. Always so thoughtful and kind and gentle. Always sacrificing himself. He knew Mr. Hammond. He knew Kayla's history. He knew how bad the situation had gotten. But she tried not to think about how scared she was for him as she dialed 911.

"Hello." She took a breath and prepared to say the hardest words she ever had to say. "There is an intruder at Farnsworth Elementary. Shots have been fired. Please send help."

The operator was questioning her, but she didn't understand a word the woman was saying, because she heard another blast from his gun. She heard Mr. Hammond's ranting voice as it got closer.

Only half her class was out the window. Only

10

half of those brave little souls were on their way down the hill toward safety. Kayla wasn't one of them. Cassandra knew he would be there before she got them all out.

She couldn't let that happen.

She grabbed Kayla and kissed the small child's head before she placed her out the window. "I want you to hurry," she told the rest of her class. "I want you to walk as fast as you can."

She handed Mrs. Simmons her phone. "Make sure they get there."

"Cassandra." The older woman's eyes flashed with tears. "You come with us!"

"I'll be there."

She attempted a smile, but couldn't manage it. And then she walked out of her classroom. Locking her door behind her. Praying she could stall him long enough till they got away.

He was just thirty feet from her door. His head turned away from her. His hunting rifle pointed at Terrance.

"Mr. Hammond." She stepped away from her door. Away from her life and toward him. Her hands raised.

"Cassandra, get away from here," Terrance hissed at her. He was holding his limp shoulder. It kind of dangled there, the blood pouring through his fingers, the pain twisting his face. Her stomach dropped, but she kept moving. Away from her door. Away from her students.

"How can I help you?"

"How can you help me? How can you help me!" He screamed the words. His eyes shook back and forth. There was a gleam to them that she couldn't describe, and she knew he was too far gone. Too broken to ever be fixed.

"You called Child Protective Services on me. You got them people in my house. You caused them to take my kids away from me."

She did. She had noticed the bruises on Kayla. The marks on her arms that looked like fingerprints. She noticed that Kayla had gone silent, too afraid to speak, to move without permission, too traumatized to be a kid. "Talk to me about it."

She tried not to look behind her, to see if they had all made it out, instead she looked at him. Studied him, unshaven, in a stained white T-shirt and cargo pants.

"You bitch!" he spat at her. "You cost me everything. My job. My family."

"Why did you beat her? She's five."

"She's a pain in the ass sometimes! But she's mine and I love her. It's none of your damn business how I discipline my children."

"What about your wife? Were you disciplining her too?"

"Cassandra." Her husband's warning tone

didn't stop her.

"She's my damn wife! Mine. I'll do what I want to her."

"But she loved you. Your kids love you. And you're here with a gun. Don't you want her back? Don't you want them back?"

"That's why I'm here. I've come to get what's mine."

"This is not the way, Mr. Hammond." She took another step closer. "We can help you. We can get you counseling. All you have to do is let us help you. You can get them back. But this is not the way."

"I know your way. You want all them people coming through my house. Watching me when I'm with my kids. Telling me how I should live my life. They don't know nothing. I'm a god-damn man! You want me treated like a boy."

No, she wanted him in prison. Where he should be. She didn't know why he wasn't there.

Terrance was inching closer, but she wasn't sure what he was going to do. He was a gentle soul. She never saw him angry. Never saw him do a violent thing, and now he was walking toward a man with a gun. She looked at him, willing him to stop, knowing he couldn't overpower this bear of a man.

The sound of sirens in the distance hit her ears. Help was coming. It was all going to be over soon. But she didn't feel relieved.

Hammond had heard them too. His eyes widened, beads of sweat dripped from his lip. He reminded her of a rabid animal that was about to be caged.

And he was about to be caged, but Terrance moved again. He reached for the gun, and in that moment she loved and hated her husband so much.

"What the fuck are you doing?" Hammond turned and fired. It wasn't a distant bang this time. It was like an explosion and suddenly all the noise stopped. Her world stopped.

Terrance fell to the floor. His hand over his heart, blood staining his white shirt. She moved toward him. Not thinking. Not caring anymore.

He was her best friend.

Her balance.

Flashes of gray and black invaded her vision. State troopers, SWAT. Help was here. But it was too late.

Hammond lifted his gun and fired it one last time. At her. She didn't feel the pain as she clutched her belly. She couldn't see the blood. But she smelled it. That metallic smell she would never forget. She felt it too, the warm thickness as it seeped through her hands. She looked up at him, at the man who murdered her family, only to see a police officer's bullet smash through his brain.

Cassandra gasped, ripping the blankets from her sweaty body as her nightmare released her from its grip.

She looked around her quiet bedroom. Looked beside her to the left side of the bed.

It was empty.

It had been empty. For almost a year now.

Terrance wasn't there.

And her nightmare wasn't a nightmare. It was her mind making her relive that day. That last day. That last day her life was livable.

Some nights, some blessed nights, she would escape it, the reliving of it, the dreaming about it. Some nights she would fall into a blank, restless sleep. But most nights she didn't get that relief. Most nights she saw it happen again, like she was a witness to that day, like she was floating over herself.

Every time she would see the pained look on her husband's face as the bullet tore through him. She could hear that his last word was her name. She could smell the scent of her own blood.

And every time, after the panic had subsided and the pain eased its choke hold, she would realize that she was alone again. That her husband was gone. That five people had died that day, including the little baby she had just found out she was carrying.

And then the numbness would take over. And then she would lay back in her bed, knowing that her life wasn't going to get any better than it was, that she no longer had anything to look forward to, to be happy about.

"Cassandra? Are you okay?"

Her mother was there, standing in her bedroom door, wearing the same pink bathrobe she had worn since Cassandra was a small girl. She was looking at her as she had done every night since she'd moved into her daughter's house two weeks ago. Staring at her with that same expression on her face that she'd had since Cassandra woke up from her coma.

"Cassandra, don't just stare at me. Answer me!"

She forgot to do that. Most days she forgot to speak; it seemed like too much effort.

She swallowed, her mouth dry, underused. "Mother."

Her mother, Cora, came over to her bedside, sitting beside her, brushing her daughter's damp hair away from her face.

"You dreamed about it again, didn't you?" Her eyes searched her face. "I heard you cry out for Terrance."

She said nothing to that. There was nothing she could say. Terrance wasn't just her husband. He was her friend. Her conscience. He died that day because she had called Child Protective Services. He died that day because Mr. Hammond was angry with her.

"He wouldn't want you to be like this."

"He would want to be alive if he had a choice." She rolled over, away from her mother's touch, her worried eyes. Suddenly the exhaustion returned again. It was the only thing she felt anymore. Tired and heavy.

"You can't go on like this. You haven't left the house in weeks. You haven't smiled since it happened. You didn't die that day. Your life is meant to be lived."

"No," she said softly as the heaviness took over her eyes. "I don't think so."

Cora gripped her face, forcing her to look into her eyes. "I won't let this happen to you. I won't let you slip away. You didn't die that day, damn it. I almost lost you. I could have lost you, but I didn't. There's a reason you lived. I'm going to make sure you know that."

CHAPTER 2

He promised himself he wouldn't come back here. To this place where he had been his happiest and most miserable. The place where he lost both his family and his best friend on the same day. But as Wylie James Everett drove up to the quiet little neighborhood where he spent the end of his childhood, he realized that he would have come back eventually. His soul, his conscience, wouldn't have let him rest until he did. He just never thought he would return here for this reason.

Harmony Falls hadn't changed much in the ten years since he had last seen it. It was one of those perfect Northeast towns. The kind of place one imagined when thinking of New England, of Connecticut. Manicured green lawns and stately Colonial homes. It seemed like a place that violence wouldn't touch; and as he passed another sign that read, GOD BLESS FARNSWORTH

18

ELEMENTARY, he knew that wasn't true.

This town was their home. Terrance and Cass had never moved from here. He should have known that they wouldn't. They *were* this town. They were everything that it represented. They were the children that every parent wanted to have. Prom queen and homecoming king. Smart, good-looking, polite kids who grew up to be smart, good-looking, well-mannered adults. They were so opposite from Wylie's trailer-park-trash beginnings. Sometimes he thought back on his life and wondered how he ended up in Harmony Falls, Connecticut. How his father, a landscaper, became best friends with the son of a judge. Before his old man died, he never got to ask how it happened, but in the end the reason wasn't important. Wylie had been a U.S. Marine. He had fought in two wars. He had been to Iraq. Lived in the mountains of Afghanistan. He had beat death a half-dozen times, but none of that stuff had half as much impact as Cassandra Miller had had on his life.

He had been on the road for nearly four hours now, but as he turned down Southington Drive, time seemed to slow down and his stomach grew tighter with every foot he drove. It was the same feeling he got the day of the rocket attack. The day he lost nearly every man in his unit. That was one of the hardest days of his life. But for some reason coming back to Harmony Falls, seeing the girl he had walked away from once again, knowing that the man who was once his best friend and brother wasn't going to be there, was harder.

He spotted Miss Cora, Cassandra's mama, waiting for him on the front porch as he pulled up to the simple white house that Cassandra and Terrance had shared.

Their house. Their life. Theirs.

He shook off his conflicting feelings and focused on the woman in the baby doll–pink sweater before him. Seeing her again was like stepping back in time for Wylie. Like he was twelve years old again and scared shitless that he wasn't clean enough, smart enough, good enough, to be in the presence of such a fine-looking lady. But unlike twenty years ago he was no longer a boy. And this time, instead of being some charity case to be looked after, he had been invited here. Called back to Harmony Falls by Miss Cora.

He stepped out of his truck, but instead of moving forward he just stood there. Stood there and stared at Cora, who hadn't aged much in the past ten years since he had seen her. Her skin was still smooth and the color of milk chocolate, her clothes still so feminine and pretty. Her hair was white now, but that only added to that air of regality that she always carried around with her. He knew that Cassandra had inherited some of that from her mother. But he also knew that there was more to Cassandra than that. There was a side of her that only he ever got to see.

"Are you going to stand there all day, Wylie James, or are you going to come here and hug an old lady?"

"Ma'am." Her words spurred him into action and his feet ate up the ground between them until he had the woman off her feet and in his arms. He missed her. Almost as much as he missed Cass. Terrance's mother never liked him, only tolerated him. His own mother had disappeared from his life when he was a kid. But he always had Miss Cora, who never seemed to think any less of him. Miss Cora who mothered him when he needed it. "You're not an old lady," he said softly after a few moments. "You still look the same."

"You are a liar, but a good one, so I will forgive you." She let go of him and stood back to study him. "My goodness, you've grown into a big man. And handsome too. Did the Marines do that to you?"

"I've finally learned to eat my vegetables, ma'am."

She smiled softly at him and touched his cheek. "How have you been, Wylie? Tell me your life has been good."

"It's been just fine," he lied. It had been a lot of things, but it had never been fine.

Tears formed in her eyes. "I'm sorry, you know. I have wanted to apologize to you for so many years."

He shook his head. Shaking off her apology. "You didn't do anything wrong, Miss Cora."

"I did. I should have spoken up, but I kept silent."

He didn't want to think about it. He didn't want to go back to that time in his life when he was pissed at the world and so lost that he never thought he was going to find his way out. "How is she?"

The sadness came over her instantly, like it was eating her up. Wylie knew it must have been bad. He knew for Cora to call him back it must have been something she couldn't handle. "Come in."

She opened the door and preceded him inside. The formal living room was the first room in the house. Tastefully decorated, understated, no signs of Cass's touch. His eyes unwillingly zeroed in on a wedding photo. It sat in a place of honor on top of the fireplace. He studied Cass in her pretty white dress, a smile that didn't quite reach her eyes plastered on her face. Terrance stood beside her, beaming. Triumphant. He should have been. He had won that day.

Terrance had asked Wylie to be there, wrote to him while he was stationed in Korea to ask him to be his best man. Wylie never answered. The request was a punch in the gut. The final nail in the coffin of their friendship, of their brotherhood. He had been so mad at Terrance for years but when he found out Terrance had been killed, he cried. He hurt. He missed the man he thought he had never wanted to see again.

"She looked for you that day," Cora said, causing his mind to turn from those thoughts. "She would never admit it, but she looked for you that day. I think Terrance did too. I wasn't sure what either of them would have done if you had showed up."

Wylie just stared, his mouth unable to work in that moment.

"I've never seen a bride so uninterested in her wedding plans. It took me some time to figure out why that was."

A funny little feeling formed in his chest, or maybe it was an easing of the tightness he had carried there all those years. He wanted to blame Cass for what happened. He wanted to blame her father, Terrance, his family and the whole damn world, but in the end he couldn't, because he was the one who had left. He left her and his friendship and the people who raised him and he never looked back.

"What's been going on?"

She said nothing, only took him up the stairs to the back of the house. On the way he saw photos of them. Of vacations and family functions. He saw their achievements. Terrance's diploma from Brown. His Ph.D. in psychology. His certificate in counseling.

"Terrance was a licensed counselor in marriage and family therapy too. He had an office in the house," she said by way of explaining the shrine to him. "He could have made more money working someplace else, but he took that job at Farnsworth to be closer to Cassandra. He didn't like to be away from her." She looked back at him. "Sometimes I wonder if she felt stifled by it. But then I remember that it had always been the three of you. I rarely saw my daughter without one of you boys behind her. I knew it was going to be bad after it happened." She stopped at the last door at the end of the long hallway. "But I never thought it was going to be like this."

She opened the door, but he could barely see into the room. It was broad daylight, just past one P.M., but the windows were covered and the lamps were off. The only light came from the television.

"She hasn't gotten out of bed in weeks."

"Start from the beginning. Tell me everything." He was away when it happened, but even when he got to a television, he couldn't make sense of it. There was so much debate about gun violence, about school safety, but all he wanted to know about was his friends, about what happened after the violence.

Cora let out a heavy sigh. "Sometimes I don't even know. She was newly pregnant. Not many people know that. She was finally pregnant after trying for three years. And he shot her in the stomach with a double-barrel shotgun." She paused for a moment, her voice choked. "She should have died that day. There was so much blood, so much damage. She went into a coma three days after it happened. The doctors couldn't explain why, but she just went to sleep and she didn't wake up for months. I was told that it was her body's way of healing itself. But I wasn't so sure she was ever going to wake up. And then one day she did. Sometimes I think it was a mistake bringing her back here. She can't leave her house without seeing one of those 'God Bless Farnsworth' signs. She can't go to the store without people coming up to her to thank her or to pay their respects. She can't even walk out of her bedroom without constant reminders of Terrance. People say time heals all wounds, but Cass's wounds seem to grow deeper with each passing day. She blames herself for his death. I know she does. She was the one who called Child Protective Services. She was the one the gunman was coming for. She still doesn't think she should live, and that scares me."

Cora went silent as she looked to her daughter, who was barely visible under the covers. "She's a hero. She got those kids out of that building. She went out into the hallway to face that man to give them time to get to safety. She's done so much good, but she's wasting away. If I don't do something, I'm going to lose her. She's my only child. I can't lose her."

The sadness had gone from her face. He only saw fear now. He had lost Terrance. He had lost Cass, too, when he walked away ten years ago, but he couldn't stomach the thought of a world without her in it.

"Can I go in?"

"Of course. That's why I asked you to

come. I think you're the only one who can get through to her."

He didn't know if that was true, but he walked in and ripped the coverings from the windows. Bright sunlight invaded the room; as he turned to face Cass, he saw her shrink from it. Shield her eyes with a pillow.

Seeing that made him pause. The girl who used to love being outside. Who spent hours walking with him, and riding bikes, and playing in the woods, was hiding from the light. It was almost too much for him to take.

He made himself move forward. He got on her bed and pulled the pillow from her face. He touched her. He cupped her face in his hands and forced her to look up at him, into his eyes. He wanted to see into her eyes. He wanted to see if there was any sign left of the girl he once knew.

Her face was pale. Gone was the gorgeous smooth brown skin. In its place was something yellow and sickly and blotchy. Her eyes were dull, not the soft brown that he used to get lost in. Even her hair seemed to have lost its will to live. Those riotous, tightly coiled curls, which she could never tame, lay flatly against her head. They looked sad. She looked sad. He never thought he would see her this way.

"Cass." He heard the catch in his throat, felt the fire burn in the back of it and the tears well up in his eyes.

"Wylie?" She came alive as the realization of him hit her. "Wylie James, is that you?" Her eyes traveled over his face as she reached up to touch his cheek. And then she did something shocking. She wrapped her arms around him and pulled him close. The last time he held her, Cass was lush curviness, at twenty-two, just coming into her womanhood, but now the body he held was thin, fading, wasting away in this bed.

"He would have liked to have seen you before he died. He missed you." She squeezed him tightly. "I missed you. I wanted to see you before I go," she said softly.

He didn't need any more clarification to know what she was talking about. Cora was right. Cass didn't want to live anymore.

"Pack her clothes." He couldn't let that happen. "I'm taking her with me."

CHAPTER 3

She hadn't met him yet. That new boy. That stranger who moved in with Terrance's family. She had been away at camp, away from Terrance for a month. They had spent every summer together since his family moved from New York five years ago. It was weird not seeing him for so long. It was even weirder seeing him play with someone else.

She sat in the bay window in her living room, just staring at them. Terrance and this boy. She could only see him from behind, but now she understood why everyone in her town was whispering about him.

He was different.

The opposite of her best friend.

He was wide. Not fat, but big, while Terrance was thin and long. The boy had brown hair, which was just a little too long, and looked kind of golden in the sunlight. His clothes were messy, worn, not quite right for the town they lived in. Terrance had short, black hair and neat clothes and those glasses she had never seen him without.

This boy was white.

And Terrance was black.

It didn't matter to Cassandra what color he was, Cassandra decided that she wasn't going to like him.

"Why are you just sitting there, girl?" Her mother nudged her shoulder. "You just got back from camp. Go see Terrance. I know you missed him."

"No, I didn't!" she said, which wasn't true. She had missed Terrance. She had been home for nearly twenty-four hours and he hadn't come over to see her. He hadn't even called to say hello. They ate dinner at each other's houses and rode the same bus to school and had gym class together. He was her best friend, but he was too busy playing with some stranger to say hello.

"Honey, I learned long ago that you can never wait for men to come around. Sometimes you just have to go out and get them." Her mother smiled knowingly and gave her a gentle push. "Go say hello to your boy before your behind fuses to that chair and I have to call somebody to remove it."

She did as her mother said, heading outside to the Millers' yard. She didn't know why she felt so self-conscious walking over to greet

Terrance. She had been to his house a million times. This time shouldn't have been any different. Except it was.

She tugged on her shirt, suddenly realizing that her clothes didn't fit her like they used to. Suddenly caring about how she looked, even though she never cared about her appearance with Terrance before.

He saw her approach just as the ball came toward him in a perfect spiral. He caught it easily and tucked it under his arm. "Hey," he said in greeting, and ran to close the distance between them.

"Hey," she said back, and that's when the boy turned around to look at her.

There was nothing about him that should have stood out to her. He had brown hair and a big chin and square jawline. Maybe he looked a little older, a little rougher, than the boys she went to school with.

But there was something about his eyes. Light brown, big, kind of sad-looking. And he was staring at her like she had never been stared at before. Her hands wanted to fly up and fix her hair and tug on her shorts and cover her body, which she had begun to feel so foreign in.

"Cassandra, this is Wylie James. He lives with us now."

Wylie James moved closer, extending his

hand. She took it, surprised by the feeling of his firm handshake. It was unexpected. No boy had ever shaken her hand. "It's nice to meet you," he said. "You can call me Wylie if you'd like."

She took her eyes off their connected hands and looked up to his face. His voice was slow. Southern. He didn't sound like any boy she had known.

And then, just like that, she decided she was going to like him.

Cassandra turned over, away from the sun, away from the light that was burning her eyes. But she didn't feel her soft bed, her safe place for the past few months, beneath her. She felt nothing but a car seat belt slide up and touch her throat. For a moment she thought she was dreaming. A dream within a dream, but she opened her eyes to see Wylie there. She dreamed about Wylie a lot. She had tried not to think about him over the years. It seemed unfair to Terrance, but sometimes he slipped into her thoughts, into her dreams.

She blinked, rubbed her eyes and stared at him, wondering how long it would take before he disappeared. But he was still there, watching the road ahead of him as he drove to some unknown destination. Then it came back to her. Her mother wiping her face with a wet cloth, telling her something about healing, telling her that she was going away for a little while. She remembered strong arms lifting her, placing her into the front seat of a large black pickup truck. But she also remembered feeling exhausted, feeling that heavy pull of sleep that never left her.

He didn't look the same anymore, she thought as she studied him. Those faint traces of boy that were still with him when she had last seen him had vanished. His body was even thicker, his jaw squarer, his face harder. Her Wylie James was a man now.

He must have felt her eyes on him, because he glanced over at her. His eyes were the same — big and light brown — and he still looked at her in that odd way that nobody else did. But this time, unlike all the other times, she saw worry there. She didn't like it and that surprised her, because she hadn't felt anything other than numbness in such a long time.

He reached over and touched her face, sliding his thumb across her cheek.

"How's my Cass?" he asked her softly, placing his eyes back on the road.

"Cass. My Cass," she silently repeated.

He was the only one to ever call her that. The only one to shorten her name. She remembered liking it. Liking the way it sounded when it rolled off his tongue, liking the person she used to be when she was with him.

Her head started to ache. Her rarely used mind started to spin with thoughts she never wanted to think again. Thoughts of Terrance and Wylie together as boys. Images of them beaming at each other during their high-school graduation. Images of Terrance looking around the church for Wylie on their wedding day. Memories of her waiting for him to come back.

She shut her eyes. Tried to shut them out, hoping her friend, sleep, would take over her again. But it didn't.

"Cass?" Wylie pulled off the road. He took her face in his hands, and as much as she wanted to, she couldn't keep her eyes closed any longer. He kissed her forehead like he was kissing her mind, willing it to soothe. And somehow it did. Somehow she stopped thinking about the past and a ruined friendship. She stopped thinking altogether, because all she could do was feel. His hands were large and rough; his lips were warm and smooth. She felt safe, shielded, protected. She felt, just a little, when she hadn't felt anything in so long.

"Drink this." He handed her a bottle of cold cranberry juice, which he pulled from a cooler in the back.

It was her favorite. He remembered. Ten years later and he still remembered. The cold, sweet juice slid down her throat as she sipped. She tasted it, actually tasted it. She couldn't remember the last time she noticed the taste of anything.

"More," he ordered, pushing the bottle toward her mouth. She obeyed, suddenly feeling thirsty again.

When all the juice was gone, he took the bottle away from her. He took her face in his hands once again, but this time he set his forehead against hers. "I should have come to get you sooner," he whispered.

Yes, a little voice whispered inside her. *You should have come to get me ten years ago.*

She couldn't believe that bitter thought formed in her mind. She had missed Terrance. She loved him. She pulled away from Wylie, looking up into his still-worried eyes.

"Where are you taking me?"

"Home." He shook his head. "To my home. You're going to live with me."

All she did was sleep. That's what Miss Cora

told him, that was what he saw during most of their journey to his home. He was almost mad at Cora for letting it get this bad, for not making her go to a doctor, for allowing her to stay in a town that held nothing but memories of her husband and how he died.

He was mad at himself too. For writing instead of calling, for waiting instead of going to see her. But the truth was he didn't know how he would be received in Harmony Falls. He had left because he wasn't good enough. He was told he wasn't good enough by the people whom he thought of as family, by the man he loved as a brother. He had only ever been a charity case to them. The one no one really wanted. He looked over to her, needing a distraction from his thoughts. Her eyes were open. For a moment he thought she was looking in his direction, but it was clear that she wasn't seeing him. There was nothing in her eyes. Not hurt, not sadness, not fear. He could have taken seeing her in pain, but this near lifelessness was too much to bear.

"We're almost there." It had been a long day, and he could feel the exhaustion tugging at his eyes. He had left his quiet town of Aquinnah, Martha's Vineyard, for Connecticut before sunrise. He hadn't planned to leave so early in the morning. He had planned to take his time, to settle things at work before he left, but he couldn't sleep that night after Miss Cora called. He could only think about seeing Cass again. "I think you'll like it here," he continued, feeling at a loss for what to say to her. "Aquinnah is on the quiet side of the island. There's not many tourists here, now that summer is ending. Most of the island kids have gone back to school, even though it's still August."

She let out a soft noise and shifted in her seat; he knew his words got to her. He hadn't meant them as anything other than conversation, noise to fill the too-quiet space of the truck. But she was a teacher. She loved kids. She loved teaching. He had helped her set up her classroom. He was with her after her first day of school. He had listened that night as she talked about her new students. He had watched her eyes light up as she recounted her day.

"Do you miss the kids?" he asked her, knowing his question was painful. "Do you miss teaching?"

She was supposed to talk about it, about what happened. It would be hard. He knew it because he had gone through it. His doctor had told him he had to talk about what had happened in Iraq or it would eat at him.

For so long he thought he should have died, that it was his fault his unit was destroyed.

But he had talked about it. He had found the good things in life. He had healed.

"Cass?" He glanced at her. She was still silent, but her eyes had sharpened. Focused on him.

It was such a little thing, but it was good. She wasn't unreachable.

"We're here." He pulled into his driveway, up to his old fixer-upper house, which he could see the Gay Head lighthouse from. He never planned on settling here, but there was something about this place that felt like home to him.

He had never had that before.

He went around to her side of the truck, reaching for her. Part of him wanted to carry her into the house, over the threshold, but he didn't. He set her on her feet. Her knees buckled a bit, but she stood. Leaning against him, she stood.

"That's it." With his arm firmly wrapped around her, they made the short trip to his door. He let them inside, nerves sneaking up on him. The house was a mess, barely livable. A circular saw sat in the kitchen, which he had just finished updating. His tools were strewn all over the living room. The only other room in the house that was fit for humans was his bedroom. He wondered what Cass was thinking about the place he had brought her to. Would she think that this place wasn't good enough for her?

But when he looked down at her, he realized that she wasn't paying attention to her surroundings at all. She was watching her feet as she put one foot in front of the other. He felt stupid then. She wasn't like that. She never thought he wasn't good enough. That was only his deal.

His bedroom was upstairs. Cass leaned on him heavily as they walked up the steps. This frail woman wasn't his girl. Wasn't the woman he thought about when he was on base in faraway countries. She wasn't the girl he had compared all others to.

Doubt started to assault him. What if bringing her here was a mistake? What if her problems were too big? What if he couldn't help her? He wasn't foolish enough to think he could save her. He knew from experience that this kind of pain was something you had to save yourself from.

"I'm tired, Wylie," she said, surprising him.

"I know, Cass. I know."

He took off her shoes and tucked her into his bed. Her eyes closed immediately, her body seeming to melt into his mattress, but she grabbed his hand. She linked her fingers with his. He had thought about the sleeping arrangements on the ride home. His couch pulled out. He could sleep there until he got one of the other bedrooms fixed up. He slept on the ground in the mountains of Afghanistan. He had survived Hell Week in the Marines. He had learned to sleep anywhere. A couple of weeks on a couch wouldn't kill him. But he didn't want to sleep on a couch, or in another bed. He looked down at her, at their interlocking fingers, at the girl he used to fall asleep with at night and knew there was no way he could leave her again.

He gently removed his hand from hers, stripped off his clothes and lay down beside her. He just wanted to be there, in case she needed him, in case the dreams got too bad. But she reached for him. And they fell asleep that night with their bodies pressed against each other.

CHAPTER 4

"Come here, Cassandra."

"No," she said to Terrance as he reached for her, with a little mischievous grin spread across his face. He was looking at her with odd determination. She knew what was coming. She also knew that Wylie was watching and Terrance's parents were watching, and it all felt kind of weird.

"You're not going to see me for six weeks." He caught hold of her hand and brought her closer.

"I know," she said as her body brushed against his lanky one. "Who's going to correct my grammar and argue with me about everything?" He was heading to Costa Rica, to be immersed in Spanish and study the culture. It was his father's present to him for his sixteenth birthday.

"My father likes to argue," he said into her hair. "I'm sure he can help you out." She had hugged Terrance before; and even though in

41

the past few months he seemed to have sprouted a foot, and filled out a bit, he felt familiar. Same square glasses. Same neat haircut. Same soapy smell. But this hug was not so familiar. He was hugging her a little longer. Holding her a little closer. Speaking to her a little more softly than she was used to.

It all felt . . . off.

"You're going to be late for your flight." She tried to push herself away from him, but he didn't let her go. Instead he kissed her. It was a loud, smacking kiss on the cheek, but he kissed her and he had never done that before.

"Yuck." She put her hand on the place where he kissed, wiping it off, still feeling the warmth and pressure of his lips. "Don't kiss me! I don't know where your mouth has been."

He grinned at her. His eyes indulgent. "I'm just giving you something to write about in your diary tonight. And something you can dream about for the next six weeks."

"You wish." She pulled away from him. "Write me, okay? Tell me about all the cute girls you meet down there. You'll be a stud when you come back to school. You know how girls love a guy who can speak a romance language."

"Yes, I will, Cassandra." He looked at Wylie, who was standing farther back, away from Mr. and Mrs. Miller, away from Terrance and her.

A part of the family, but always apart from the family.

"Brother." Except to Terrance. He reached out his hand to Wylie, who shook it before they both came together briefly in a manly hug. Wylie had been in Harmony Falls for four years now. Since he arrived, there had hardly been a time when she saw one without the other.

She thought Wylie's constant presence would bug her, but it never did. Wylie had always been this quiet, calm force surrounding them. She didn't think she would feel right without him either.

"I want to know about the girls too," he said softly, but Cassandra still heard him. "You come back here a man, you hear?"

Terrance smiled as he pulled away. "You'll be the first one to know."

Terrance hugged his weepy mother and said his good-byes. Soon he was gone. His father had taken him to the airport, while his mother retreated to the house to compose herself. They were alone, standing next to each other in silence for a few moments. It wasn't often that there was just the two of them, but there were times. And whenever there were that odd little feeling bloomed inside her.

"I'm not sure I know what to do with myself," he admitted with a bashful smile.

"I know. We're kind of pathetic if we can't figure out how to spend our summer without Terrance. Maybe we should go fling ourselves in the lake?"

"Dramatic." He lightly bumped her shoulder with his own. "It's hot as hell out here. Come sit with me in the gazebo."

They walked slowly behind the house to the little shaded area where the gazebo sat, their arms brushing as they went.

"I still can't believe you built this." She ran her fingers along the white railing as she looked at Wylie James.

"I didn't do it by myself." He shrugged, still bashful. "Terrance and Mr. Miller helped."

"Terrance ended up in the hospital when he hit his thumb with a hammer, and Mr. Miller hired the gardener's son to replace him. I would use the term 'help' loosely."

Wylie grinned at her, his head down, like he wanted to hide his amusement. "That thumb of his swelled up three times its normal size. He stayed in bed for two days." He sobered. "I shouldn't laugh. He was miserable."

"You should laugh." She sat down beside him on the bench; even though it was hot, her body wanted to be near his. "Terrance is so good at everything. It's kind of nice to know he sucks at something."

"I'll never be as smart as him, and I'll never

be able to run track like he does, but I got a few things to keep my head up about."

"Wylie James!" Patricia Miller's voice rang out through the yard. They both looked up, inched apart as she walked toward them. "There you are." She glanced from Cassandra to him, trying to determine what was going on. Mrs. Miller always looked at them that way when Terrance wasn't around. "I'm heading to Avon to spend the day with my sister. While I'm gone, I want you to tidy up this house. Vacuum the den, wash all the dishes and toss out all the leftovers in the refrigerator."

"Yes, ma'am."

"I also want you to mow the side lawn. I don't like the way the lawn service people did it. You're going to have to go over it with the push mower."

"Yes, ma'am. I'll have to put gas in the mower. We don't have any in the garage."

"You'll have to get some, but don't worry about it today." She looked at Cassandra. "I know Terrance wanted you to look after Cassandra while he was away. You two can spend some time together."

Cassandra sat up straight. " 'Look after'?"

Wylie touched her leg. It was a sly touch, not one that Mrs. Miller could see, but enough of a touch to deliver a message.

He wanted her to shut up.

"Thank you, ma'am."

"You're welcome. I won't be home until late. I'm not sure when Eric will be home. You are on your own for dinner tonight."

He nodded. "Have a nice time with your sister."

She looked at him for a long moment, as if she was confused by him, as if she was trying to figure him out. "I will."

"Why does she treat you like her servant?" Cassandra asked when Mrs. Miller was gone. "She has a cleaning woman. You're not it."

"I've got to earn my keep somehow. They took me in when nobody else wanted me, and that means I got to do what they say. Besides, I had to work a hell of a lot harder when my daddy was alive. Mowing her lawn isn't much of a thing."

She shook her head, not understanding how he didn't feel slighted. "They could have sent you to Costa Rica with Terrance. Your grades were good this year. You do so much to help them."

"I've got that job at the hardware store that I don't want to give up. And I couldn't have gone." He grinned at her as he studied her face. "There would have been nobody around to 'look after' you if I did."

"I don't need anybody to *look after* me!"

"But you're Terrance's girl. I've got to keep

46

the other boys away," he said in his soft, slow voice.

His words caused her head to snap up. "I'm *not* his girl. It's not like that. Terrance is just my friend. You know that."

"I know." He turned his big brown eyes on her. "I know. But they think you're going to end up with him."

"Who thinks that?"

"Everyone. Don't you know, Cass? Terrance loves you."

"He's my best friend." She tried to shrug off his words. "Of course he loves me."

"Not like that. Not the way you love him."

She sat still for a moment as his words sank in. Things were mostly the same between her and Terrance. He never tried to make a move. He never gave any hint that he wanted to be her boyfriend, but lately she had noticed a slight change in their friendship. He didn't tease her so much. He touched her a little more. She wanted to think it was because they were going into their junior year, and it was because they were growing up. But she couldn't convince herself of that.

"Did he tell you that he loves me?"

"He doesn't have to," he said heavily.

"But, Wylie . . ." She slid her fingers through his, moved closer to him. Wanting to close the space that always seemed to be between him.

She rested her head on his shoulder and looked up at him. Wylie James, who was always so hard to read, always so guarded, was like an open book in that moment.

He looked a little tortured.

"Please," she whispered.

He moved his head closer, brought his big, rough hand up to her face to touch her cheek. They had never spoken about that strange little pull they felt around each other.

"Cass . . ." He choked on her name. "Don't ask me."

"Please." There was nothing wrong with what they felt. They were sixteen and seventeen. They were unattached. They knew each other so well, and being near him made her feel good and jumpy and soothed, all at the same time.

But it also made her feel guilty. Like liking him so much was wrong.

"Please," she asked him one more time. She saw the moment something inside him broke. His eyes went soft again as he pressed his lips to hers. Her first kiss was gentle and too quick and so sweet.

"Hell!" He cursed himself and lowered his mouth to hers again. He moved his mouth over hers, prompting her to open her lips a little wider, teaching her how to kiss him back without saying a word.

"Damn it, Cass." He broke the kiss. "I can't. I can't do this to him."

Cass awakened. She didn't open her eyes, but she was awake. It was a long time since she dreamed about her first kiss. It was a long time since she had thought about Wylie like that. But she had been dreaming about him all night. She dreamed that he was with her, that he held her while she slept. She never saw him in that dream, but she knew it was him. She felt it was him.

Terrance popped into her mind. Thinking about Wylie, dreaming about him, was unfair to Terrance, especially since Wylie had left her without a word. Terrance really loved her. He treated her well. They had a nice marriage. She turned over, blindly reaching for him, wanting to show him that she appreciated him. But the bed was empty. Even the scent of his shaving soap was gone.

And then she remembered.

He was gone. It had been a year without him. Over a year. She opened her eyes, waiting for the panic to come, waiting for the desolation and then the numbness to overtake her, but she realized that she wasn't in her bed, in the house she shared with her husband. There was sun pouring through an open window, hitting her face. She smelled the ocean.

"You're awake." Wylie James was standing by the door. It all came back to her. Her mother's words, the long car ride. Him telling her that she was going to live with him.

She never thought she would see him again. And now he was back.

He was shirtless, only wearing a pair of blue-checked boxer shorts on his hard body and a worried expression on his face.

He sat beside her on the bed, smoothing her hair away from her face, touching her cheeks with his rough hands. She was having a hard time believing this. That she was here with him. She had long ago given up hope that she would see him again. "You look like hell."

For a moment she was lost in the sensation of being touched, of having Wylie James run his hands across her skin. But then what he said hit her. *What?*

"You're wasting away. You're trying to let yourself die, and I'm not going to let it happen."

She opened her mouth to speak, but no words came out. She had nothing to say. Wylie wasn't wrong. Her husband was gone. The baby she wanted had died that same day. There wasn't reason to get out of bed anymore.

"I want you to get up today. I want you to get up and get dressed."

"There's nothing left for me." She turned away from him.

She missed his warmth as he walked away. She shut her eyes, burrowing farther into the mattress. He was gone.

Good.

It was what she hoped for.

The sound of a running shower registered in her brain. She couldn't remember the last time she had truly bathed, when she last had a long, hot shower or bath. She couldn't remember the last time she wanted to get dressed and walk outside.

Her mother had tried to baby her, then badger her, and then bully her to live again. But her father couldn't even look at her. She couldn't remember the last time she had spoken to him. Terrance's parents had stopped coming by the house shortly after she had come home from the hospital a month after she had awakened from her coma. Patricia cried whenever she saw her, wept over her son's lost life. Told her it was too bad that she lost the baby, that she had lost the only piece of Terrance that was left. Eric wouldn't even look her in the eye, too uncomfortable with her life.

She could read their minds.

Why did she live when their son had to die?

She had the same question.

Wylie's footsteps pounded back into the room, distracting her from the thoughts that never left her. He grabbed her shoulder, turned her over to face him. He was angry. His eyes were determined and she was lifted from the bed and into his arms.

The sound of water grew closer. He took her to his bathroom. Before she could think, before she could process where she was, she was beneath icy cold water. She gasped. Gripping Wylie, trying to get closer, trying to get out of the way of a cold blast. But he wouldn't let her. He held her there in his arms and she realized that she was too weak to fight him.

"You feel this, don't you, Cass? You feel this and it means you're still alive. You can still feel. You can still breathe." He set her on her feet and turned her to face him. "You want a reason to get out of bed? I'll give you one. *You lived.* You can move on and start a new life. You're young and beautiful and there are people who love you. There are people who want you to be happy again. You're thirty-one years old. You've got your whole fucking life ahead of you. And if those aren't enough reasons, here's one more. Terrance would have hated this. He would have hated to see you this way. He would have been so disappointed in you."

Disappointed. That word hit her hard.

"How the hell can you know how he would have felt?" She found her voice. She found her anger. She found it was still in her to yell at him. "You left. Remember? You left him and you left me. And you never came back. So don't you tell me how my husband would feel."

He looked at her for a long moment. There was sorrow in his eyes. She knew it because that's what she felt every single moment of every single day.

"I left." He nodded, his anger seeming to evaporate. "I left, but I loved him. He was my best friend too. He was my brother. We were closer than you'll ever know. And if you think that your grief is any less than mine, you're kidding yourself."

Wylie stepped out of the shower and its icy spray and stared at Cass as the water pelted her. Her hair was plastered to her face. Her dress was stuck to her body.

But she was alive. It was past time she realized it.

He turned the hot water on and stepped

closer to her so that he could peel her clothes from her body. He had undressed her before. He had seen her naked body so many times during their secret relationship, but none of those times compared to this. She was skinny and her ribs poked out from her body. Her hip bones jutted out. Her skin almost hung from her bones. She didn't look like the beautiful girl he used to be in love with. Still, he found himself aroused at her nudity. Because he still had vivid memories of the girl she used to be, and he knew that deep down that girl was still there.

He climbed back into the warm water with her, reaching for the shampoo. "Close your eyes," he ordered as he squirted a handful into her hair. He tried to distract himself as he washed her hair. He was beginning to feel panic gnaw at him again. He had taken her away without thinking. Without a plan. He had acted on feeling. He had only done that a few times in his life and knew from experience that never ended well.

He rinsed her hair and she opened her eyes to look up at him. She said nothing, making him wonder what she was thinking. Did she understand how much he loved Terrance, or would she always hate him for walking away?

He grabbed his soap. It wasn't the pretty

floral scent that he was used to smelling on her. He was going to have to go shopping for her. No — he was going to make her go shopping with him, to get things she needed, to make her stay here as comfortable as possible.

He soaped her neck and shoulders without thinking about what he was doing, but as his hands moved down her chest, his mind focused on his task. He was touching her, washing her. Memories of the last time they bathed together entered his mind. He could still remember the way her thighs felt wrapped around him, still remember how he felt buried so deep inside her. And how his name sounded on her lips when she moaned it. And her smell. And how she tasted. And felt.

His heart pounded harder, his breathing grew a little sharper, and it snapped him from those memories. He wasn't with the girl he spent hours making love to. He was with a woman who had married another man. Who had married his best friend and broke Wylie's heart.

And he was soaping her breasts. Her nipples had hardened to little milk chocolate brown beads. He wasn't sure what came over him, but he ran his thumbs over them. She shivered. She shivered despite the heat of the shower. He went completely hard in that moment. In the ten years since he had walked away, he never wanted another woman as bad as he wanted this one right now. It didn't matter that she was skinny and depressed and the widow of his best friend.

He took his hands off her breasts, moving to clean the rest of her body. His hands came to her belly. His thumb hit her scars. A circular one from where the bullet hit her. A long, thin one from where the doctors had to operate to save her.

He stroked those scars, the physical reminders of the day that would never leave her. She jumped at his touch. She put her hands over his, trying to push him away, but he wouldn't let her. He got down on his knees and kissed her there. He pressed his lips along the length of her scar and kissed, silently sending a prayer of thanks to God for saving her.

She let out a choked sound. For a moment he thought she was going to cry, but she held it in, forced it down. Crying would be a good thing. Crying would prove she wasn't so dead inside. Miss Cora said she hadn't cried once since she had woken up from her coma from the hospital nine months ago. She hadn't cried since they told her they buried Terrance without her being there.

He stood up, looking her in the eyes, knowing this process would take a long time, knowing from experience that wounds like hers couldn't be healed in a few days. "I want you to get up every morning. I want you to get out of bed and get dressed. If you don't, we'll do this every day. I'll come after you every day."

She blinked at him and he wasn't sure he reached her until he touched her belly again.

"Okay," she finally said.

"Good." He shut off the water and inwardly breathed a sigh of relief.

It was a start.

CHAPTER 5

Cassandra felt . . . *Better* wasn't the right word, maybe *different* was a better choice. She felt different. She didn't remember feeling dirty or so weighed down, but as she sat at Wylie's little wooden kitchen table, she realized that she felt the opposite of those things. She was clean. Her hair had air-dried to its naturally curly state. She smelled like Wylie, like his lightly scented spicy soap. She felt lighter, and — for the first time in a long time — the urge to crawl back into bed and sleep until her thoughts disappeared didn't overwhelm her.

"How do you like your eggs?"

She heard the question, but it took a while for her to process it. She was with Wylie James. She had just been in the shower with him. He had run his hands all over her body. He washed her. Yelled at her. He cursed. He threatened. He had kissed her scars. It didn't seem real. He'd left without saying good-bye. Without saying a word. She never thought she would see him again, but she was in his kitchen watching him as he cooked.

He wore a gray T-shirt, low-slung cargo pants and work boots. The last traces of innocence she saw in him ten years ago had faded away. He looked like a U.S. Marine now, even out of uniform. She could see it in him. She had been scared for him when he first told her he wanted to enlist. She didn't want him to; she had asked him to wait. Marines went to war. Marines died in combat. But he told her that he wasn't Terrance. He couldn't see himself sitting in a classroom, or working at a desk for the rest of his life. He was right.

It was funny how Terrance, who went to school, who always took the safe route, died by a bullet, and Wylie was still alive and well.

"Did you go into the Marines after you left?"

He looked over at her, seeming surprised by the question. "Yes, I did. The very next day."

"Are you still a Marine?"

"No, ma'am." He paused for a moment and glanced at her. "I got out after my last deployment. How do you want your eggs?"

His accent was still strong. He had moved

59

from Alabama nearly twenty years ago, but she still heard it in his voice. She was glad it was still there. He wouldn't be Wylie without his deep Southern inflection.

"Where . . ." Her mind was a little sluggish. Her mouth was unable to keep up with the questions her brain produced. "Where were you deployed?"

"I've been to lots of places. Most recently Iraq and Afghanistan." He turned away from the stove and looked at her. "I'm making my eggs over easy, Cass. How would you like yours?"

"With yolks," she said without thinking. "I like the yolks. Terrance only ate egg whites."

"Do you miss him, Cass?"

"It feels like my whole left side is missing." She looked into Wylie's eyes. "Does that make sense?"

"It does." He nodded.

"He was always there. Too much sometimes and I got annoyed with him for it." She paused. "And now he's gone. I never thought he'd be gone. I took him for granted and I hate myself for it."

"It's okay to talk about him with me," Wylie said softly.

She hadn't talked about him since he died. It was too much. There was so much she couldn't say. "I don't want to talk about him anymore right now. Can I have my eggs sunny-side up?"

"Anything you want, Cass." He turned away from her briefly to put bread in the toaster. She looked around his kitchen, around the parts of the house she could see from her spot at the table. She would have never pictured him here, in this seaside house that was little more than a cottage. She could tell he had been renovating it, for there were little touches of Wylie in the woodwork. But there were no decorations to speak of, no personal effects, nothing to suggest that this place was his home. But then again, as long as she had known Wylie, he had never had a real home. His room was sparse at the Millers'. The tiny attic apartment he lived in was bare. He had been deployed all over the world. He hadn't had a home since his father died.

"You like fruit in your oatmeal?" He slid a bowl in front of her. The smell of butter and brown sugar hit her nose. Her stomach spoke, causing her to jump. *Hunger.* She hadn't felt hungry since . . . She didn't remember. Lately she had been eating only when her mother forced her.

"There are apples, cranberries and raisins on there. Eat up now." He handed her a spoon and slid a large glass of orange juice in front of her. "Eggs will be ready in a minute."

She lifted the spoon to her mouth. The oatmeal was hot, thick and sweet. The cranberries were sour, and the apples crisp. She put another spoonful in her mouth, and then another. Just as her spoon was scraping the bottom of the bowl, Wylie placed two eggs and what looked like an English muffin before her.

"These are Portuguese sweet muffins," he told her, reading her mind. He sat across from her with his own plate. "They are like English muffins, but they're doughier and they don't have any of those nooks and crannies. They're popular here on the island." He took one off her plate and slathered it with butter and strawberry jam before handing it back to her. "Go on."

She bit into it. Chewed it. Tasted the yeast and melted butter and the sweetness of the jam. Bread. She remembered loving bread, warm French bread with butter. Croissants from the local bakery. Bagels from the bagel shop on Main Street. Terrance had brought her a bagel that morning. He brought it to her classroom, scolding her because she didn't eat before she left the house. Reminding her that she had to take care of their growing baby. She remembered being annoyed with him that morning. But that bagel was his last sweet gesture and she hadn't even thanked him for it.

The muffin slipped out of her hand, dropping onto her plate, into her still-warm eggs.

Wylie reached for her, grabbing her arm, keeping her upright. She felt dizzy. She felt dizzy and guilty, and nauseous. She missed the numbness that had been her constant companion for the past few months. She'd rather have that any day.

"What is it?"

"I don't feel well. I want to go back to bed."

"No," he said softly. "I can't let you do that."

"I want to! I need to!"

"No," he said again, and she knew he wasn't going to let her have what she wanted. And in that moment she hated him for it.

Wylie looked over at Cass for what must have been the thousandth time that day. He made her sit outside while he worked on fixing the porch railing so he could keep an eye on her. But he spent more time paying attention to her than the task at hand. It was still surreal to him that she was there, that she was with him again. But it wasn't a dream. She was there, curled up on his porch swing, a blanket wrapped tightly around her, despite the seventy-five-degree weather.

He almost wished he had let her go back to bed that morning. It was hard to see her like this. So hurt. But seeing her hurt was better than seeing her near lifeless, and he knew if he let her crawl back into bed, she would never want to get out. He knew because there had been a time in his life when he felt the same way. Post-traumatic stress disorder, the doctors called it. He was diagnosed with it after he survived the rocket attack that had killed nearly his entire unit. Friends that had become like family had died. Men he'd served with for years were disfigured beyond recognition and yet he had walked away unhurt. Physically. There were times when he thought he was back there, when he heard a car backfire or when he smelled fire or felt intense heat on his face.

But he came here to Martha's Vineyard to work and met the little boy, the family that he hadn't known about. And things got better.

He needed to see Teo again. He hadn't gone more than a day without being with him since he found out about his existence. The boy reminded him that there was always something to look forward to, that there was always going to be someone there who loved him no matter what.

"You keep looking at me," Cass said softly, surprising him. "I won't disappear."

"No?"

She shook her head. "No. Not today."

He put down his saw and abandoned the piece of wood he had been cutting. He sat next to her on the porch swing. "You promise?"

She didn't answer him, instead she looked toward the ocean in the distance, toward the lighthouse that he had never been to. He couldn't accept her silence. He touched her wild curls, pushing them away from her eyes so he could see her face.

She looked at him, her eyes less hollow than before. So much better than yesterday, better than that half-dead woman he saw when she woke up this morning. But she didn't look like Cass. Not yet. He wouldn't let up until she did.

"Come with me. I want to show you something." He jumped to his feet, slipping his hand into hers. Her eyes widened slightly, but she didn't question him. She just rose to her feet and followed him down the path.

"There's a little beach here," he told her, not knowing why getting her to move in that moment was so important. "Just enough sand to put a few chairs on. Sometimes the local kids ride their bikes here to go swimming, but nobody else comes. This is my little beach. Deeded to me with the house. I grew up so poor, Cass. Even when I lived with the Millers, I never had nothing. But I've got a house now, and this little beach to call my own. Sometimes I just come here to think. You can come here too, if you want."

He looked back at her to see if she was listening to him babble. He just wanted to reach her.

He must have, because she was staring at him with interest as they crossed the sandy path to the ocean.

"You can come here anytime you want, Cass. Just as long as —"

"I promise not to drown myself?"

Her words jarred him. They reminded him of his darkest days after the rocket attack, when he wondered if things would be better if he were dead.

"No." He pulled her close to him, feeling her too-thin body as it pressed against his. "I was going to tell you to clean up before

66

you go. There's a five-hundred-dollar fine for littering."

She wasn't expecting his words. Confusion passed through her eyes. He let her go, set her away from him, as he sat on the sand to take off his boots and socks.

"Just before dusk is the best time to come. The sand is cool and damp. Feels good on your toes."

"Wylie . . ." She looked lost. Lord knew, he felt lost. He had no idea if he was doing the right thing with her, but he had to try.

"Take off your shoes, Cass. You always liked the beach. Remember when we used to go to the lake? Remember how you used to bury your feet in the sand?" He reached for her leg, grabbing her foot to pull her sandal off. "Feel that?" He pressed her foot into the cool sand. "Doesn't that feel nice? Little things can be nice, Cass. Little things can bring us happiness. You need to remember that."

Her eyes filled with tears and she started to tremble. He reached for her, pulled her into his lap and held her. "I'm not going to tell you not to end things, because I know that won't make one lick of difference. All I'm asking you to do is remember how it feels to live. The girl I knew loved life."

"I'm just so tired."

"I know, baby. But you can't sleep anymore."

Cassandra gasped, clawing the heavy blankets away from her body as she tried to escape another dream. For once, she didn't dream about the event, but she did dream about her husband's killer, about his daughter and about how she got those bruises on her little body. It wasn't the first time she dreamed this dream, but it was the first time she hadn't woken up alone.

Wylie was there. He pulled the blankets from her body, laid her back down on the bed and fanned her overheated skin, just like he had done every night for the past three nights.

"It's okay, honey." He spoke into her ear, crooning in that still-thick Alabama accent. "You're not there anymore. You'll never be back there again."

She listened to his soothing words, inching her body closer to his, wanting to feel his warmth, wanting his hard body to serve as a constant reminder that she wasn't in Harmony Falls anymore. That she wasn't in the house she was sharing with Terrance, which was slowly becoming her tomb.

He must have known that, because he pulled the blankets around them and gathered her closer. Her head on his chest, she heard his heart beating. They used to fall asleep like this. Years ago, during those few stolen nights when they got to be totally alone. She didn't want to think about why he was back in her life now, after ten years. She didn't want to think about her past. She just wanted to get through this moment.

The past few days she had been living moment by moment. She didn't feel good. She wasn't sure she would ever feel good again, but she was feeling better. Like her brain wasn't asleep anymore. Like she wasn't stuck in that horrible nightmare.

His hand came up; his fingers burrowed in her thick curls. "You want to talk about it?" he asked her. His voice was thick with sleep. Her nightmares were keeping him up. Her presence was keeping him from his life. He never complained or made any excuses to be anywhere else, but she knew that he must have a life here.

She had hoped Wylie James had found happiness, even though he left her without a word, without a good-bye.

"No. Go back to sleep."

He lifted his head to drop a kiss on hers. "Only if you do."

"I will. I'm better. I promise."

"Good." He shifted her body, turning her on her side, bringing her even closer so that he could rest with his lips buried in her neck. It shouldn't have been a comfortable position, but it was. She felt sleepy again, and safe. She felt close to him, something that she never felt with anybody else before, even her own husband.

The next morning she woke before he did. She slipped out of bed, prepared to do what she had done every morning since she arrived here. Shower. Eat. Live. But for some reason her feet wouldn't move more than a couple of feet from the bed. She looked down at Wylie. He slept with his mouth slightly open. There was a pillow crease on his face and stubble on his cheek. But he was beautiful. And the urge to get back into bed and snuggle into his warmth came over her so quickly that it nearly knocked the wind out of her.

"You all right?" He opened his eyes, feeling hers on him.

"Um . . . yes. I was just going to get dressed."

He nodded. "I want to take you into town today. We need to go shopping. We just about ate everything in the house. Are you okay with that?"

"Would it matter if I wasn't?" she forced herself to ask. Ever since the day he had taken her to the beach, she made an effort to speak, to respond, to be present. Wylie reminded her that she had lived once, that there was life beyond Terrance. Even if the thought of that life was terrifying to her.

"No, ma'am." He gave her a sleepy, almost mischievous smile and folded his arms behind his head. "It's time to get you out of the house." For a moment they stared at each other. He was bare-chested and rumpled. Stretched out on the bed in his boxer briefs, he looked better than any underwear model that she had ever seen. An uncomfortable feeling passed through her.

Recognition.

Through her numbness and pain she realized that he was a man. And he was beautiful. She wasn't immune to that.

"Are you all right?" he asked, sitting up. There was that worry in his eyes again and she couldn't help but think back to their time together, when he was unguarded and showed her exactly how he felt.

"I'm okay," she said quickly, trying to cover up her new feelings. "I just can't seem to get moving this morning."

"You want me to help?"

Immediately his question brought back

memories of that first day. Of him in the shower with her, of him washing her body and touching her breasts and kissing her scarred skin. It wasn't sexy in the moment, but thinking back on it now, she realized how much she had felt then.

How his touch reminded her that she was still alive.

How his touch could be a powerful thing.

"No. No." She shook her head, taking a step toward the dresser, where he had neatly placed all her clothes. "I'll be out soon."

She escaped to that bathroom door, locking herself inside. She caught a glimpse of herself in the mirror. She had avoided it, not wanting to see herself. She wasn't sure why. Maybe it was because she had no idea who she was anymore.

She couldn't avoid it today and so she stepped closer. She didn't recognize herself. Her skin was lighter from not seeing the sun. Her face was thinner, and the bags under her eyes were bigger. She had known her hair would be in its natural curls from not having been straightened in a year, but she hadn't seen herself this way since . . . before she was married. It seemed like a lifetime ago.

Wylie was right. She did look like shit. And after nearly a year of not caring what she looked like, she realized that maybe she should. It was past time she returned to the living.

It was still early that late August morning, but the sun was warm. Cassandra closed her eyes and let it bake her face as she waited for Wylie. She liked the feeling. The heat on her face. The warm wood of an Adirondack chair on her back. The smell of the ocean air.

This place smelled so different from her house, from her bedroom, and the sheets she never washed because she thought they still held her husband's smell. She let herself think about him, not the guilty memories that usually invaded her, but of the happy times. The time Wylie and Terrance took her tubing on the Connecticut River, and the time they convinced her to jump out of a plane. She thought about the times Terrance and she had talked all night before they were married. He was her friend. He was her husband, but she had always thought of him more as her friend.

"Are you ready?"

She looked up at Wylie as he stood over her. Mirrored sunglasses shielded his eyes and on his body he wore a black T-shirt, blue jeans and boots. His style hadn't evolved much over the years, and she was glad for that. Because as much as she wanted to forget parts of her past, she needed something familiar to ground her.

He held out his hand to her. She reached to take it, only to realize her own hand was shaking. "I haven't been out of the house since . . ." She trailed off. She couldn't remember the last time. It had been a year since her husband died; it had been nine months since she had woken up and seven months since she had left the hospital. She hadn't cared for herself at all in that time. She had tried to, but she had failed. Miserably so.

The thought of it made her feel sick.

She rose to her feet. "I'm ready."

"It's okay to be nervous."

"Is it? I'm ashamed of myself, Wylie James. I can't believe I let it get so bad. Everyone must hate me." She looked away from him, unable to meet his eyes.

"Hush now," he said softly. "Nobody blames you for feeling how you do. Nobody hates you. I don't want you to think about that. All I want you to do is think about what we need at the store."

"Okay." She nodded and took a step off the porch and toward his truck. As she opened the door, it came back to her, the last time she had gone to the store. The daughter and husband of her principal had been in the produce section, going about their business until they saw her. They froze. His wife, her mother, had been one of the five people that died that day. The girl's eyes filled with tears, sadness crossed the man's face and guilt slammed into Cassandra. She lived when all those people had died. She lived when it was her fault the gunman entered the building. She left her cart in the store, too guilty, too shaken to continue shopping. Somehow she had gotten herself home and into bed.

Every time she left her house, she saw reminders of that day. Kids who were in her class, a family member who had lost a loved one. People who just wanted to tell her how much they loved her husband. She slowly stopped going out, getting out of bed, living.

"I was thinking about grilling up some steaks for dinner," Wylie said, breaking her from her thoughts. "Baked potatoes, sour cream and butter. Maybe some pie for dessert. How does that sound?"

"It sounds nice, Wylie." She reached for his hand and squeezed. "Thank you."

"For what?" He gave her a quick grin. "You're doing all the cooking."

A Jeep flew down the road and into Wylie's driveway. There was no top, no doors; the radio was blasting Eminem.

"Shit," Wylie cursed. "Not now."

Cass hadn't seen a soul since she had been at Wylie's. Not a neighbor or visitor. He hadn't even received a phone call in the last few days, but it seemed that quiet had come to an end.

Out of the Jeep came a woman wearing a low-cut black tank top and tight dark denim jeans on her abundantly curvy body. She was beautiful, but in a wild way. She had straight, black hair, which was so long it stopped just past her behind, pretty light brown skin and delicate features that made it impossible to identify her ethnicity.

"Wylie James Everett, you get your sorry ass out of that truck right this minute!" She had an accent too. Southern, but not like Wylie's sweet, soft one.

Wylie's jaw hardened. He cursed again and got out of the truck. He grabbed the woman by her elbow and pulled her toward the house. "What the hell are you doing here, Nova? I texted you that I wasn't going to be around this week."

"Yeah, you texted. Thanks a lot for that. You tell me how I explain that to a five-year-old. You promised you would help me with him. You said you were going to be around."

"I am helping you with him. I give you a check every damn week. I was at every soccer game. I'm around. I called him the other day, so don't act like I've been ignoring him."

"Calling him ain't enough, Wylie James. He's been asking for you and bugging the hell out of me. And take off those stupid sunglasses. I feel like I'm talking to a damn robot."

"I'll come for him tomorrow. Where is he right now? And why haven't you put the doors back on that thing? I told you I don't want him riding around in the Jeep like that. It's dangerous."

"You ain't my daddy. You don't get to tell me what to do." She crossed her arms over her chest and lifted her nose in the air.

"Where is he?"

"With his great-grandmamma. He was bugging me so bad that I had to send him for a sleepover."

"It seems like he spends more time with his great-grandmother than you."

"Are you criticizing my parenting?"

"Yeah, I am, Nova. I'm criticizing you as a person too. You don't get to come over here just to start trouble. I told you I had something important to take care of. The world doesn't revolve around you."

"Is that her? Your important thing?" Nova motioned to the truck where Cass sat. "That's the one you just about lost your mind over? Isn't it?" She looked at Cass, and even from a distance, Cass knew she was being scrutinized. "Well, she's skinny. Looks like a chicken that ain't fit for Sunday dinner."

"Good-bye, Nova." He walked away from her. "I'll get Teo right from his great-grandmother's house after school. I wouldn't want you to lose any of your beauty sleep."

"Wait! You aren't going to introduce me?"

He got back in the truck, slamming the door. He started the car and drove onto the grass and sped down the road, not waiting for Nova to move her Jeep.

"Spoiled, jealous pain in the ass," Wylie spat.

Cass sat silent. Her head spun. But she shouldn't be surprised. She had gotten married. If things had gone differently, she would have been a mother by now. Her life had moved on. It only made sense Wylie's would too. It made sense for him to have a son.

CHAPTER 6

Cassandra sat in Wylie's bed later that night, watching him run a comb through his wet hair. He was shirtless again, dressed only in a pair of gray boxer briefs, his skin still damp from his recent shower. This was her fourth night here. Her fourth night sharing a bed with him. Her fourth night sharing a bed with a man who was not her husband. That thought struck her. A little over a year ago she couldn't envision a world without Terrance. A year ago she would have never thought about sharing a bed with another man, especially the first man she had shared a bed with.

Any moment now, Wylie James was going to crawl into bed next to her, and would spend the night sleeping beside her. She would feel him next to her and smell his scent and be comforted by his warmth. He would be there when she was trapped inside her bad dreams. He would be there in the morning.

He would be there.

She wouldn't be alone.

But she knew infringing on Wylie's life was wrong. She was going to have to leave him soon.

"You did good today, Cass," he said as he crawled in beside her. "At the store, I mean."

"Thank you, Wylie, but I just pushed the cart."

"I know, but you did better than me my first time back."

She looked at him, only to see pain cross his face.

"For years I was deployed. Afghanistan, Iraq, even did a stint in Guam, but I lived on bases mostly in war zones. I'm a Marine. I'll die a Marine. I never thought I would return to civilian life. I didn't think I would ever adjust."

"Why did you leave?"

"My unit was hit with a rocket attack when we were on patrol in Iraq. Most of them died. My commander was injured so bad I couldn't recognize him. My friend Cooper suffered head trauma so bad he couldn't remember who he was."

"And you?" She felt her heart in her throat, those same feelings coming back that she had ten years ago when she first learned that he was enlisting.

"Not a scratch. I got caught up talking to a local kid and was far away enough that I didn't get hurt. I was messed up after the attack. I couldn't walk down the damn street without expecting an explosion. I couldn't see fire without thinking of all the men we lost that day. But despite that, I loved serving. I'm proud to be a Marine. I just realized that I didn't want to die not having led a normal life. I didn't want to die without owning a home and raising a family. I was on my fourth tour. I had come close to death more times than I can count. I knew it was only a matter of time."

She nodded, sorry that they had lost touch for so long. She knew Terrance had thought about Wylie often. He would have been so worried about his friend. "Nova is very beautiful. I'm sure she must have delivered a beautiful baby."

He frowned at her in confusion. "I guess. If you can look past her personality."

"You must have found something good in her if you spent time with her."

"Yeah, she cusses better than any truck driver I know and she fights more efficiently than most men in the armed services."

It wasn't exactly bitterness in his voice

when he spoke of her. No pain either, only frustration. Annoyance. It told Cassandra that Wylie didn't still love this woman, and for some reason that made her feel better. She couldn't get the fiery Nova out of her mind since she confronted Wylie that day. Wylie had met somebody beautiful. Wylie had fallen in love. Wylie had made a baby.

"I'm sorry I've taken you away from your obligations. I'm going to call my aunt in California. Maybe I can stay with her. I don't think I can go home yet."

He shook his head firmly. "You're not leaving here, Cass. Not yet."

His jaw was set stubbornly. Her easygoing Wylie rarely dug his heels in, but she knew that when he did, he was serious. She felt guilty enough she couldn't let him choose her over his son. "But what about . . . your work? What about the little boy? I'm getting in the way."

"I'm heading back to work tomorrow. I'll see Teo then. You're not leaving. Do you realize how bad you were? How bad you still are? I can't let you go again."

"I'll be okay." Those were her words, but even to her ears they didn't sound believable. "I don't want to make things tougher between you and Nova." She believed that. She had come between him and Terrance.

She never wanted to come between him and another person again.

"Things are always going to be tough between me and Nova. You staying here is not going to make a damn bit of difference."

"What about your son, Wylie James? I never thought you would put anybody ahead of your own child. Especially me. I'm the last person who deserves to come ahead of anybody."

"What?" He looked bewildered. "You think Teo is my son? You think me and Nova . . ." He looked horrified. "Nova is my sister. I'm not anybody's father yet."

He had decided to take Cass to work with him. The thought of leaving her alone even for just a few hours didn't sit well with him. On the surface she seemed to be getting better. She was getting out of bed. She was eating without prompting, but she was still so detached from the world. He could still see the heavy sadness that covered her like a blanket. And he knew when she stared off into space that it wasn't happy thoughts filling her head.

He thought it best to show her his world, the little community that had become his family, even though he wanted to keep her to himself, in their safe, quiet bubble. But that wasn't what was best for her. She needed to see that there was life outside Harmony Falls.

"Nova and I don't have the same father," he said to her as he drove to his work site the next morning. "My mom took off long before Nova was even thought of. That's why I never told you about her. I'd only met her a couple times before I moved to Harmony Falls."

"You don't have to explain anything to me." She looked at him for a moment before turning to look out the window.

"I do. You thought I was a father. You found out I had a sister last night and all you did was roll over and go to sleep."

She blinked at him, remaining silent for so long that he thought she wasn't going to say anything. "I was pregnant, Wylie, when that bastard shot me in the stomach. I really wanted that baby, more than I've ever wanted anything in my whole life. You want to know what I was thinking? I was glad when you told me that you had a nephew and not a son, because I don't think I could have taken seeing you love a baby you made with another woman when mine was taken from me." She turned away from him, looking out the window to the beauty of Aquinnah. "It's an ugly, bad thought that I had. I couldn't be happy for you. I didn't want to be happy for you. So you don't owe me anything. Not an explanation. Not your time. Not anything."

He pulled off the road suddenly, his tires kicking up the dust and rocks, making it so cloudy he couldn't see the world outside his truck. "You think you're the only one full of hateful thoughts? When I heard that you had accepted Terrance's proposal six months after I left, I hated you for it. I wished he had cheated on you. I wished that you would grow to hate each other. I wished that lightning had struck the church you were going to get married in. I wished you had failed." He gripped her face and pulled her closer so that his lips were just brushing hers. "He was one-half of me and you were the other. You were my family and I didn't want to be happy for you. I couldn't be happy for you. So I do owe you."

Her eyes were wide, startled as she searched his face for truth, but he could barely pay attention to that because he was too focused on how sweet her lips looked up close. Soft. Pink mixed with brown. He was the first man to kiss her lips, to touch her body. And that filled him with pride and devastated him at the same time.

He spent too much of his life wondering

how things might have been if he hadn't walked away.

He had no right wishing failure on them. He had failed. The only one he could blame was himself.

He had spent too many years thinking that. So he cleared his mind, closed the gap between their mouths and kissed her very softly. His instinct was to open his mouth over hers and suck her in, taking out every ounce of the years of pent-up anger and frustration he had on her lips. But that wouldn't be fair to her, so he just pressed his lips to hers, hard enough she could feel him, long enough that the shape of her mouth imprinted on his brain again, slow enough that the memories of all the past kisses they shared returned.

He broke the kiss, looking down at her. Her mouth was slightly open, slightly damp from his kiss, but this time it was her eyes that captured his attention. For the first time since they had met again, he saw something in them other than hollowness and despair. He couldn't name the emotion, but he knew it was a start. It gave him hope. And that was all he needed.

A few minutes later, Wylie pulled up to his work site. He was proud to be a Marine, proud to have served his country, but this project was by far what he was most proud of.

"After I got out, I wasn't sure what to do with myself. I had a friend who told me I could make good money being a government contractor. I wasn't sure what the hell that meant, but I knew if I could work with my hands that I would be all right."

"You're a carpenter." She looked around the site. "You're building houses."

"Yes. Nova is half Native American, and her tribe — our tribe, because they took me in — lives here, or they are going to live here as soon as we finish. Me and a couple of guys are training some of the members in construction and carpentry, and they are helping to build low-income housing here for their people. As of now we have completed four houses. We'll have fifteen by the time the project is completed."

"And then what?" Cass looked away from the window and at him.

"Excuse me?"

"What will you do when you finish building all the houses?"

It was a good question. It was one he thought about from time to time, but hearing it from her caught him off guard. "I don't know. I'm just going to take things one day at a time."

That's all he could do. He was never a man who was sure what his future would look like, but he couldn't see himself living any other place but here.

He stepped out of the truck, looking around the site to see what progress had been made. He had been gone for a week, but he trusted his small crew to do good work in his absence. The foundation had been laid on the next house; electrical work was being done on the current one. People were working. Altogether there were thirteen members on their crew. A carpenter, a plumber, an electrician and ten members of the tribe who wanted to learn the construction trade. A few of them were young men like him, not cut out for academia but hard workers and good with their hands. They just needed a chance.

Wylie had been given more than his share of chances. First with the Millers, who took him in, sight unseen. Then with his eighth-grade shop teacher, who first noticed his talent. And there was Cass. He walked over to the passenger side of the truck to open the door. She was the first person to make him feel like he had something to offer the world. She was the person who made him want to be a better man. That's why this place was important to him. He wanted to give a chance to those boys who were just like him.

"Yo, Wylie! Welcome back," one of his crew called to him.

He nodded his greeting and then turned his attention back to Cass, who was still sitting quietly in the truck, taking it all in.

"Come on, Cass." He held his hand out to her. "Let me show you around."

He didn't have to glance at his staff to see that everything around him had stopped; every eye went to Cass as she stepped out of the truck.

"Hey, Wylie. Glad you're back." Tanner Brennan, former Army Ranger and his head electrician, greeted them as he walked out of the house they were just finishing up. He didn't stare at Cass like her presence there was anything out of the ordinary. He just extended his hand and smiled easily. "I'm Tanner, the electrician here."

"Hello." Cass was slow to respond as she looked up at the lanky six-foot-six former ranger, but she took his hand and shook it. "It's nice to meet you. I'm Cassandra. I'm . . ." She looked at Wylie for a moment. "I'm Wylie's friend."

"She's going to be staying with me for a while."

"Are you?" Tanner grinned. If he noticed any awkwardness, he didn't let on, and Wylie respected him for it. "I thought for sure that place was going to be condemned. Heard there was no running water and that Wylie had to chase a whole herd of raccoons out of there a couple of weeks ago."

"If they haven't condemned your truck, they sure as hell ain't going to condemn my house. You got so many empty water bottles in there I was sure you were going to start a recycling plant."

"A man's pickup is supposed to be messy. It's supposed to smell like sweat and dirt and hard work." He playfully flexed his bicep for them. "Oh, by the way, your loudmouth sister was here this morning." The look of distaste that crossed his face was hard to miss.

"Nova? Shit. I told her I was going to get Teo today. She just does this to get under my skin."

"Teo is still here. She dropped off some more clothes for him. She said that she was going to be working late at the salon tonight and that she would be home after his bedtime and to tell you not to bother bringing him back to her house." He shook his head. "She might be working late tonight, but one of the guys told me that he heard she had a date with his cousin. If you ask me, you need to wrangle that girl and teach her how to act."

"I can't." Wylie shook his head, feeling weary. "But you're welcome to try. I'm likely to string her up by her red toenails."

Tanner laughed. "Anybody ever tell you that your accent gets thicker when you talk about your sister?"

"Whenever Wylie gets passionate about something, his accent grows thicker," Cass said, surprising him. "My husband used to tease him about it."

" 'Used to'?" Tanner said innocently. As soon as Wylie heard the words, he froze and looked at Cass. Terrance was too painful a subject.

"He passed away," she said quietly. There was a tiny bit of a waver in her voice. "Wylie was his best friend. He loved him like a brother."

"Yeah." Tanner set his hand lightly on Cass's shoulder and squeezed. "I guess he's all right for a Giants fan." He gave Cass one last grin before taking a step back. "I've got to get back to work. But it was nice meeting you, Cassandra. I'm sure I'll be seeing you around."

Tanner walked away and Wylie looked down at Cass, not knowing what to expect.

"He's a nice guy," she said softly. "Cute too. Is he single?"

He stood there, staring at her, his mind unable to process what he heard. "What?" Her voice was soft, her expression neutral. If anyone else had asked that question, he would have taken it seriously. "Was that a joke?"

"My husband is dead. I'm crazy depressed and you just kissed me. You think I'm looking for dates?"

Wylie smiled at her, one of those full happy smiles that she had seen only once in a while in all the years that she had known him. He pulled her into a rough hug and laughed. It was warm that day, but her body unconsciously snuggled closer to his to feel the laughter that vibrated in his chest. People said smiles were contagious. Maybe that was true, because seeing Wylie smile made her want to smile. Feeling his laughter made her want to laugh too, but she couldn't yet. But she wanted to. She couldn't remember the last time there was anything to smile about.

"I like it when you're sassy. My grand-mamma would say you were acting salty."

"How is your grandmother?" She remembered Wylie talking about her, going away for a few days every Christmas break to see her.

"She passed away."

"Oh. I'm sorry. I know you loved her."

"I did." He released her. "But she had a good life and stayed salty to the end. It was her time. Come on. Let me show you around."

Wylie slid his fingers between hers as they walked around the little village. Wylie explained more about the project and the people he had come to like so much during his time there. She heard every word he said, but the front of her mind was focused on their interlocking fingers. His hands weren't smooth; they weren't manicured. They were thick and hard and rough, but the texture of his skin didn't bother her. She enjoyed the feeling of his palm flat against hers. Their hands were as close as they could be. The feeling was familiar, but her mind had been bogged down with so many memories lately that she couldn't conjure up a picture of them doing this — just walking with their hands pressed together.

The last time she was with him, they couldn't hold hands, except for when they were alone, in private, or away from Harmony Falls, where everyone knew them. But not here. Here he walked around holding her hand, like it was nothing, like he didn't care who saw. And everyone did see them here. Every eye went to her, wondering who she was and why she was with Wylie. He must not have told his friends about her, that he was going to get his pathetic, too-depressed-to-function old friend. If they had known, she would have seen pity in their eyes and she couldn't have taken that. It would have been just like being in Harmony Falls all over again.

They came to a little house on the outskirts of the development. It was the sweetest of all the houses. It had a tiny porch that held two white rocking chairs and a half-dozen hanging plants. "This house is a little different from the others," he explained to her as they walked up. "Have you ever been to Martha's Vineyard before?"

She shook her head. "I've wanted to come. Terrance said his aunt loved to spend her summers here, but we never made it."

He nodded. "She stayed in Oak Bluffs. There's a lot of history on this island. There's a place called the Campgrounds, where there are a whole bunch of gingerbread cottages like this one. A lot of them are painted pink or lavender, and they've got latticework that makes it look like they were painted with icing. The woman who lives here always wanted a house just like that, so we built her one. The actual construction of the house wasn't all that difficult. It's all the details that make this house special."

"Are the owners allowed to pick the designs of their houses for this project?"

"No, but I know the owner." He led her up to the front door. "She's someone that I want you to meet."

He knocked on the door. "I would like to take you to see the Campgrounds one day. There's so much to this island. It's not like anyplace I've lived before." As soon as the last word left his mouth, the door flung open and a little brown body flew into Wylie's arms.

Wylie's smile came immediately as his arms caught the little boy. "Hey, buddy! I missed you."

"I missed you too. I wanted to show you the new car Mommy bought me. She said you was busy and that I can't bug you every day. She said you have a life, but I don't think so. I never seen you with a life." The boy's words came out so fast that Cass almost had a hard time understanding him, but she did. She had spent a lot of time with fast-talking little boys.

Teo looked to be around kindergarten age. He had overly long, shaggy, curly hair, a sweet, round face, which looked like it had been smeared with chocolate pudding, and a body that was covered in scrapes and bug bites. Almost every year she had at least one boy in her class like this one. A boy who liked to dig in the dirt, jump out of trees and run wild. Teo looked like one of those boys, and looking at him hurt her. This was the first year since she was twenty-two years old that she hadn't set up her classroom, the first year she didn't stand at her door and welcome seventeen little beings. The first year she hadn't sung the good-morning song, or saw a child start to read. Those kids were her life and she missed them so much in that moment that it stole her breath and made her dizzy.

She gripped the railing of the porch as memories of that day came back to her. She could still clearly see every one of their little worried faces. She could still see them climbing out the window. She never learned what happened to them after that day. She never knew if they all made it out of the classroom that day. She never got the chance to check on them.

She never thought she would have the chance to check on them, because a little part of her thought when she stepped out of her classroom that day, she was never going to be able to step foot back in it again.

"Sometimes I have a life. Not always, but sometimes. You can still bug me."

"Mansi says I can't play with the car in her house. It's got a remote. She said I'll drive it into the walls." He suddenly looked over at Cassandra. "Who are you?" he asked her. "And what's wrong with your face? You look sick."

"Teo!" Wylie and another voice scolded.

There was an older woman standing in the doorway. She was tall, probably close to six feet, and had silvery white hair, which was loose down her back. Nothing about her was petite, and she had one of those soft-looking bodies that any little child would like to snuggle into.

"What?" Teo shrugged. "She looks sick."

Wylie set the boy on his feet and went to Cass, sliding his hands up her cheeks, stroking them with his thumbs as he studied her. "You okay?"

She nodded. She knew she wasn't. She knew that she was nuts. Seeing a little boy shouldn't send her into hysterics. "I'm fine." She forced herself to look at Teo. "I'm Cass, and I'm not sick. I just don't like little boys. They've got germs and are always sticky."

She could see the shock that crossed Wylie's face.

But Teo didn't seem to mind her dry humor. He grinned at her, showing off his missing teeth. Kids knew bullshit when they heard it, and right now she couldn't pretend that she was the sweet, content kindergarten teacher she used to be. She was sad and bitter and it was too much to hide.

"I don't like girls either," Teo told her matter-of-factly. "They are drama."

" 'Drama'? You're five," Wylie said. "How the hell do you know about drama?"

"I know!" He nodded emphatically. "My mother tells me all about it."

Wylie sighed heavily. "Of course she does." He looked to the woman standing in the door. "Hello, Miss Mansi." Wylie kissed the woman's cheek. "How are you?"

"I'm just fine, Alabama." She patted his cheek. "I'm glad to see you back."

"Thank you, ma'am." He motioned to Cass. "This is Cassandra. She's going to be staying with me."

"Welcome, Cassandra." She turned away and headed back inside her home. "Now come in and let me feed you. You are far too skinny. We don't like skinny around here."

CHAPTER 7

"I can't believe you've never seen *Star Wars*! Any of them! How is that possible?" Terrance plopped himself next to her on the couch in the Millers' plush finished basement. "How are we even friends?"

"We're friends because I can't get rid of you. You're like a virus or a roach. There'll be a nuclear holocaust and you'll still be bugging me."

"You're right." He wrapped his arms around her and gave her a loud, smacking kiss on her cheek, but he didn't let her go afterward. For a few moments they stayed close like that. For the past couple of years she had noticed his attempts to get closer to her. She hadn't missed the hints that he thought of her as more than a friend; she ignored them. She loved Terrance, but he was like a brother to her. Yet they both had just turned eighteen, and in less than a month they were about to go their separate ways. Not forever. She couldn't imagine him gone from her life forever. He was going away to college in California. Stanford. The same school his father had attended. He was going to be three thousand miles away and she was staying here, going to a local university to start her teaching degree.

She was going to miss him.

"You really are lame though. You were calling Darth Vader 'Dark Vader.' I don't think I can stomach that."

"I'm not lame." She playfully elbowed him, causing him to let her go. "You're a nerd. And when you go away to school, you'll probably meet a bunch of other nerdy people who enjoy *Star Trek* too."

"*Star Wars,* not *Star Trek!*"

"Whatever. I hope you meet your dream girl there and she knows all about Darth Vader and Luke Solo"

"Luke Skywalker," he corrected with a groan. "My dream girl doesn't have to know about *Star Wars*" — he locked eyes with her — "but a willingness to learn would be nice."

"We should watch *Pretty Woman.* I love that movie." She left the couch, feeling a little uncomfortable, and went to the massive tower of movies kept in the entertainment center.

"*The Princess Bride* is in there." She heard Wylie's voice and turned around to see him entering the room. Her heart lifted. She hadn't expected to see him tonight. "It's girly enough for Cass and manly enough for Terrance."

"She's never seen *Star Wars!*" Terrance complained. "There's a love story in there. Perhaps the greatest love story of all time."

"I'll tell you what. Before you head off to that fancy school of yours, we'll have a marathon and watch all three. We'll tie Cass to a chair and force her to watch it."

"You don't have to force me, boys. Just make sure you supply enough pizza and gummy bears to last six and a half hours."

"Done," Wylie said as he sat next to Terrance on the couch.

"You're back from your date early," Terrance said to him. "What happened? You sneezed in her food or something?"

"No. We just went out for ice cream. It wasn't a big deal. What about you? Aren't you late for your date?"

Cassandra turned completely away from the movies she was studying. "You have a date tonight?"

"Yeah with Terry Jones. But I was thinking about blowing it off."

"Why?" Both Cassandra and Wylie asked.

He shrugged. "I wanted to hang out with you guys tonight."

"You can't miss an opportunity with a girl as

fine as Terry Jones. The worst part of graduating from high school is not being able to see that fine girl walk around in her cheerleading uniform. We can hang out tomorrow. I don't have to work. Tonight you are going out with that girl."

"She does have amazing legs and arms and everything." Terrance nodded.

"You ever see her do a full split? I bet she's real flexible. Bend-y." Wylie grinned and then caught Cassandra's eye. "Sorry, Cass. I shouldn't talk that way around you."

"Why not? I'm not a baby. I know what goes on with you guys and your dates."

Wylie and Terrance exchanged a look that spoke a thousand words. Unfortunately, she couldn't hear any of them. There were times when she felt left out around them. Like they had their own little secret club that she wasn't a member of. But she couldn't be upset about it: Wylie made Terrance popular in school and Terrance pushed Wylie to do better. She wasn't the only one who was going to lose her best friend when he went off to school. She wasn't sure how the two men would function without each other.

"I'm going to go." Terrance got up. "Don't wait up. We'll hang out tomorrow. Let's head to the beach at Hammonasset."

"And get lobster rolls at the Sea Food Shack."

"And corn dogs," Cass added. "I can't leave without a corn dog."

"You got it." He winked at her. "We'll leave at nine tomorrow."

He ran up the stairs, leaving them, and that brief moment of awkwardness took over as it always did when they were alone together. Maybe *awkwardness* wasn't the right word. *Awareness* was. She was more *aware* of Wylie James Everett than any other person on the planet.

"Do you want to watch *The Princess Bride*?" she asked, feeling a little silly, a little jumpy. "There's *Die Hard* here too. Or maybe I should just go home."

"It's eight o'clock on a Friday night," Wylie said in his slow Southern drawl. "Why aren't you out on a date? And *The Princess Bride*. I like that giant guy."

"I'm not on a date, because nobody asked me." She popped the tape in the ageing VCR and sat next to him on the couch. "Why aren't you on a date? Boys who look like you, Wylie James, don't just go on short ice-cream dates."

"Yes, they do. All the time — especially if they want to stay out of trouble. She had a vanilla cone with rainbow sprinkles and I had one of them twist cones. We talked about her grandmamma and her little brothers and I took her home."

"So you're telling me you didn't lick ice cream off her naked body in the back of your truck?"

"Cass!" he scolded. "Don't talk like that."

"Why not? I'm eighteen years old. I'm going away to college too. If you and Terrance can talk that way, why can't I?"

"Because you're a lady, and where I come from, ladies don't talk like that."

"You're *not* where you came from. You're where I came from, and I want to know what's up with this girl. You've been out with her three times and your dates are never more than an hour or so. Isn't she flexible enough?"

"I did *not* sleep with her, Miss Cass." He frowned at her, his neck getting a little red. She knew she hit a nerve with him. "I want her to go home and tell her daddy that I am a gentleman. So that's why nothing has happened."

"You are for the most part. Why is it so important for this girl to believe it?"

"You know that around here I'm just one step away from being considered white trash."

"That's not true!"

He looked her in the eye. "You know it is, Cass. Besides, her father is a carpenter who does really solid work and I want to learn from him. He won't teach me if I'm screwing around with his daughter."

"So you don't even like the girl. You're just using her to get close to her father."

"No. I like her just fine. She's fun to hang out with."

"Oh." She didn't know why, but his answer made her heart feel a little sore. Like it always did whenever he was dating someone.

" 'Oh'? There's a hell of a lot you just said with that *oh*." He took her hand in both of his and stroked his thumb across her palm. It was a simple touch. He didn't even look at her as he did, his eyes focused on the TV before them, but the touch awakened all her nerves and she felt those tingles that only he ever made her feel. "She's fun to hang out with, but I really wanted to be here tonight."

"Why?"

He didn't answer. Instead he pulled the old blanket the Millers kept on the couch over them and her closer in the process. "Do you have to be home soon?"

"No. My father is away on business and my mother went to Hartford with her friends. She'll be home late. She has a better social life than I do."

"I'm sorry about that." He placed his hand on her bare knee, just inches away from the hem of her sundress.

She swallowed hard. "Don't be. It's not your fault I'm dateless."

"It might be. I might have scared some guys away."

"You what!"

"Hush." He pulled her closer, his hand slipping up her dress to her thigh. She nearly jumped at the sensation of his large, rough hand on her skin. He had never touched her like this, never allowed himself to be this close to her. "How do you think I got you to go to senior prom with me?"

"You could have asked!"

"Shh," he hissed. "We both know I couldn't have. I had to make sure that no one asked you."

"Why?"

They heard footsteps on the stairs and jumped away from each other, putting more and more space between them as the steps got closer. Both Mr. and Mrs. Miller appeared, dressed in evening wear.

Mr. Miller was grinning, but Mrs. Miller wasn't. She had that suspicious look in her eyes, the same one she always had when she found Cassandra and Wylie alone.

"What are you going on about down here, Cassandra?"

"Oh, nothing, Mr. Miller. Wylie just told me

he's a Red Sox fan. I can't take that."

"You're in trouble now, son. Cassandra's father is a New Yorker, and this is Yankee country. You'll get your butt kicked around here."

"I won't make that mistake again, sir."

"Where's Terrance?" Mrs. Miller asked.

"On a date, ma'am. He left just a little while ago."

"Oh. Okay. We're going out to dinner in New Haven. We'll be back late. I would prefer you didn't leave the house tonight."

"I won't, ma'am."

"And set the alarm after Terrance comes in. He never remembers to."

"Yes, ma'am. I will. I hope you have a nice time."

"We will." She nodded. "Let's go, dear. It's a long drive."

Wylie let out an audible breath when they were gone and left her alone on the couch. "Maybe you should go home, Cass."

"Why?" She followed him across the room. "We were talking."

"No. I was about to say something stupid."

She went to him, wrapping her arms around him, pressing herself against him like she had always wanted to do every time she was near him. He stiffened at first, but only for a moment, before he wrapped his arms around her

107

waist. "I have never wanted to hear something stupid so badly before. Be stupid. Why do you keep guys away from me?"

"You know why."

"I don't."

"I don't want to see you with anybody else."

She leaned into him, pressing her lips to his mouth. He kissed her back, letting himself go, sweeping his tongue into her mouth and kissing her so deeply she forgot where she was.

"We can't do this," he whispered after breaking their kiss.

"Tell me why we can't. You're not serious with that other girl."

"No, but I can't do this to Terrance."

"Do what to him? We are not a couple. He dates other girls all the time. It's not fair to me. He gets to go out and have fun, but I can't date anybody because he likes me. He's going all the way across the country to college, where he'll meet other girls."

"You're right. He will, but he doesn't just *like* you. He *loves* you!"

"But I love *you.*"

"Don't say that, Cass." He shut his eyes as if her words hurt him.

"Why not? It's true. I love you and I know you love me too. You can't hide it."

"I can't, but I can't do this to him. We can't be together."

"Terrance is my best friend and I love him, but I don't love him like I love you. I want to be with you."

He looked at her for a long moment. "It would hurt him."

"Just for tonight then." She softly kissed his mouth. "Please. Only we have to know."

"You're killing me."

"And you kill me every time you go out with another girl."

"I'm sorry. I wish things were different."

She pulled away from him and grabbed his hand, leading him back to the couch. "Make it up to me. Be my first."

"What's wrong?" Wylie wrapped his arm around her, resting his lips on her shoulder.

"Did I wake you? I'm sorry. Go back to sleep."

"You didn't wake me up. I can't fall asleep until you do. What are you thinking about?"

"You." She turned over to face him. He was bare-chested, slightly bearded and much bigger than the nineteen-year-old boy who made love to her for the first time. But he had been gentle that night and sweet, and even though she felt guilty about thinking about him when she was married to his best friend, she never regretted any bit of their time together.

"Me? I was worried about you today."

"You're always worried about me."

"I am. Even when you were with Terrance, and I knew he was taking care of you better than I ever could, I was worried, but now I'm worried that today was too much for you."

It was, but she didn't want to tell him that. "I'm okay. I want to know about your sister. I thought I knew everything about you, but I don't know anything about her."

He sighed, turning over on his back to look up at the ceiling. "The damn girl hates me."

"You don't seem too fond of her either."

He looked over at her, one side of his mouth turned up in a slight smile. "Can't say I am."

"But you live here to be near her. You must love her."

"She's got Teo. That's why I'm here. They're all I've got."

She rolled closer to him, about to reach out and touch him. She heard pain in his voice. It might go unnoticed to another person, but she knew him. She knew that Terrance was like his brother, that the Millers were his family, that she had been important to him — and in one day he lost them all.

But he walked out, without a good-bye, without an explanation, without looking back. For so many years she'd hated him for that. So she didn't touch him like she had first wanted to, because she had always wondered how things would have been if he had never left.

"I've been here over a year, but I still don't know very much about my sister."

"Did she grow up here?"

"No. My mama dragged her all over the place, trying to find her a new daddy. I don't know Nova's history with this place for sure. She was born here. I think she came back here a few times when life with Mama became too crazy. She came here for good when she left Teo's father. He used to smack her around. I'm glad I never knew about it. Nova bugs the shit out of me, but if I knew that bastard was beating up my sister, I would have killed him."

"I know you never grew up together, but now that you've found each other again, why don't you get along?"

"I loved my mother, but she was a drunk. The best thing she ever did for me is walk out. My pop may have been poor as piss, but he worked hard and he loved me. And when he died, he sent me to the Millers. I had a better life than Nova and she hates me for that. I don't want to think about what happened to her when she was a kid. My mother had a lot of boyfriends. . . ." He trailed off, shaking his head. "I make sure she doesn't bring any jerks around Teo. The kid has a decent shot at being normal. It could be a first for our family."

"You're *not* normal?"

"Aw, hell no, Cass." In the moonlight she could see his mouth spread into a full grin. "I'm as fucked up as they come."

"True, you volunteered to babysit the mentally ill, depressed, aging widow of your former best friend. There must be something seriously wrong with you."

He let out a soft sigh and rolled over so that their bodies were so close that he was nearly on top of her. His lips brushed her forehead, his hands on her back. "I took in my former best friend's depressed widow, not because I wanted to babysit her, but because I missed her and I wanted to see that girl come back."

Wylie pulled into Mansi's little driveway with Cass by his side. He was going to leave Cass here today while he worked, and he felt nervous as hell about it. He knew she would be fine with Mansi, that the strong woman had raised a truckload of kids and was helping to raise Teo now. But he didn't want Cass out of his sight.

He had let her go ten years ago. He had walked away from her, from his family. and now she was back in his life, and in his bed at night and at his side all day. It was illogical to think that something was going to happen to her in the few hours he would be working. But he never thought a gunman would go into an elementary school and kill his best friend either.

She might leave him again, when she got better; she might decide to pick up her life and move on somewhere else. He would have to let her go if she wanted. He'd lost all rights to her when he walked away; but right now, while he had her back, he wanted to keep her close as possible.

"I'll be on the job site all day. I'm teaching some of the guys to make cabinets, but I'll have my phone on, if you need me. I know Mansi will probably be wanting to feed you herself, but I packed you some snacks and stuff." He handed her the small, soft cooler, which he sometimes packed his lunch in. "I'm going to come see you around lunchtime. Okay? My number is written on a piece of paper in that bag. Mansi has it too. You call me if you need me."

She looked at him for a long moment, her face devoid of emotion like it usually was. "I taught kindergarten for nearly ten years and you remind me of all the mothers sending their babies to school for the first time. I'll be fine, Wylie James. I won't call you while you're working."

It had only been a week since he took her from her house, since he forced her out of her bed, that prison she had confined herself to. She wasn't herself. She was too skinny and too sad. And too fragile still.

But she wasn't a baby. And he wasn't her mother. He was going to have to trust her to be okay.

"What if I want you to call me while I'm working?"

She surprised him by leaning over and pressing her lips into his cheek. "I will then."

She opened the door and got out, giving him one last look before she took her cooler and walked herself to Mansi's front door. He had planned to walk her in, to talk to Mansi, but he stayed in his truck and watched her as she knocked on the door.

Cassandra was right. He was just as bad as those kindergarten mothers watching their kids go off to school. And just like a mother he was proud to watch her leave him, but sad to see her go.

Her heart was racing faster and faster with each step she took away from Wylie. She wanted to go back to bed and bury her head under the covers and stay there. She didn't know how to talk to people anymore, how to be around them — when she was with Wylie, she didn't have to. She could stay safely cocooned in the tiny world he had created for her, but that was no life at all. She may not want to return to the world of the living, but she was going to have to. She couldn't stay here with Wylie forever. She had learned that as much as he cared for her, it wouldn't stop him from hurting her. It wouldn't stop him from leaving. Terrance left her too. Not on purpose, but she realized that no matter how loyal she was, no matter how much she loved a person, there was no guarantee that they would always be there.

Mansi opened the door just as Cassandra had lifted her hand to knock. The older woman again wore her thick, pin-straight, gray hair loose today. It fell down her back, just hitting the top of her flowing, colorfully printed skirt.

"Good morning," Cass cleared her throat

to say. "Wylie sent me here so that you can babysit me."

Mansi grinned at her. "I hope you're potty trained, because if you're not, that's going to cost the boy double." She stepped aside. "Come in, girly. My shows are just starting. I hope you like talk shows. And if you don't, I hope you brought a book."

Mansi's home was an eclectic mix of fifties-style furniture and beautiful artwork that she collected over the years. The little gingerbread cottage was nothing like the stately home she was used to in Harmony Falls, and it was nothing like Wylie's beachy house, but it was warm. The pictures of the children she raised lined almost every inch of the wall.

Cassandra absently touched her belly, her mind going back to the moment she placed the framed picture of her first sonogram on the wall in Terrance's office. She had told him that was going to be the first of many pictures. She had joked that she was going to take his diplomas down just so they could have extra picture space.

"I had four children," Mansi said as she settled into her easy chair. "Two of them ended up in California. My oldest boy is in the Navy, and my youngest, Bobby, Nova's father, is dead. I loved that boy, but he was no good. Got that from his father's side. If he had taken after me, he would have been up for sainthood by now. But that's life for you. You hope and plan for things, but they never turn out the damn way you expected. Now hush. My show is starting."

Mansi only said a few words to her in the next few hours. She fed her popcorn and kept her glass filled with sugary iced tea, but she didn't talk much. She didn't ask her why she was here, or how she knew Wylie. She didn't attempt to make awkward small talk. The woman was just there and it was nice. Nice not to be alone that day. It was nice to be in a new place, doing something different.

"Alabama is a good man," Mansi said out of nowhere after one of her court shows had gone off the air.

"He is," Cassandra agreed.

"He built me this house, you know."

"I know. It's very beautiful."

"I think he did it because he's worried about that sister of his. He's worried she'll take after her mother and leave Teo. So he built this house for me so Teo can have a nice place to grow up, just in case she takes off."

"Are you worried about the same thing?"

Mansi looked toward an old picture of a

little girl in pigtails hanging on her wall. "Sometimes. Nova is young. All the women in my family had their babies young. I was seventeen when I had my first. But then again, I was married and I wanted a baby. I wanted to be a mother. Teo was an accident. A beautiful little accident, but an accident created by a rebellious girl and a man who shouldn't be around wild animals, much less children. But Nova loves her boy. She's a hellion, but she loves that boy deeply. She loves Alabama too. She'd rather pull her toenails out than admit it, but she loves him and she trusts him. And she don't trust anybody."

"He loves her too," Cassandra said softly. "I'm glad he has her. He needs a family."

"He's got one." She nodded. "He's not my blood, but he's my grandson now too. Call him." She handed her the phone. "And go take a nap. You look sleepy." She turned her attention back to the TV. "*The People's Court* is on next and I can't have you snoring through it. There's a little bedroom in the back."

Cassandra knew when she had been dismissed, so she left the living room and found the tiny bedroom in the back of the house. It was only big enough for a twin-

118

sized bed and a sewing table, but it had a view of a little garden. In the distance she could make out the ocean through the trees.

She wondered if Terrance would like it here. For a split second she had forgotten that he wasn't alive anymore, that she couldn't pick up the phone to reach him. He had so many plans for them. So many places he wanted to take her and their child.

He had the plans, not her. When she married him, all of her plans went out the window. Because she had never planned on marrying him. Or staying in Harmony Falls. Or having his baby. She had walked down the aisle in love with somebody else. But he left her. And Terrance had stayed. And Terrance had loved her so much and had treated her so well. She owed it to him to be a good wife and to go along with his plans and support his dreams. She owed it to him because even though she loved him, she didn't love him like he deserved to be loved.

The guilt had eaten at her for years, but it had disappeared when he died, only to be replaced by heavy despair. Now that the despair was lifting, she felt the guilt returning because Wylie had returned. She couldn't help but wonder what Terrance would think about that.

The phone rang, making her jump. She forgot she was holding it. She was too caught up in her own thoughts. She absently answered it after the first ring.

"Cass?"

"Hi, Wylie."

"Were you ever going to call me?" he complained. "I feel like a teenaged girl waiting for a boy to call."

"Good. I want you to suffer a little."

"I bet you mean that too."

"I do."

"You're a little edgy," he said, then paused. "I've always liked that about you. How are you, Cass?"

"I'm fine, Wylie James. Mansi is being good to me."

"I know she is. I'm going to come round and see you later."

"You don't have to."

"I know. But I want to."

"Okay then."

"Okay then," he said back softly. "Good-bye, Cass."

He disconnected and she kept the phone to her ear for a few moments after he was gone.

Wylie James had come back. Wylie James was treating her so well. She lay down in the little twin bed and drifted off to sleep, thinking about him.

Wylie slipped his phone back in his pocket and returned his attention to cabinets that he was making, only to see Tanner there studying his work.

"These are solid. They'll last this family a hundred years, but it would have been a hell of a lot faster, not to mention cheaper, if we just bought a set and put them up."

"I know, but I make these cabinets so the guys can learn the skill. We're not here just to put up some houses."

"I know. We're here to teach. It's just not like any other construction job I've worked. I've been here a few months now and it's still hard to get used to everything."

"It's hard as hell going from seeing action in Afghanistan to doing electrical work on an island in New England."

Tanner stared off into space for a moment as if he were reliving something. "For years I was off American soil. It's always good to be home, but I kind of miss being away. You ever get that feeling? I got so used to my life being abnormal that normal doesn't feel right anymore."

"Hell yeah, I know what you're talking about. Regular just don't feel quite right."

Tanner nodded. "You were talking to Cassandra just now?"

"Yeah. She's going through a rough time. I was just making sure she was doing all right."

"She's that teacher, isn't she? The one who was shot in that school."

"How did you know?" He never told anyone about his connection with Cassandra and Terrance. It had been too hard to talk about.

"Her face was all over television after it happened. She looks different now, but she's got the kind of eyes that are hard to forget."

"Yeah," Wylie said, thinking about them. Her eyes used to have a spark in them. *Happiness.* Now they were mostly blank, and when they weren't, they were sad, haunted.

"Your sister told me that you grew up with rich folks in Connecticut, but you never went back there because of some girl. Is Cassandra that girl?"

"You were talking about me with Nova?" Tanner and Nova were like oil and water. Couldn't be around each other without some kind of argument breaking out. What the hell were they doing, talking about him?

Tanner shrugged. "She's got a big mouth, and, frankly, there's not much to do on this island. Listening to her complain about you is entertaining."

"If you don't like it here, why don't you move on? Go back home?"

"Nah." He shook his head. "I'm not going anywhere until every one of these houses is complete. Plus I think I need quiet for a while. I never had much quiet in my life. Even my childhood was noisy."

"Hey, Tanner," one of their youngest workers, Jimmy, called to him. "There's an outlet sparking in Mrs. Wright's house. Can you come check it out?"

"Did you turn off the power?" he asked as he strode toward the door.

"Yes, sir."

"Good." He touched the kid's shoulder as they walked out. "You're about to fix it."

Tanner was a good electrician and an amazing mentor to the men who were in the program. But Wylie didn't know much about the man. Nothing about his family or his service or where he came from. He only knew that just like Wylie, Tanner had some invisible scars from war. And beneath his good nature lay a man with demons that would be hard as hell to get rid of.

CHAPTER 8

Cassandra awoke when she felt something touch her hand. She didn't open her eyes at first. She didn't want to. The sun was warm on her face. The air coming from the open window smelled faintly of the ocean. It was the first time, in a long time, that she didn't want to wake up because she was comfortable and warm, rather than not wanting to wake up because she had nothing worth waking up for.

"Are you sure you're not sick?" she heard a young voice ask. She opened her eyes to see Teo sitting on the small twin bed beside her, hugging his thin little legs to his chest. He still had his shoes on, his knees were scraped and a Band-Aid half hung on one of them. Immediately that awful pang hit her in the chest, and her stomach lurched. He reminded her so much of one of the little boys she had in her class. He would be starting second grade. Her whole class would be going into second grade. She had missed a whole school year of teaching.

"Get your dirty feet off the bed." She closed her eyes and rolled over, away from him.

"Oh, yeah." She heard two thuds on the wood floor, and instead of Teo going away, she felt his small, warm body press closer to hers. "Mansi will swat me if she sees me with my shoes on the bed. She don't even let me sit on the good couch. Said I can't sit on it till I'm sixteen."

"That's because you'll get it dirty. You should probably take a bath."

"No thanks. Uncle Wylie is going to take me swimming. I'll get clean in the ocean."

"Soap. Shampoo. Toothpaste." She said this without opening her eyes. "Children need to use those things."

"I use them. Sometimes." She felt his hands on her side and then his knees on her hip. When she opened her eyes, she found him curled up before her, staring up at her like she was some kind of mutant. "You didn't answer me. Are you sure you're not sick? My mom says you're not supposed to ask people that. She says it's rude. But I don't know why. When Mr. Otis got cancer, everybody was whispering about it and treating him so nice. They wasn't nice to him before, because he was a mean old jackass. But he got cancer and everybody's nice, and they always whisper about him being sick."

"Don't say 'jackass.' "

"My mom used to call him a shithead. She said I couldn't say that, but I could say 'jackass' because it's not so bad."

"You can't say either!"

"Okay," he relented. "I can't say them because you're sick."

"I'm not sick! I already told you that."

"Yeah, but you said you just didn't like little boys. I know that's not true. Everybody likes me."

"Oh, really?"

"Yeah, my mom told me."

There was something charming about this kid. There was something about him that she couldn't yet put her finger on.

"Why do you think I'm sick, Teo? Do I look that bad?"

"Let me see." He took her face in his hands and peered into her eyes. "You should wear some makeup. My mom says all ladies over a certain age need some makeup, but you're not ugly or nothing. I was asking because Mansi says not to bother you because you're going through something now."

"If your great-grandmother told you not to bother me, why are you here?"

"Because I wanted to know about you. I've never seen Uncle Wylie with a lady before, and you live with him, and he's never told me about you."

"We grew up next door to each other. Your uncle was my very good friend. You've never seen him with a girlfriend?" She hated herself for asking, but she couldn't help it. How Wylie had spent his time after he left was a total mystery to her.

"Nope. He's not like my mom. She goes on dates sometimes."

"Does she tell you about them?"

"No, but I think that's why she leaves me with Mansi all the time. She says she works, but I heard Miss Taylor say she needs her nights free so she can go on dates."

"Oh. Are you sure you're not forty-five years old? You sound like a very mature man."

"Yeah." He grinned at her, showing off his missing teeth. "I'm just five, you know."

"I'm not sick, Teo. I'm sad. My husband died and I'm very, very sad. That's why Mansi told you to stay away from me. That's why your uncle brought me here. He doesn't want me to be sad anymore."

"Oh. My dad is dead, but I'm not sad

about it. He was a bum."

"Did your mother tell you that?"

"Yeah. She tells me a lot of stuff. She calls me at night when I stay here."

"Do you stay here a lot, Teo?"

"All the time. I get on my mom's nerves. Mansi don't mind me so much."

She didn't know what to say to that, but she got a glimpse into Teo's relationship with his mother — and she wasn't sure that she liked it.

"Teo!" Wylie barked. He was standing in the doorway, frowning down at them. "Your great-grandmamma told me she sent you outside to play. What are you doing in here bothering Cass?"

"I'm not bothering her. Right, Cass?"

"You call her Miss Cass, boy. Where I'm from, you don't call adults by their first names. You understand?"

"Yes, sir."

"Now go outside like Mansi told you."

"Yes, sir." Teo's face fell a little. Cassandra had wanted him to go. Children and being around them — it was too much for her, but Cass was almost sad to see Teo go.

"Teo," she said softly as she grabbed him and pulled him close so that she could speak into his ear. "You don't have to stay away from me just because I'm sad. It's okay to see me."

He looked up at her, with his deep brown eyes wide. "I don't want to make Uncle Wylie mad."

"Don't worry about him. Just don't stay away."

"Okay, Miss Cass. Good-bye."

He jumped off the bed, grabbed his shoes and ran out the door.

"Are you all right, Cass?" Wylie came to sit next to her on the bed, the concern in his eyes hard to miss. For the first time she felt herself a tiny bit annoyed by it. She wasn't going to break. But then she remembered, she did break. She spent so much of the past year broken. But she knew that time had come to an end.

Wylie watched Cassandra that night as she smoothed lotion on her legs. She wasn't being intentionally seductive. In fact, he was positive that she didn't even notice that he couldn't take his eyes off her as she rubbed the cream into her pretty brown skin. She was still too thin for his taste, her eyes too sad and her hair still hung limply around her shoulders, but she turned him on. He felt guilty for wanting a grieving woman so bad his teeth hurt. He felt guilty that he was going to bed each night with the widow of his best friend. But it never left the back of his mind that he was her first love, her first time with a man. Before there had been Terrance and Cassandra, there had been Wylie and Cass. Before the world told him he couldn't have her, he had planned never to let Cass go.

"Will you take me to the store tomorrow?" She placed his lotion on the nightstand and sat back against the headboard.

"Of course. I'll bring you right after work. What do you need?"

"Lotion. I don't smell like me anymore."

"No." He crawled onto the bed next to her. He couldn't help himself. He placed his nose in the crook of her neck and inhaled her. Her skin was so soft, so smooth, that his lips just glided over it. "You smell like me. That's not a bad thing."

He placed his hand on her thigh, knowing he was going just a little further than he should. He wasn't sure if she noticed the effect she had on him. He had slept beside her every night for over a week. He'd spent every moment of the day with her, but he hadn't seen her today. Not for long hours — and he couldn't shut off his mind. He couldn't stop thinking about her. He had missed her for ten years. There was a time when he thought he would never see her again, but now that she was beside him, he didn't want to give her space or let her go. He just wanted to do all those things he had thought about doing with her for the past ten years. He wanted to get back those feelings he had when they were together so long ago. When he was with her, it was the only time in his life when he was ever truly happy.

He slid his hand under her nightgown, just so he could feel her skin. She stiffened very slightly, but didn't react otherwise.

Calm down, he ordered himself. *Stop it. She loved Terrance. She loves Terrance.*

And so do you.

She looked up at him, into his eyes. "I think I would like to get some makeup too."

"Why?" He slid his hand to her cheek, brushed his thumb over her cheekbone. "You don't need any."

"I look like shit." She said it so matter-of-factly that it caused him to laugh.

"No, baby." He pressed his lips to her cheek. "You don't. You're beautiful."

"You're the one who said I looked like shit."

He kissed her again. "I just said that because I hated to see you so damn miserable."

"Teo asked me again if I was sick. He sug-

131

gested some makeup. I think he's right."

Wylie let out a soft curse. "I'm sorry he bothered you today. I won't let it happen again."

"He was fine. You were the one that was bothering me. I think you were too hard on him today."

"What?" He narrowed his eyes at her. "That boy needs to learn to mind his elders and show adults some respect. If I don't teach him the right way while he's young, who will?"

"You're right. But Teo thinks I'm sick because you are so protective of me. When you and Mansi tell him to stay away, he thinks I'm frail. You're treating me like I'm frail."

"Damn it, Cass. When your mama called me, you hadn't been out of bed in weeks. You were ready to die. If that ain't frail, I don't know what the hell is."

"You're right." She nodded. This time, though, when she looked him in the eye, he didn't see that sad, empty look. He saw a little bit of determination. "Teo makes me uncomfortable," she said softly. "He reminds me of my students. He reminds me that I not only lost my family, but I lost a job that I loved. Yeah, he bothers me. But I think it's past time I feel bothered."

He gripped her hand and squeezed. There was nothing he could do but agree with that.

The roar of an engine passing by distracted Cassandra from the cards in her hand as she sat at Mansi's small kitchen table the next day. She didn't need any distractions. She was already losing badly at rummy; her brain was sluggish and slow from not using it for so long.

"Come on, girly," Mansi urged. "It's your turn. You didn't throw out."

"I know. I'm still trying to figure out what to do."

"Show me your hand. I'll tell you what you should get rid of."

Cass looked up at the older woman and frowned. "I may be depressed, old woman, but I'm not stupid."

Mansi grinned widely at her, showing off that little gap between her front teeth. "I'm the best at this game and could beat the pants off you any day, but I do enjoy when people make it easier for me."

"Yeah. She beats me all the time," Teo said from the other side of the table. The little boy had mostly kept his distance since he got home from school. However, when they started to play, he pulled up a chair next to Cassandra and quietly watched them.

"You play cards with Mansi?"

"All the time. She's good."

"Do you ever win?" She looked from the boy to his great-grandmother.

"No. I can't. It's impossible. She won a lot of money at a casino once, but my mom said she can't go there no more."

Cassandra looked at the woman, who shrugged at her. "It was blackjack. I have a system."

"It's called counting cards, you crazy old thing!" They all looked up to see Nova walking in. Cass had seen the woman before, but it still struck her how beautiful Wylie's little sister was. Her long hair was loose and wild around her shoulders. Her pretty, light brown skin looked healthy and sunbaked at the same time. She wore a thin, spaghetti-strap tank top and a denim pencil skirt on her ultracurvy figure; chunky, wedged heels covered her feet. There was nothing neat or demure about her, but she was somehow put together in a wild way. Cass admired that. Every item of clothing she had owned for the past ten years she bought because it fit an image: schoolteacher, resident of Harmony Falls, wife of Terrance, daughter-in-law of one of the most respected men in the town. She never wore anything bright or short or tight. She never wore anything solely because it made her feel good. And now as she looked at Nova, she felt dowdy, dim-looking, unpretty. She was glad that this woman was Wylie James's sister and not the mother of his child, as she'd originally thought.

"Mommy!" Teo bounded from his chair, heading toward his mother, but stopped short before running into her arms, like some kind of invisible wall had blocked him from making contact.

"Hey, kid." Nova gave him a quick smile and a soft pat on the head.

The exchange was awkward for Cassandra to watch, but it must have been the norm for them. Cassandra remembered her mother as being different. Always one to give long hugs and squeezes. Cassandra wanted to be the kind of mother Cora had been.

"So here you are." Nova narrowed her eyes on Cassandra. "I'm surprised that my brother hasn't locked you in a gilded cage. His fancy girl from Connecticut. You're not what I pictured, that's for sure. I imagined someone more like Gwyneth Paltrow."

"You mean, you didn't think I would be black? I like to think of myself as a cross between Lena Horne and Kerry Washington, only with a better butt."

Nova stared at her for a moment and then threw back her head and laughed. "What brings you to the island?"

"Dead husband."

Nova glanced at her son for a moment. "I got one of those, too. Come shopping with me, Miss Cassandra. My brother is going to have a shit fit when he finds out, but we need to be getting to know each other."

"Okay," she said without thinking. It was time for her to venture out.

He was going to kill Nova. Put his hands on her shoulders and shake her till sundown, or at least until she got some common sense. He had pulled up to Mansi's house a little after three, after spending all day away from Cass, not talking to her, not calling to check up on her. Because she was right, he had brought her here to heal, to move on. She didn't need him hovering, but he sure as hell hadn't expected her to go off with his sister. His sister who had disappeared for the past three hours and wasn't picking up her cell phone.

"Why are you worried, Uncle Wylie? Mommy goes out all the time."

Wylie glanced at Teo, who had put his small hand on his jiggling knee to calm it. "I know." He ruffled his hair.

"She always comes back. And if she doesn't, she calls. She's good like that."

"I know." He gathered his nephew in his arms and gave him a squeeze. Teo was used to his mother taking off. It shouldn't be something that a five-year-old was used to, but Teo was good about it, better than he should be. And it made Wylie want to shake his sister even more. "Are you busy after school tomorrow?"

"Nope. No plans."

Wylie grinned at his nephew's adult answer. "Well, since you have room in your schedule, why don't we go for some ice cream?"

"Are you going to bring Miss Cass?"

"If she wants to go."

"Oh."

"What's wrong?" He looked into Teo's face. It was normally so open, but it had become unreadable. "You don't want her to come?"

"Are you going to marry her?"

The question took him by surprise. There was a time in his life he would have answered with a "yes," without hesitation. "I . . ."

The loud engine of Nova's Jeep prevented him from answering. He put Teo down and made his way out the door and toward his sister and Cass.

Nova was laughing as she got out. His normally abrasive sister looked happy, but he could barely focus on her because his eyes went to Cass. She looked no worse than she did this morning when he last saw her. In fact, she looked a little better. Her cheeks had some color. Her curly hair was windblown. Her eyes didn't look as sad, as empty, as he was used to seeing them.

"Where the hell have you been?" He directed his comment toward his sister, but his gaze went to Cass. He knew she was okay, yet he couldn't stop himself from touching her face and looking into her eyes. "Are you okay?"

She nodded, then leaned in to kiss his cheek, lingering there for a moment. For the second time in the past few minutes, he found himself surprised. "Relax, Wylie. We just went to the store."

"Yeah, Wylie. I can't believe you have this woman locked up in that house with no makeup or girly things." She walked over to him and slapped him on the back. "I had to take her to Target. You owe me a hundred bucks, by the way."

"You took her off island! Without telling me? What the hell is your problem?"

"Of course I took her off island. Where

else were we going to get this kind of stuff? What crawled up your ass anyway?" She rolled her eyes. "She's a grown woman, and unless she is under house arrest, I don't see why she can't go off island."

"Something could have happened. I didn't know where you were. I couldn't get in contact with you. The world doesn't revolve around you, Nova. You can't be so damn inconsiderate all the time."

"Shut up, Wylie James. You're such a controlling son of a —"

"Nova!" Mansi appeared on the porch. "You stop it right now. Your brother is right. You should have told one of us that you were going off island. You should have picked up your phone. Not because you had Cass with you, but because you left your boy here and something could have happened to him and we wouldn't have been able to get in contact with you. You are a mother. You need to think like one."

"You're my grandmother. Why do you always take his side?"

"I'll take your side when you're right."

"Whatever." She rolled her eyes, reaching into her Jeep to hand Cass some plastic bags. "I've got to get out of here." She gave Cass a quick hug. "Let me know if you want to get away from the overbearing son of a bitch."

"Mommy!" Teo called to Nova just as she was about to get back into her car. "Can I sleep at home with you tonight?"

Nova froze, and for the briefest of moments a tortured look crossed her face. "Not tonight, baby." She scooped him up and kissed him all over his face, which was unusual for her. Wylie rarely saw Nova be that openly affectionate with her son. "You're better off here," she said into his ear. "I'll see you tomorrow."

Cassandra's hands felt clammy as she listened to the phone ring for the third time. She must have called her mother thousands of times, but she couldn't remember the last time she really spoke to her. She hadn't felt anything but misery for so long, but now a dozen emotions ran through her. She didn't know how to process them.

"Hello?"

"Mom? It's me."

"My love." Immediately she heard the catch in her mother's voice and it caused her eyes to tear. "How are you? Is that a stupid question? I'm just happy to hear your voice."

"I love you." There were so many thoughts

clamoring around in her head, but the first one was that. "I feel stupid, embarrassed that it got so bad. That I let it get so bad. I'm so sorry you had to put up with it."

"Don't. I don't want to hear that from you. I can't imagine how you felt. Nobody knows what you went through, and nobody blames you for the way you felt. If you want to talk about it, I will, honey, but can we talk about something else for a little while? I just want to know what you've been up to."

"I'm getting to know Wylie again. He's got a family here and seeing them made me realize that I have a family too. I want to know how they have been."

"Of course. Let's start with the good stuff. Your cousin Marsha is getting married again. This makes her third trip down the aisle and I'm having the hardest time picking out a wedding gift for her."

Cass hung up an hour later, and for a long time she sat at Wylie's kitchen table, just thinking about her mother, how happy she sounded on the phone, how normal their conversation was. She hadn't felt normal in so long. She hadn't talked, slept or eaten *normally* for so long that doing average, ordinary things that other people did felt odd. Living life felt odd, but for once, just feeling odd was a welcomed sensation.

Wylie walked into the kitchen and pulled a frying pan out from under the counter. "I thought I'd fry up some chicken for dinner. Is that okay with you?"

"It is." She stood up and went to him. He was still angry. He hadn't said anything since they left Mansi's house, but she could tell. His body was stiff; that pretty, full mouth of his was held in a tight, straight line. There was this kind of heat rolling off him as he stalked around the house that evening.

And she couldn't help but think how damn handsome he was. She placed her hand on his shoulder, unsure of how to touch him. He touched her every night, all the time. She went to sleep with his big, hard, warm body wrapped around hers. At first he was her safety — her big, live security blanket — but now each day, as the life returned to her, she was becoming more and more aware of him. During the past two nights, instead of going to bed looking forward to sleep, she had gone to bed looking forward to feeling his hands on her body.

He turned around to face her, his intense brown gaze bore into her.

"I talked to my mother," she said, not knowing what to say.

"I know. I heard you." The stiffness never left his body, but he took her hand in his and slid his thumbs slowly over her palm. The touch sent tingles along her newly sensitive nerves. It made her heart beat faster and her mouth go slightly dry.

"I asked her to send me my wallet and some of my things," she continued, trying to ignore the effects of his simple touch, trying to pretend that it didn't feel so good. "I owe Nova money."

"No, you don't." His eyes flashed.

"I do. Besides, I think I should have some of my own money. I don't want you to have to take care of me."

"I want to, and I give Nova more than enough to help out with Teo, so you don't need to give her a dime. She's making damn good money at that hair salon now. The least she could do is buy some damn lotion and mascara."

"Did she ask you to give her money for Teo?"

He paused for a moment, his lips smoothing into that fine line again. "Not in so many words. But she asked me to help out with him. And that means paying for T-ball and summer camp, and making sure the boy has new shoes and books and the same stuff every other kid on this island has."

"Why?"

"Why what?"

"Why do you do it if it makes you angry?"

"Giving to my nephew doesn't make me angry. I want him to have everything I wanted as a kid and couldn't have. I promised myself a long time ago that when I had a family, I would make sure none of them would want for anything. It's my damn sister who makes me mad."

"Because she leaves Teo with Mansi?"

He nodded. "He's probably better off there. At least I know none of the guys she's dating will be around him. He doesn't need any more of her bad decisions affecting his life. She doesn't think about anyone but herself."

"I don't think that's true."

"You spent three hours with her. You don't know her."

"You don't know her either," she countered. "I like Nova. I think she's sweet."

"And I think you're crazy." He let go of her hand, only to grab her waist and pull her closer to him. Her breasts settled against his chest. As his hands smoothed their way up her backside, her nipples tightened, her breath quickened and her knees went a little bit weak. She kept her face neutral; at least she tried to, because she had so many unresolved feelings about him. He walked out on her. That thought circled around in her head at night as they lay entwined in his bed. He broke her heart. No word. No reason why. No explanation.

Before, she was too devastated to be angry, but now when she thought about it, the hurt snuck up. The anger, the bitterness over having all her plans changed, came up again.

His lips settled on her cheek and he kissed her there before sliding his mouth down to her jaw, where he left a half-dozen soft, sweet kisses until he reached her ear. "You feel so much better against me," he whispered.

She pried her eyes opened, not realizing that they had closed. She couldn't melt in his arms like she used to when they were together. She didn't want him to know how much his touch affected her. She had married another man. She had created life with a husband that wasn't Wylie. She still wore that man's ring on her hand. He was gone, for over a year now, but a little part of her felt like she was still married to him. It was as if Terrance was going to walk through the door any moment now. And that was why a part of her felt guilty for enjoying Wylie's touch so much.

His hands slipped up the baggy, shapeless shirt she was wearing. He touched her belly, rubbed his thumb over the lumpy scar, where she was shot. She stiffened then, but he didn't stop. She didn't want him to stop. His hands kept traveling up her torso, stopping at the band of her serviceable white bra. She wanted him to keep going, to feel her breasts, to rub his thumbs across her nipples. But he didn't. He stopped where he was and leaned in to kiss her. She didn't kiss him back. She just kept her mouth soft and open for him to invade. It was almost as though she didn't know how to react, as if she had forgotten how, like she was sixteen years old again and this was her first kiss. But it wasn't her first kiss. She had been kissed countless times by him, but it had been so long since she had been kissed by him like this. All those feelings rushed back, every heady moment, every explosive sensation she'd ever had, came back.

He broke the kiss, hugging her close and resting his lips on her forehead. "You want cheesy garlic mashed potatoes or ones with plain old-fashioned brown gravy?"

It took her a moment to process what he was saying, to recover from that kiss. "How about we go wild and you let me make some with bacon and cheddar?"

"You want to help me cook?"

"Yes. I do."

Wylie woke up with a start later that night. He almost forgot where he was. He forgot he was in his bed, in his little house by the sea. He forgot Cass was there, warming him up and driving him crazy every time her body brushed his as she slept.

He'd dreamed about them again. About his unit that barely survived that rocket attack. Time had faded the intensity of the dreams. After it first happened, he couldn't close his eyes without seeing the explosion, without smelling his friends' burning flesh, without hearing their screams of pain. It had been a while since he dreamed about them, about the reason he had finally chosen not to reenlist. Aquinnah soothed him, being a place that was so different from Iraq, from Afghanistan. A place that had never been touched by war helped his still-fragile mind.

But tonight he dreamed about them again, and as Cass shifted herself closer to him, he knew she was the reason why. Whenever things weren't going smoothly, or he was stressed, his dreams would return. His PTSD would sneak up on him and screw with the life he had carved out for himself.

It had gotten really bad after he found out Terrance was dead, and that Cass had been shot.

"Wylie." Cass half moaned his name. He had inched away from her in his sleep, now on the other side of the bed. "Come back." She reached out for him and he obeyed her call, gathering her close to him. He hardened as soon as she had come into contact with him. This was the problem. Controlling himself around her. It would be so easy to turn her on her back, slip her panties down her legs and push himself inside her.

She would let him offering up no resistance, but making love to her like that would only offer limited satisfaction. He would never know if she was making love to him or to the memory of her husband. She still wore Terrance's ring. Every time he looked at it, every time he felt that little piece of metal on his skin, it served as a barrier, a reminder of what the world told him could never be his.

He was smart enough now to know that the world didn't control him. But Cass did. He could never be with her unless he knew she wanted it.

This arrangement wasn't going to work. He couldn't continue sharing a bed with

her each night. It was the worst kind of
torture.

CHAPTER 9

Lightning flashed before her just as she pulled into the driveway that led to Wylie's new apartment, causing her entire car to light up and making her jump nearly out of her skin. It had been torrential downpours the whole two-hour drive from her campus. The nasty weather made her nervous, but what she was about to do next made her hands sweat and her heart pound more than anything she had ever done before.

Nobody knew she was here. She had lied to her parents, telling them that she would still be up at school for another few days, that she had finals to finish. But she was done with all her tests that afternoon, and as of four P.M., done with her third year of college.

In school she had her freedom. No one to watch over her. No parents to tell her what to do. No unspoken rules to live by. Each time she returned home for break, it became harder and harder to live under her parents' roof, harder to live in Harmony Falls. And as time went on, she was starting to think that she might like to start out her life somewhere else. Another city. Another state. Maybe she would go to grad school on the other side of the country.

She wasn't sure what she wanted to do with her life, but she knew she wanted to spend time with him. Wylie had been on her mind lately. Much more than he probably wanted to be.

She left the safety of her car, with overnight bag in hand, and dashed up the flight of steps that led to his apartment over the garage. He finally had moved out of the Millers' house this year. She was proud of him. She knew holding down two jobs and going to school full-time couldn't have been easy, but he needed to carve out his own space in the world.

She raised her hand to knock, worried that he wouldn't hear her over all the rain and thunder, but the door flew open just as her hand was about to connect with it. Wylie stood there, just in a pair of blue boxers.

"Cass?" His eyes widened with recognition. "What are you doing here?" He yanked her inside, pulling her dripping-wet jacket off her body.

"You didn't go to your graduation, Wylie James."

"What?"

"It was this past weekend. You got your degree. You did it. Why didn't you go?"

He looked bashful. "It's just an associate's degree in business. And it took me a hell of a long time to get it. It's nothing to compare to the degrees you and Terrance will be getting next year. Ouch!"

She pinched him. She wanted to slap him, but she couldn't bring herself to hit him. "What the hell is wrong with you? Why can't you be proud of yourself? It's not just an associate's degree. It's something you worked hard for. It's something you did while holding down two jobs and paid for all by yourself. I'm proud of you. I'm sure Terrance is proud of you, and if nobody else would have been at your commencement ceremony, we would have been there cheering you on. We would have been there to celebrate you."

He blinked at her; and then before she knew it, he had her backed against his door, his lips sealed to her mouth, kissing her until she had no air.

"Did you come here just to tell me that?"

"No. I came here because I love you and I wanted to see you."

He groaned, resting his head against hers.

"What did I tell you about saying that to me?"

"That you hate it when I do."

"No." He kissed her forehead. "I don't hate it. How could I hate hearing that?"

"I want you to let me love you." She cupped his face in her hands and kissed his pretty, full mouth before stepping away. The apartment was small; it was an in-law suite over a garage. It was sparse, but it seemed warm and homey on the cold, rainy spring night. She peeled her sweatshirt off, over her head, and stripped off her jeans. She could feel Wylie's eyes on her as she did. She was so nervous. So afraid he was going to reject her, but she wouldn't be able to live with herself if she didn't try.

There was a blanket on the couch. Her mother had crocheted it for him as a housewarming present. She wrapped it around herself as she sat on the couch and then she held her hand out to him. "Come."

He hesitated, but did as she asked. She opened the blanket, inviting him into her embrace. For a long time they just lay there together, skin pressed to skin, bodies hugged close together. "I want to be with you," she finally said.

"You are with me."

"You know what I mean, Wylie James. There's been no one else since you took my virginity three years ago."

"No?" He trailed his fingers down her neck. "I had wondered. Especially after the last time we were together. You definitely didn't seem like a girl who'd only made love twice before."

"When you're only with the man you love once a year, you try to make it count." She dropped a slow kiss on his lips. "But I can't do it anymore. I can't be with you just once a year."

"This time will be twice this year."

"Wylie, you know what I want from you."

"Yes." He shut his eyes. "I know what you want. You think it's been easy for me? Every time I see you, I want you. Every time I have you, I don't want to let you go. But I have to, because you're not meant for me."

"If you say this is about Terrance, I'm going to punch you. There is nothing between us. He has a girlfriend. He's —"

"I'm going to enlist."

"What?" Her eyes locked on his, not sure if he was serious.

"In the Marines. I have to do something with my life, and if I stay around here, I'll be stuck. I'll always be that poor boy the Millers took in. I need to do something with my life that I can be proud of."

She nodded, understanding how difficult it must have been growing up with no parents, in a house where he was almost treated like a second-class citizen. She was scared for him. Terrified. Marines died. So many men and women never came back. "If you want to enlist, I'll support you, but I don't see what that has to do with me being your girlfriend."

"Cass." He grinned at her, one of the big, beautiful, open grins that she had seen so rarely from him. "What am I going to do with you?"

"Love me." She kissed his throat as her hands explored his chest and torso. Each time they were together, she could feel the changes in his body. Less of a boy, more of a man — it excited her. Sex was still so new to her and she wasn't sure how to interpret all the sensations that crashed down on her when he was near. She was growing damp; that throb between her legs growing more and more persistent. Her nipples scraped against the fabric of her bra and all she could think of was how much she wanted to be free of the little bit of clothing she had on. She wanted to feel his hard body on top of hers, inside hers with no barriers between them. "Please don't go yet though."

"You got me, Cass, but if we are going to do this, we have to be quiet about it."

"Why?"

"Because I'm the last man anybody wants

for you."

She wanted to protest that, but she couldn't. She knew what her parents expected from her. She knew the kind of man her doctor father wanted her to bring home. "You're what I want for me."

She slid her fingers into his boxers, taking his manhood in her hand. It hardened instantly, and she couldn't help but glide her palm up and down it. She loved the little pained noise he made, the way his breath quickened. The way he said her name.

"Cass!"

Her eyes flew open and she realized that she wasn't twenty years old and lying on Wylie's couch about to make love to him. She was thirty-one and in his bed.

"Please," Wylie begged her, his face pained. "Let go before I do something I regret."

His swollen manhood was in her hand. She wanted to say it was sleep that had addled her mind, made her slow to respond, but it hadn't. She liked the way he felt in her hand, the thickness of him. Immediately she wondered what it would feel like against her lips as she kissed it, how the long, slow slide would feel when he pushed inside her.

"Cass!" he barked. She let go that time,

missing the weight of it in her hand.

"I'm sorry. I was sleeping. Did I hurt you?"

"Did you hurt me?" His expression grew bewildered and then he was on top of her, his hardness pressing against her underwear. "You want to know if you hurt me. How the hell do you think it's going to feel to have this thing swinging between my legs all day? There aren't enough cold showers in the world."

"Oh." She stopped herself from moving against him. Her body wanted to, and it was screaming to relieve the pressure that was building between her legs. But her head made her pause. "You've got a hand. You could use it."

He flung himself off her and onto his back; a loud bark of laughter escaped his chest. "If you ever wanted to know why I'm so crazy about you, it's that, right there. You always take me by surprise."

He left her then, getting out of bed and into the shower. She hoped he took her advice, and she hoped that while he did so, he thought about her.

Wylie drove to his work site after dropping Cassandra off at Mansi's house that morning. He hadn't said much to her. He could barely look her in the eye, not because he was embarrassed, but because he wanted her so bad. The fact he woke up to her stroking him was fate, or karma, or God plotting against him. He had told himself that he couldn't go on sleeping in the same bed with her, but until she slipped her hand down his boxers, he really didn't think he could send her to sleep in another room. But he was going to have to now.

She was looking better. Every single day he saw it. Her face wasn't gaunt. Her body was filling out nicely. She was starting to care about what she looked like. She wore makeup today. Just a little. Mascara. Maybe a little lip gloss. She had pinned her hair up and out of her face. She was always beautiful to him, but today she looked pretty.

She was healing. Still sad, but healing. It was all he could ask for.

He got out of his truck and found Tanner showing John, one of their older workers, how to wire breakers to a circuit. "You've seen me do this enough times. I want you to do the rest by yourself, okay?"

John looked at him. "You sure?"

"What kind of question is that? You think I'd risk the safety of this family if I thought you couldn't do it?"

"I don't know. You might if you were a

dumbass."

Tanner laughed his loud, happy laugh and slapped John on the back. "Get to work, old man."

John picked up a wire, ready to perform his task, but paused. "I'm not so old, you know. I was on drugs for a long time. I drank too much. I screwed up too much. Not a lot of people trust me. I thought I ran out of chances a long time ago. But you trust me, and I appreciate that."

"You think you're the only one who drank too much? I screwed up too. A hell of a lot more than anybody knows. How do you think I ended up in the army?"

"That wasn't a choice?" Wylie asked, letting himself be known.

"Nah. It was the army or prison kind of thing," Tanner said, turning to him. "Why did you join up?"

"To impress a girl." He shrugged. "Same reason every man joins the Marines. I need you to come with me today, Tanner. John will be all right by himself. He was the handyman round here for years. Plus the rumor is this man was the king of hot-wiring cars."

"Haven't done that in years. These new cars are a bitch to get going now."

"Get to it, man," Tanner said to John as

he walked with Wylie out the door. "What's up? Do we need to go pick up supplies?"

"Yes and no. I need to fix up the house for Cassandra. She needs her own bedroom."

"Tired of sleeping on that old lumpy couch of yours? I'm surprised you lasted this long."

Wylie shook his head and got back in his truck. "Wasn't on the couch," he said once Tanner climbed in on the passenger side.

"You made that sad widow lady sleep on the couch. I thought they said Southern men had manners. You seem like a dick."

"Of course I didn't make her sleep on the couch!"

Tanner looked at him, disgust, confusion, then understanding, crossing his face. "Um, you sleeping in the same bed as your dead best friend's wife?"

"Yes, and I can't take it anymore." He pulled off, going over the mental checklist of things he had to do to make the room livable.

"No. I guess you can't. I don't want to pry, but you want to tell me what the hell is going on with you and her?"

"Nothing," he said, which wasn't strictly true. "Cassandra was married to my best friend. But she was my girlfriend first. We were together for over two years."

"And this best friend of yours stole her?"

"No. I left." He shook his head. "It's complicated. My father and Terrance's father were good friends as kids, and before my pop died, he sent me to live with him. Cassandra was their next-door neighbor. I was thirteen years old when I first met her, and she got me right then and there. She smiled at me and I was done. But so was Terrance. He always loved her. He had known her since they were little kids. She was *his* best friend. She was meant for *him*, and the whole damn town knew it. I grew up my whole damn life knowing that they were going to end up together. The doctor's daughter was supposed to marry the lawyer's son. There was no place for me in that equation. I knew that and I tried to stay away from her. Only Cass wouldn't let me. She didn't give a damn what anybody thought."

"So why is she your best friend's widow and not your wife?"

"We kept it quiet for so long, but somehow Mr. Miller, Terrance's father, found out. He's a good man. He took me in without a thought. He raised me. He was good to me, but he showed up at my apartment one day with Cassandra's daddy and they sat me down. They told me I had nothing to offer her. No money. No future. I was a nice kid, but Cassandra deserved better. She deserved Terrance. She was too smart to make a life with a kid who literally had come from pig shit. And even if we were happy for a while, she would end up resenting me for making her miss out on the things she could have had."

"I hope you told them to fuck off."

"I did in so many words. But part of me knew they were right. Terrance had everything. Big, fancy degree. Money. A job right out of school that I could never get. And people respected him. I knew I wasn't good enough. I knew the moment I met her."

"So you left then."

"No. I left after Terrance found out. I left the night I almost killed him."

Cass watched Teo from her spot on the couch. He was sitting at the dining-room table, a worksheet before him and the contents of his pencil box spread across the table. His little shoulders were hunched and she could see by the amount of times he erased his writing that he was struggling with his homework. She looked at Mansi to see if she had noticed, but she was dozing, oblivious to her great-grandson's problem.

Cass didn't want to get up. She didn't want to go over there to see what he was working on, but she did. So many people discounted what kindergarten teachers did, but she knew if a child had a bad experience in kindergarten, it could affect his whole school career.

"What's the matter, kid?"

He looked up at her, his face full of frustration. "My letters don't look right and I'm supposed to practice reading my sight words, but I don't know what they say. I never know what they say." He shoved the crinkled homework calendar at her.

"It says you're supposed to practice with an adult. Does your mom practice with you?"

"Not really."

"What about Mansi?"

"She needs new glasses. She can't see words real good."

"I can help you."

A little bit of hope sparked in his eyes, but then it faded. "Uncle Wylie says I'm not supposed to bother you."

"Hush up about your uncle. He's not the boss of me."

"That's what my mom says." He grinned at her. She felt that little painful twinge in her chest as she looked at his adorable but dirty face. She got up, needing to get away from him for a moment. But she only got as far as the kitchen before she returned with some wet paper towels and a felt-tip marker.

"You're a mess." She cleaned his face. He squirmed a bit, but she was determined to get the ketchup off the corner of his mouth and dirt smear off his cheek. "And you smell like a funky little boy."

"What do 'funky little boys' smell like?"

"Dirt and cooties."

She took his hands in hers, studying his fingernails that needed to be cut. "Tell me," she said, wiping his little fingers. "What do you do to get all scraped up?"

He shrugged. "I play."

"Well, it's easier to write with clean hands. Can you show me how you write?" He gripped the pencil hard, forcing it across the paper, but his problem wasn't uncommon. Some kids found it hard to write with pencils. There was too much traction on the paper. "Try with this marker. Just don't hold it so tightly. If it explodes, Mansi will kick your butt for sure."

He did as she asked and, sure enough, the marker glided across the paper and his messy letters became more clear. "Beautiful work. I think that is just about a perfect letter *H.*"

Teo beamed at her and that little painful twinge bloomed into a full-blown one. She ignored it. She had to. She had been avoiding feeling this kind of pain for so long that she ceased to feel anything at all.

"Okay. Write four more and then let's practice reading these words."

"How did your husband die?" he asked out of nowhere a few minutes later.

"What a morbid question for a five-year-old. Why do you want to know?"

"Mansi says it makes a difference how people die when they are young. Mansi's brother died in the war, so he's a hero. My grandmother drank too much and died because of that, and that's a bad way to die. My dad is dead too. My mom says he got hit by a Mack truck and that he probably had it coming, because he was an asshole."

"You shouldn't curse." Cassandra shook her head, uncomfortable with the conversation, with how and why Teo knew so much. "And they shouldn't talk about such things with you."

"Why not? I'm going to find out anyway. How did your husband die?"

"He was shot," she told him because she couldn't lie to him. "He was trying to save me."

"So he was a hero?"

"Yes."

"You're proud of him."

"I am. Very."

"See? That's a good thing."

Wylie arrived at Mansi's house a little later than usual. He and Tanner had worked all day to make the room he chose for Cass habitable. They had to replace one of the windows and clear out what must have been forty years of old junk, but the room was looking better. Not ready for her, but better. He wanted to give it a fresh coat of paint and get her a nice bedspread and new sheets before he showed it to her.

He was kind of glad that Cassandra had burrowed herself under his skin. It gave him the push he needed to fix up the rest of the house.

"Thanks again for today, Tanner. It would have taken me weeks to get it done alone."

"No problem. I was thinking it was time we start to give the guys a little more freedom. I think they can handle it. I can help you tomorrow too."

"That would be great. I was going to take Teo and Cass out for ice cream, but let me take you all out to dinner."

Nova's Jeep came roaring up behind them, blasting some Beyoncé song. She locked eyes with him through the windshield as she put her car in park. He was pretty sure she only blasted the music for his benefit. He had said something to her once about it. That turned out to be a mistake, because now every time she saw him, she turned her music up.

"She's such a goddamn kid."

Tanner said nothing, but Wylie couldn't help but notice how the man's eyes never left Nova as she jumped out of her Jeep and walked toward his truck. She had on a tight white T-shirt and tight black pants; her heels were so high, he was surprised she hadn't broken her neck. Part of him wanted to smack Tanner for staring, but he couldn't blame the man for looking at his sister. All men looked at his sister.

"Hey, bro," she said to him as he got out of his truck. "Hey, tall, dark and dummy," she said to Tanner as she looked him over.

"Real mature, Nova." Tanner shook his head. "How old are you anyway? Wait, don't answer. I shouldn't have asked. I know you can't count that high."

"I'd slap you for saying that, but I don't want to be arrested for animal abuse."

"Ouch, Nova, that one stung. I'm impressed. I've never met someone with such a small mind inside such a big head before."

"I don't have a big head!"

Wylie walked away from them and went inside the house. He had witnessed their arguments before. They could go at it for hours.

"Hello, Miss Mansi. How are you today?" He bent to kiss the older woman's cheek.

"Just fine, Alabama."

"Would you like to come out to dinner tonight? Nova just pulled up, so she's probably going to come along, but I was going to take Tanner, Cass and Teo."

"You know I don't like to go out to eat. Gives me indigestion. But take the boy. He took Cass to the beach about an hour ago."

"Cass went out with Teo?"

"He said he wanted to show her something. They left through the back door."

There was a tiny strip of a beach about a ten-minute walk from Mansi's cottage. In his mind he knew they would be fine when he found them, but he couldn't stop his heart from racing at the thought of Cass and Teo alone. Teo was high energy, and while Cass said she was ready to take on more, he wasn't sure the company of a kindergartner was what she needed right now. But as he came up to them, he realized he had no idea what Cass needed right now. They were sitting in the sand, side by side,

Teo leaning against Cass. The last time he had found them together, it had been in bed, Teo curled against Cass, like he had known her forever.

Kids had always been drawn to her. She had this way about her that seemed to invite them and make them feel welcome. He knew she was one hell of a teacher. And he knew she would have made a hell of a great mother, given the chance.

"The belly goes the other way on a lowercase *b*," Wylie heard Cass say. As he got closer, he could see that Teo had a stick and was writing in the sand. That alone made him pause. Getting Teo to do his homework was like pulling teeth. His mother couldn't get him to do it without a fight. Mansi didn't take any fooling around from Teo, but even with her, Teo struggled to get things done. But here he was with Cass, voluntarily writing letters.

"I get confused sometimes. I never know which way is right."

"Want to know a trick?" She took the stick and drew an uppercase *B* in the sand. "If you get stuck write an uppercase *B* and erase the hump on top. And ta-da!" She erased the hump. "Lowercase *b*."

"That's cool. How do you know so much stuff?"

"I was a teacher, but I don't do that anymore."

"Why not? You're good."

"Thank you." She tousled his hair. "I got sad when my husband died and I didn't want to do it anymore."

"I don't wanna do stuff when I'm sad either. Maybe one day you won't be sad no more."

"Maybe I won't. Being sad kind of sucks."

"Hey," Wylie said, making his presence known. "You guys want to go out to dinner? I think your mom and Tanner are going to come."

"Mommy's going to come?" Teo looked up at him so hopefully that it almost broke his damn heart.

"Yeah. I'll make sure she does."

"Did she say that?" Teo knew his mother, and while Nova wasn't one to break promises to him, she wasn't prone to make them either.

"She's at the house. You tell her that I said I'm taking you all out to dinner and she'd better be ready in ten minutes."

"Okay." He grinned at him. "She doesn't like it when you boss her around."

"Well, I'm the big brother, so I get to. Now go on and tell her what I said."

Teo took off, leaving Wylie alone with

170

Cass. She was quiet, staring thoughtfully at the letter *B* still left in the sand.

"Are you all right?"

She stood up and hugged him tightly, burying her face in his chest. As soon as her body came into contact with his, that same rush, that heat, that excitement, which he always felt, came over him. Thank God he was fixing up her room. He wasn't sure how much longer he could stand her closeness. Once again he was questioning his judgment in bringing her here. He knew he hadn't done it just for her. He had brought her here for himself, and he knew his self-control wouldn't last long.

"Talk to me, Cass." He slowly ran his hands down her back.

"I like him," she said softly.

"Who? Teo?"

"Yes, but he knows too much."

"Was he being fresh? I'll get on him for that."

"No." She shook her head and looked up at him. "He wasn't being fresh. He knows too much about life and death and loss. He's only five. A baby. He shouldn't know so much."

"No, but I think growing up too fast is one of the hazards of being born into my family. What were you two talking about anyway?"

"He asked me about Terrance. He wanted to know how he died."

Wylie swore under his breath. "What did you tell him?"

"The truth. He died trying to save me. I feel bad. Not for telling him, but for how he responded. He made me feel comforted and sad all at the same time. There is so much of him that reminds me of the boys I taught, but there is an old soul in him too." She buried her face in his chest again and sighed. "I don't know what the hell I'm talking about. Ignore me. I'm being crazy."

"You're not." He kissed her nose. "Let me take you to dinner. What do you feel like eating?"

"Ribs and French fries. And beer. Dark beer, like I used to drink in college."

"That's doable." He grinned at her. "In fact, that sounds amazing."

Cassandra stared at the wall very early that next morning, sleep escaping her. The previous day's thoughts filled her head in a never-ending flow. She had gone out to dinner. She had sat at a table in a low-key barbecue joint and ordered the most decadent thing on the menu. She drank beer. She had dessert. She listened to stories. She had enjoyed herself.

Really and truly enjoyed herself.

And she couldn't remember the last time she had done that. Terrance and she had a small group of couples they sometimes socialized with. They went out to quiet dinners at five-star restaurants, saw plays, had wine tastings and toured museums. They had conversations about politics and cultural happenings. She liked those people. She liked Terrance's friends. She found them interesting, but she always felt a little out of place with them. Like the simple schoolteacher was putting on airs just to keep up with the cool kids.

Then there was tonight. Everyone ate with their hands and laughed freely and loudly. They talked about television shows and action movies they had enjoyed. She watched Tanner and Nova trade barbs across the table and look at each other with hot looks that were barely disguised. Teo babbled happily about nothing and knocked his apple juice all over the table. She left there sticky, and tipsy and overfull. She had a good time, even though that cloud of sadness never fully lifted from her shoulders. She enjoyed herself and she never once felt out of place, or worried about her elbows on the table or what she said or what anybody was thinking of her.

And she felt guilty for that. She felt guilty for having a better time with a messy five-year-old, two bickering adults and the man who broke her heart than with Terrance, her best friend and the man whom she chose to devote her life to.

She snuggled closer to Wylie. He hadn't come to bed until late; when he did, he stayed far away from her, his back turned to her, as if he didn't want to touch her at all. She was confused by that, by him. He touched her, whenever he was around her. He touched her like he couldn't help but touch her.

Last night at dinner his fingertips had grazed the bare skin of her arm; his hand had settled on her knee; when he spoke to her, it was always close to her ear, his breath always tickling her skin. Every touch, every Alabama-accented soft word he spoke, sent a dozen sensations along her nerves. It reminded her that she was alive, that it felt good to be able to feel.

Then there was tonight, when he lay on the other side of the bed, when she couldn't feel his warmth, when she had to reach out to touch him. It was like her security blanket was gone. But he was back now. His body wrapped around her, his hands underneath her nightgown, one cupping her belly, the other her breast. He was hard. She could feel his erection prodding her backside. She thought back to yesterday morning, when she held him in her hand, when she dreamed about them on his couch, making love. She remembered how he felt on top of her, the way he pressed his hardness into her to show her how much he wanted her. Or maybe he didn't want her. He had flung himself away from her. He didn't try to make love to her. He turned away from her last night. He had walked away from her ten years ago. Maybe she was just another woman in his bed. Maybe he was a man who reacted like any other man when in close proximity to a nearly naked woman.

Still, she pushed herself closer, wanting to feel more of him, wanting to feel more of his arousal because it mirrored her own. She was damp with want, throbbing between her legs; her nipples were hard little points, begging to be touched.

She had always liked sex, to be touched and kissed and loved, the closeness with somebody else. But she hadn't had sex in so long, even before Terrance had died. And she knew the last time she was made love to, because it was the day she had conceived her baby.

She shut that thought out by wrapping her hand around the one that was cupping her breast. The feeling of his rough skin, scraping her sensitive flesh, made her desire spike a few notches. He let out a little moan in his sleep and squeezed her breast. His lips came to rest in the crook of her neck; the hand that was on her belly slipped down to her hip, where he shifted her. She knew what was coming. He would peel away her panties, so that she would be bare to him, and he'd touch her, rubbing her in that aching spot with his thick fingers, making her even more ready for when he slid inside. They had made love like this before. Sleepy, slow, languorous, luxurious.

Luxurious because it was a luxury to be so close, so intimate. It was luxury because she only ever felt that good with him.

He rubbed against her, seeking her opening, only to find that there were barriers between them, her panties and his boxers.

"Fuck," he swore violently. "Shit." He tore himself away from her completely, leaving the bed. He stood over her for a moment, just looking, and in his eyes she could see anger, regret and pain. There were too many emotions there and she wondered what was going on in his brain.

And just as she was about to ask, he grabbed his discarded clothes from the night before and stormed out of the room.

CHAPTER 10

Wylie rolled down the windows in his truck. He had been overheated for hours, but that had nothing to do with the temperature outside. Cass had made him hot. But now as the sun went higher in the sky, he was starting to feel the actual heat of the day. It was hotter than normal for mid-September; the temperature was creeping up to nearly eighty and it wasn't even nine A.M. yet. It was going to be a warm day, but he didn't care how hot it became in the room he was fixing up for Cass. He needed her out of his bed as soon as possible.

He couldn't blame her for what almost happened that morning. He had his hands on her breast; his erection had been poking her backside. He had crossed the boundary that he had set for himself last night. He found her in his sleep. He started to make love to her in his sleep. They were like magnets — always attracted to one another, always a little difficult to separate, always giving in to that pull.

He left the house before sunrise. He had to. He had to get away from her. Jumping into a cold shower and stroking himself to completion wasn't enough. He had been in a dangerous mood. If he was close to her, he knew he wouldn't have been able to stop himself, so he drove around the island. He stopped at Mansi's house, because he knew the old woman was up by five. He showered there. Saw that Nova had spent the night there and dropped Teo off at school. All of that. All of the distraction and distance didn't help. He still wanted her. He hurt with it: his teeth, his head, his heart.

And the only thought that kept going on in his head: *Things would be different if I hadn't left.*

He finally returned to his house. He had to get Cass and drop her off at Mansi's so that he could meet Tanner at ten to work on the house. But when he went upstairs, she wasn't there. Not in the bathroom, kitchen or any of the spare bedrooms. He ran down the stairs, with his heart knocking against his rib cage.

Had she left him? Had she walked away? Her mother had overnighted some of her things: her wallet and her cell phone. When he walked toward the door, he saw that they were still sitting in the box where she had left them last night.

He went outside, standing there for a moment, trying to fight the fear that was choking him. She was healing, growing stronger every day, but she wasn't strong enough yet. And he had mistreated her. Touched her body like it was still his to enjoy; then he walked away from her again, but this time it was for hours and not for years.

Maybe she was smarter than he was. Maybe she knew that this situation, her living with him for an undetermined amount of time, was a stupid plan. But then he noticed the footprints. There were bare footprints on the sandy path that led to the little beach he owned.

He forced himself to calm, for the panic to seep away as he followed those tracks. He found her, splashing in the water, just dressed in her simple white bra and little cotton panties. He grew hard all over again. Overheated. He knew he should give her this time, give her some privacy, and then wait for her back at the house, but he didn't want to. He couldn't. His feet forced him forward, toward her.

She heard him approach and froze, before slowly turning around to face him. "Hi."

She folded her arms across her chest as if trying to hide from him.

He sat on the sand, slipped off his socks and boots so he could feel the cool, still-damp earth beneath his toes.

"You said I could come here if I wanted," she said defensively. "That this could be my place too."

"I did," he agreed. "Do you want to be alone?"

He wanted her to say no. He willed her to say no; but if she asked him, he would leave. He didn't deserve to be around her in that moment.

"I didn't want you to see me in my underwear."

"I've seen you naked," he reminded her. "Recently too. Why are you worried about your underwear?"

"They look bad." She looked down at herself. "I'm awake enough to realize that now and I'm thoroughly embarrassed by it."

"They don't look so bad. And even if they do, who cares?"

"I do." She stepped out of the water, coming closer to him, but then she stopped herself, looking unsure. "Where did you go this morning?"

"I — I had errands this morning."

"Oh? I thought it was because you woke up with your hands on my breasts. I know they aren't what they used to be, but they shouldn't have scared you away."

Her words made him smile, made him get off his feet and go to her. "They're bigger now than the last time I touched them." He wrapped his hands around her waist, pulling her closer, knowing it was a mistake the moment he felt her soft skin.

"Age and two pounds of ribs will do that to a girl," she said, her voice a little breathy. "I had fun last night at dinner. I didn't tell you that, but I did. Thank you for that."

"You don't need to thank me."

"I do." She nodded. "I need to start doing that — telling people how I feel in the moment — because I never know if I'm going to see them again. Losing Terrance so quickly taught me that."

It was a beautiful sentiment and a horribly sad thought all at the same time. "How are you feeling right now?" It was a dangerous question, an unfair one, because he wouldn't be able to answer it truthfully if she asked the same of him.

"Confused." She looked him in the eye. "Uncomfortable. You touched me this morning."

"I'm sorry."

"Why?" She searched his face. "I don't want you to be. I need to be touched. It reminds me that I am still alive."

Alive . . . and so very lovely.

Her words, it seemed, were all the invitation he needed. He wanted to touch her and she wanted to be touched. He moved his hands from her waist to her belly. He touched her lumpy scar, the one that reminded him how close he was to losing her, and how badly he wanted to keep her now that he'd found her again. She stiffened a little, but she allowed him to touch her. He moved from that spot soon and brought her fully against him. He could feel her nipples through her wet bra, hard and aroused. He wanted to free them and touch them, roll them between his fingers, suck them into his mouth, but he didn't. There were so many other things he wanted to do to her too. He settled for her throat. He kissed it, with slow, dragging, soft kisses. Her breathing quickened; she let out little pants and moans as he made sure that every spot of skin on her neck was touched by his lips.

"This feels good," she told him. "Thank you."

Her words made him grow a little harder, drove him to touch her a little more boldly. He smoothed his hands down her backside, cupping her behind in his hands, squeezing it.

Calm down, he warned himself. He had barely touched her and yet he felt like he was going to explode.

He forced himself away from her, not completely away but enough to slow him down.

She must have thought he was finished, that this interlude was over, because she took his hands and kissed each one. Then she turned to walk away from him.

"No." He grabbed her, pulled her against him so that her back touched his front. "Not yet. I'm not done."

Excitement flooded through her as she heard Wylie's accented voice whisper those words in her ear. He was hard. He was hot. He wanted her. His lips touched the back of her neck, just lightly, making her jump with anticipation. His fingers curled around her breast as his other hand did a slow slide down her stomach. "Let me make you feel good." His voice had grown rougher, strained; she recognized the tone. It was the tone he always had when arousal was making it too hard for him to speak. "Please. Let me make you feel good."

She just nodded, unable to speak at all.

His big hand slipped into her underwear and he let out a hiss of pleasure when he found her wetness. He just felt for a moment, touching her mound, getting re-acquainted with the shape of her lips. The simple touches set her further on edge. She moved against him, trying to seek relief from the throbbing that he was causing.

"Let me," he urged as he grasped her hip to keep her still. She relented, allowing him to be in control. He entered her with the slow slide of one thick finger. Her knees buckled, but he caught her, taking her weight on with his body. He rubbed her in slow circles: once, twice, three times, before she came totally apart. Three times before the waves and waves of orgasm hit her, taking her breath and making her want him all over again.

She turned to look at him, taking his face in her hands. He stiffened slightly, disappointment crossing his face.

"What? What's wrong?"

"Nothing." He kissed her lips once. "Let's get back to the house. I have to go to work."

He would have made love to her. He would have laid her down in the sand and made love to her until he made up for every one of those ten years that he spent away from her, but she touched his face. She touched his face and he felt the slightly cool metal of her ring. Her wedding band reminded him that she had married Terrance. She probably still felt married to him. She still loved him. He was just a stand-in for the man she wanted to be with.

"You look like hell," Tanner said in greeting when he found him later that morning.

"You ain't so goddamn gorgeous yourself."

"Whoa!" Tanner held up his hands in defense. "And I thought you were nicer than your sister. I see cranky pain in the ass runs in the family."

"It does." He wiped his hand over his face, as if that could wash away his mental exhaustion. "And I know I'm being an asshole, but I don't care to stop being one at the moment, so you are just going to have to deal with me being unpleasant for the whole damn day."

"It's Cassandra, isn't it?"

"Damn girl has been screwing with my life since I was thirteen years old. Probably going to screw with me long after I'm dead."

"I like her," Tanner admitted. "She's seems all quiet and sad, but she's a smartass. And I like a little bit of a smartass in a lady."

"She's different than she was when we

first met. How could she not be different after all she's been through? But I like her just as much as I did before I left."

"So what's the problem then?"

"She married him."

"You walked away, and if he loved her like you said, what did you expect her to do?"

"I don't know. I walked away. I know this is my fault, but I wish she hadn't married him. I wish she had married anyone but him."

When Cassandra arrived at Mansi's house that morning, she found the older woman sitting in her usual spot. There was a giant glass of iced tea in her hand, and a bowl of chocolate ice cream was in her lap.

"Ice cream in the morning?" she asked as she sat beside her.

"Yeah." Mansi raised one of her white brows and pinned her with a rebellious stare. "I'm old. I'll eat what I want, when I want. If you got a problem with that, write to your congressman."

"I don't have a problem with it." Cassandra wanted to laugh. "I was just wondering if I could have some too."

Mansi grinned at her. "Of course. I've got four kinds in the freezer. Just don't eat the cotton candy. It's for Teo and it's disgusting."

"I won't. Can I do anything for you today? Do you need weeds pulled or laundry done? I can cook pretty well. Can I make you something?"

"You're getting bored with me, girl?" Mansi nodded. "Good. You're getting better. I don't need any help, but Nova does. She's in the kitchen."

"Nova's here?"

"Yes. She spent the night here with Teo. I think she's putting away groceries."

When she walked into the kitchen, she found Nova at the counter, placing sliced carrots into a plastic container. She watched her silently for a moment as Nova meticulously placed each piece. Curious, Cassandra walked closer to see that Nova was turning those carrot sticks into whiskers.

"You're making a cat!" Cass stood beside her, studying the sandwich she was turning into an art project. "Wow, Nova! This is beautiful."

"Thank you." She watched the normally bold woman become bashful. "I saw these bento box things on the Internet and thought I would try to make them for Teo. Silly kid won't eat a vegetable normally, but if I slap some eyes on it and stick it in a box, he eats them all up." She slipped her phone out of her back pocket. "He flipped over this one. I made birds out of rice balls mixed with chicken. The flowers are made from broccoli. There is no way I thought he would eat it," she said softly, a sweet smile crossing her face. "But he did. He called me at work just to tell me how much he liked it."

"That's very sweet, Nova."

"Yeah." She put her phone away and shrugged. "He's all right for a kid that came from me."

Nova was sweet. The more time Cassandra spent with her, the more she saw that, but Cassandra was confused by her too. She saw that when Nova was with her son, she kept her distance, kept Teo at arm's length. The boy spent more time with Mansi than he did with Nova, but those beautifully made, intricate boxed lunches were a sign of love.

"Mansi said you might need help. Is there anything I can do for you?"

She motioned to the basket of clothes on the dryer. "You can help me fold Teo's clothes. I'll do forty-five loads of laundry. I'll scrub a latrine, but I hate folding clothes."

"I love to fold."

"You're crazy."

"It's not the first time I've been accused of that." She picked up one of Teo's shirts, the one she saw him in yesterday, which had been covered in chocolate syrup and soda and whatever else he came in contact with that day. It was now free of stains, devoid of any signs that it had ever been worn by a messy little boy. "How did you get this so clean?"

"I filled the machine with cold water and let the detergent dissolve before I put the clothes in. Then I added a booster. Trust me, Teo goes through more clothes than a Kardashian, but this helps keep them a little longer."

"My husband would have loved you."

"I doubt that," she answered with a snort. "If he was anywhere near as quiet and proper as you, he would have gone running for the hills as soon as he saw me."

"I'm not proper. Terrance was, but you would have been his type. He was a neat freak and you know your way around a washing machine. Plus you've got the type of body that would have made his mouth drop to the floor. He had a major thing for women who looked like pinup girls."

"Your husband told you that?" she asked in surprise.

"Of course not. But I'm not oblivious. A wife knows what her husband likes, and Terrance liked bad girls. Besides, it's hard not to notice when your husband almost breaks his neck looking at a woman with breasts the size of my head, but he was a good man, so I forgave him that."

"And your guy was Wylie's best friend?"

"They were closer than friends. They were like brothers, even though they were so different."

"What was he like?"

"Terrance is . . ." Cassandra paused, realizing that she was talking about him as if he were still here. "Terrance was the type of guy who was good at almost everything he tried. He was brilliant and handsome and funny and tall and athletic. He could talk to anyone about anything. But he was a dork too. He liked comic books and sci-fi movies and —"

"Supercurvy bad girls. You're not a bad girl. How did he end up with you?"

"He loved me. And I was the type of girl he was supposed to marry. My father is a doctor. My mother was a debutante. His father was a lawyer. His mother was the daughter of a diplomat."

"And where did my brother fit in, in that family?"

"He didn't. Wylie was the opposite of everything the Millers were. Terrance was always in the middle of it all, while Wylie stayed in the background. But he was sweet and polite and kind and thoughtful, and he worked hard for everything. Plus he was thankful for whatever he got."

"You loved your husband. But you loved Wylie, too."

"Yes. I loved him very much."

"Then how did you end up with your husband?"

"Because your brother was a giant dumbass who left me and broke my heart."

Nova threw back her head and laughed. "You're right. You're not so proper. And my brother is a giant dumbass. And I always thought you were the one who broke his heart."

"What did he tell you about us?" She had always wondered — wondered why he left, wondered why he walked out without a word.

"Nothing. Less than nothing. I was constantly busting his stones about why he never had a girl since he's come to the island. He told me because there was someone he had to leave behind in Connecticut."

"What the hell did he mean by that?"

"My guess is as good as yours." Nova left

her spot and stopped in front of Cassandra, surprising her by sliding her hands along her face and studying her closely. "Do you think I could . . ."

"What?"

"Cut your hair. I'm sorry, girl, but you look like a hot mess."

"You need jewelry. And not pearls either."

"I like pearls," Cass protested.

"They are for fifties housewives and socialites, and you are neither. Here." Nova pulled a pair of diamond studs out of her purse. "Try these."

"I couldn't. They are too nice."

"Do I look like the type of woman who owns a pair of real diamonds? Put them on and stop questioning me all the time."

"You're bossy," she said as she studied herself in the mirror. She couldn't stop looking because she didn't recognize herself. She wasn't the girl she was ten years ago. She wasn't the woman who spent so many years devoted to her job and husband. She was totally different. She felt lighter. She felt new.

"But you'll forgive me because you look much better than the walking corpse I first met. Now I can see why my brother had such a thing for you."

" 'Walking corpse'? That's not a nice thing to say to a grieving widow."

"Who said I was nice?"

The sound of Wylie's truck pulling into the driveway made Cassandra's heart pound a little faster. Thoughts of him flooded her mind all day. He touched her, slid his hands all over her body, kissed her until the numbness went away, and brought bliss to her body without asking for anything in return.

He was hot and cold with her again — just like when they were kids — kissing her and then walking away, making love to her and then telling her they couldn't be together. It used to drive her crazy then, and it bothered her now. How could he do that to her? How could he be so tender and sweet and then not say anything else to her that morning? How could he act like none of it happened? It made her question why he brought her here.

She knew why. Her mother had asked him to; and deep down, Wylie was still that same boy who always wanted to please.

She should move on, go away, find a new place to make her home. She couldn't go back to Harmony Falls, but she couldn't leave this place yet either. Not when her life was starting to feel hopeful again — and not like such a burden.

The front door burst open. Teo was the first one in the house. "Mommy!" He skidded to a stop in front of her, staring up at her in surprise. "You're still here?"

"For a little while. I have to go in to work soon."

"You do?"

The disappointment on Teo's face was easy to read; surprisingly, Nova's face looked the same way. "There's a fancy wedding on Vineyard Haven and they picked me to do everyone's hair, but I'll come get you tonight."

"When I'm sleeping?"

"Yes, when you're sleeping."

Teo shook his head. "I'll stay here instead."

"You don't want to sleep at home with me?"

He shrugged. "I sleep here more anyway. Uncle Wylie is going to pick me up from school again tomorrow. Miss Cass is going to help me with my homework again." Teo looked up at her. "Whoa."

"Holy shit." They looked over to see Tanner standing just inside the doorway with his mouth agape. "You look hot. Like amazingly hot."

Pleasure flooded Cass at the outrageous compliment. Her face felt odd, warm, like

195

her cheeks were stretched; she realized that she was smiling. Not thinking about smiling. Not wanting to smile. Actually doing it. Actually smiling. "Blame Nova. She did this to me."

Tanner came closer, passing her and going straight to Nova. His expression changed when he looked at her. His eyes grew soft and hot, all at the same time. Nova looked up at Tanner, eyes bold, her body leaning toward him unconsciously. There was heat there and Cassandra wondered if the two were as aware of it as she was.

"I'm impressed, Nova. You're actually good at something more than being a loud-mouthed pain in the ass. Maybe I'll have to come and sit in your chair sometime."

"You do need a haircut." She reached up and ran her fingers through Tanner's over-long dark hair. "But I'm warning you. My scissors are not a magic wand. I can't fix ugly."

Tanner leaned closer to Nova, his lips just grazing her ear. "Bitch," he whispered.

"Smug bastard," she returned. "Come by the shop Friday. I'll fix you up."

Tanner nodded and the two stared at each other for a moment, oblivious to the other people in the room. It was Wylie's heavy, booted footsteps that broke the heavy tension between the two.

"Uncle Wylie." Teo ran up to him. "Do you see? Miss Cass got a haircut."

Wylie looked at her for a long moment; for some reason Cass felt breathless as she watched him study her.

"Well, say something, you knucklehead!" Nova yelled at her brother. "We spent all day doing this."

"It looks . . . You look . . . just fine. Where's Mansi?"

And just like that, disappointment flooded her. "She's — she's taking a nap."

"Okay. I need to talk to her. You want to wait for me in the car?"

"No," she said, shaking her head. "I would like to stay here tonight."

"What?" His eyes widened.

"I'm going to stay with Teo tonight." She turned away from him.

He grabbed her shoulder, forcing her back around. "Why?"

"Because I want to." She removed his hand from her shoulder and walked completely out of the house, leaving everyone staring after her.

"Dude." Tanner rounded on him, anger rolling off him. "What the hell is your problem? Were you trying to be a dick, or did that come naturally for you?"

"Yeah." Nova punched his arm. "You couldn't have pretended? You couldn't have told her she looks pretty? She was finally feeling good about herself, and with two freaking words you took that away from her. I would have walked away from you too. In fact, if I was her, I would be looking for a giant stick to whoop your ass with."

"Did you go shopping today?" he asked, ignoring the angry looks from his sister and friend.

"How the hell do you think she ended up in that dress? Magic?"

"Where is her stuff?"

"Why do you want to know? Are you going to try to return it? She bought it with her own money, you know. Her mama sent her a wallet full of her money. Are you mad that you don't have control over her anymore?"

"I'm not explaining myself to you, Nova. Where is her stuff?" he barked the question, making her jump.

"It's in the spare room." He went there, grabbing the five or so heavy bags and dumped them in the back of his truck. Then he was on Cassandra's heels, following the dainty tracks her sandals left on the path to the beach.

She hadn't made it far, only halfway there, when he caught her. "You are not staying away from me." He lifted her up, slinging her over his shoulder and carrying her to his truck.

"Put me down!" She punched his back hard, but he barely felt the pain. He carried her back to his truck, dumped her in and sped off before she had a chance to escape.

She was pissed. He could feel the anger rolling off her, burning him as he sped back to his house.

"Just fine."

He knew the words were impossibly stupid as soon as they left his lips. There had never been anything *just fine* about her. If there had been, he wouldn't have risked losing his brother, the only family he had known, to be with her.

He pulled into his driveway, throwing the car into park and locking the doors so she couldn't get away from him.

"I want to leave, Wylie James."

"You want to leave and I want you to stop being every goddamn thought that runs through my mind."

She looked at him then. Her eyes narrowed in confusion. He couldn't explain what was going through his mind when he first saw her that afternoon. It was like he was meeting her for the first time again. It was like he was thirteen and tongue-tied and unsure of himself.

Because she was more than beautiful. More than perfect to him. Her hair was gone. Shorter than he had ever seen it, but instead of the wild mess of waves, she had short, soft curls. The kind that he wanted to touch, to run his fingers through. The style highlighted her graceful features, her pretty, high cheekbones and her wide eyes. It made her neck look longer. More skin, which he could stroke his fingers over, more space for him to kiss.

She wore a dress, a simple little green dress. It was the color of spring, the color of growth, the color of renewal. It was a color that looked so good with her pretty brown skin. The dress just fit her, not just her body but her personality, the happy, sassy girl he had loved. The little dress showed off her legs and bared her shoulders. It defined the flare of her hips that so often drove him to distraction.

So, no, she wasn't *just fine.* She was something he couldn't describe. "I'm not good with my words, Cass. I never was. I'm not like Terrance. I don't know how to tell you how beautiful you are to me," he said, looking straight ahead. "But you are. You are so beautiful. You always have been. A haircut and a pretty dress don't change that for me." He leaned over and took her hand. He lifted it to his mouth, knowing if he got any closer, if he tried to kiss her lips, he wouldn't be able to stop himself. "You do look very nice."

He left her then, walking back to his private little beach, where he had almost made love to her that morning.

CHAPTER 11

Her mother had taught her how to cook when Cassandra was fourteen years old. She had always helped her mother in the kitchen, but when Cassandra was fourteen, her mother decided it was time for her to learn what all the women in her family knew.

Her mother said it was "woman training." Her mother was from the South, and she was lovely and proper. She had been raised to believe that a woman took care of the home while the man made the money. She also taught Cassandra that even though the men made the money, the women did all the hard work. This meant that women really had all the power. She taught her daughter that knowing her way around the kitchen was part of that power.

Cassandra smiled at those good memories of her and her mother in the kitchen. As she placed the balls of dough into the pot of chicken and dumplings she was making,

Cassandra recalled how they used to argue playfully about women's roles. Cassandra was cooking again. She, who had told herself that she would never cater to a man, never spend her nights in the kitchen, was enjoying this. She was enjoying making something from scratch again, enjoying making something she knew that Wylie would like.

Her mother taught her how to make all the Southern classics. Smothered meat loaf, biscuits with sausage gravy, slow-cooked beef stew and perfectly fried pork chops. Wylie used to love coming over for Sunday dinners when they were kids. This kind of food reminded him of home, of the South. Cassandra sometimes forgot that he had to leave his home at such a young age — that his mother had abandoned him, and his father had died abruptly. He was so quiet when he first moved to Harmony Falls, people thought he was slow or couldn't talk. He was always so stoic. She had forgotten how hard things must have been for him.

She had been mad at him today. No, more than mad. She was hurt — hurt after feeling numb for so long. After a year of not giving a shit, not caring if she lived or died, she wanted to be pretty for herself, but a big part of her wanted to be pretty for him.

And when he said nothing, when he said *"just fine,"* it took her back to those days right after he had left her, left Harmony Falls. It was like when she had felt raw and empty and wondered why she wasn't enough, wasn't lovable enough, or worthy enough for a simple explanation or a good-bye.

She still wondered about that, about how one moment he treated her like the world, and the next moment he was gone. How even now, he brought her close to him and then pushed her away. She had hated him for that for a long time. She was still mad about it now. Hurt by it. But then he said things like he said in his truck and she was reminded that even though the outside packaging had changed, Wylie, in large part, was still the thirteen-year-old shy boy who had been through too much, too young.

The kitchen door opened and she heard his booted footsteps on the hardwood floors. She didn't turn to look at him. She didn't know what to say. He had been gone almost two hours. At first she hadn't known what to do with herself. She rarely found herself alone since she had come here. She had been alone so much of the time since she had come out of her coma: alone be-cause her friends and family got sad when they looked at her; alone because being around people who knew Terrance was too much to stand; alone because she no longer cared to be a part of the life that was still going on around her.

It had fooled her into thinking she liked being alone, that she needed to be alone. But she liked noise and conversation and just feeling another person's presence. Being around people reminded her how much she had once enjoyed life.

"It smells good in here," Wylie said, coming up behind her. She could smell the ocean air on him, feel the warmth from the sun on his skin. It made her want to move closer. "You didn't have to do this."

"I did. I wanted to. I put a load of laundry in too. Everyone has been taking care of me since Terrance died. I should be taking care of myself. I should be doing more."

"But you don't have to do more. You know that, don't you?"

"Yes. I know that. I also know that you walked out on me. Twice today."

She couldn't see his face, and she felt him go stiff, but she didn't care if her words made him uncomfortable. "You walked away from me ten years ago too. I'm not sure what I did. I'm not sure what happened, but you hurt me and I've decided I don't want to be hurt anymore. I appreciate what you've done for me these past few weeks, Wylie. I can never thank you enough for bringing me here, but if me being here is too much, I'll understand. I'll leave so you don't keep having to go away."

He was silent for a long moment. "I — I . . . I like having you here."

She turned around to face him, to look into his soulful eyes. "Then don't walk out on me again. Next time you do, I'm leaving. For good."

"What?" His eyes went wide. "But, Cass . . ."

She turned away from him, checking on her chicken and dumplings, finding comfort in their familiar smell. "Set the table," she told him. "Dinner is almost ready."

She had to know why he left. She had to. Wylie had often blocked out that night. It was his worst memory — the night he completely lost control and beat his best friend bloody. She had to know that Terrance came to his apartment, pissing mad and feeling betrayed. She had to know about the fight that broke out, about the words that were exchanged.

Terrance must have told her. He must have gone to her that night to show her what kind of out-of-control animal Wylie could be. That's why she married him, accepted Terrance's proposal so soon after Wylie left.

Right?

He never contacted her besides the one note he left for her on the morning he left. He never went back to Harmony Falls because he assumed she hated him. He assumed that the entire town hated him for nearly killing their favorite son.

But what if it didn't happen that way?

He shook his head. No. It had to have happened that way. Because if it didn't, that meant he had thrown away the only woman who ever really made him happy.

"What is it?" Cass asked him from her side of the porch swing.

"Dinner was good," he said instead of asking her. The need to know right then and there was clawing at his chest, but he couldn't bring himself to ask her. "Thank you. I haven't eaten so good since . . ."

"The last time *you* cooked. You cook way better than I do." She inched closer to him on the swing, so close that their sides were brushing.

He had slept in bed beside her every night since she had been here. He had made love to her before, but sitting next to her like this — alone on a late summer night —

made him feel like he was sixteen years old again, wanting to kiss her so bad his chest ached.

"How did you learn? I know Terrance's mother expected a lot from you, but I don't recall her making you cook," she observed.

"She didn't. I spent a lot of time with my granny when I was a little kid. "My mama was never around and my daddy worked long hours in the fields. He never wanted me to help so I stayed with my granny and she taught me how to cook. I took over making dinner when I was ten."

"You were so young."

He shook his head. "I never felt that way, but I guess spending all your time with an old lady does that to you."

"Why didn't your father want you to help him?"

"He didn't want me to be like him. He said I needed to be smarter, so I didn't have to work farm land. He said I was going to be the first one to finish school."

"And you did." She inched even closer to him, so that their sides were fully pressed together. The breeze had kicked up. The night was growing cooler, and the heat of her body felt like a blanket around him. "He would be so proud of you."

"I got my bachelor's while I was in the

service. I did it for him," he partially lied. His father would have gotten a real kick out of seeing him get his degree, but he got it for himself too, and for the Millers and for Cass and Terrance, just to prove that he could. "He died of a heart attack. He was thirty-eight. Everybody always says how sudden it was, but I think he knew he had a bad heart. I used to see how his legs and feet would swell. I used to hear him wheeze and cough this nasty, loud hacking cough at night. He said it was from smoking as a kid, but I knew it wasn't. The man never smoked a day in his life. Toward the end he couldn't even make it to his truck without getting exhausted. He knew he was dying. I just don't think he did anything to stop it because he wanted me to have a shot."

"You really think that's true?"

He looked into her eyes, wide with concern. "He knows I would have dropped out of school to help him."

"You would have given up your future to help him live longer."

"Yeah, and he gave up his future so I could have a good life."

"Do you have a good life, Wylie?"

"Define 'good'?"

"Are you happy?"

He smiled at her, at the expectation on

her face. "Define 'happy'?"

"All right. Don't answer me. I don't care anyway." She turned her face away from him, staring out at the setting sun.

"I could ask you the same thing. I could ask you if you were happy before Terrance died. I could ask you if you thought you had a good life."

She turned back to him, surprise etched all over her features. He'd caught her off guard and he was glad for it. He was glad when her mouth opened and no answer immediately came.

"I loved him, you know," she said firmly, like she was almost trying to convince herself. "I still love him."

"So do I," he said truthfully. He was so mad at himself that they never spoke again, that he ignored Terrance's attempt to reach out to him. But in the end he couldn't see him with her. He couldn't go back to Harmony Falls and see them together, knowing he would never be able to look his best friend in the eye while he was still in love with his wife. "I have something to show you." He got off the swing and extended a hand to her. "And after the crazy day we had, I'm not sure I want to show you."

"Why?" She took his hand, sliding her

fingers between his.

"I don't want you to leave."

Cass wasn't sure what Wylie was going to show her, but her heart pounded as he took her up the stairs, past the bedroom they had been sharing. She had only been in the back of the house once. It was filled with old furniture, a lifetime's worth of stuff from someone else's life.

"How did you get this house, Wylie?" she asked him as she looked around the beautiful old house. She was trying not to think about what was going to happen next. She was trying not to think at all. When she did think, she realized how crazy it was that she was here, especially when she knew it would probably be better for her to go. "I know you've done well for yourself, but having a house this close to the ocean must cost a fortune."

"It would, even in this condition. The man who sold it to me was a Marine too. He saw action in Vietnam and has PTSD also. Art helped me get through mine. We got close, and when he lost his wife, he called to tell me he wanted to give me the house. Said he didn't have a son and would rather let a fellow leatherneck have it than some uppity stranger. I was honored, but I knew I couldn't accept the house. It was too much. So I went and bought a boat, a real nice one that you could live on, and we traded. He once told me that he wanted to sail around the world with a beautiful girl. I couldn't find him a girl, but I got him the boat. He took it down to Florida."

Wylie was sweet and so thoughtful. She still couldn't wrap her head around why he left. Even though they rarely spoke of Wylie, she knew Terrance felt the loss of him too. For so long it didn't feel right to be together without him there. "I bet he met a beautiful girl in Florida."

One corner of Wylie's mouth curved into that soft half smile that always made her insides feel wobbly. "He did. Her name is Edna. They drink piña coladas and sail around Key West. He invited me down. I was thinking of going this winter."

"You should go see him," she urged him as they stopped in front of the last bedroom at the end of the hall. "He's your family now."

"I need all the family I can get."

They went quiet for a moment, staring at each other, their hands still linked as they stood before the closed door. "Is this the room where you kept your secret collection of body parts?" she joked, trying to ease the tension that had crept up between them.

"You've become morbid in your old age."

"Getting shot will do that to you."

He shut his eyes for a moment as if he were in pain. His hand went to her belly, to right where the bullet had entered her body. He stroked his thumb over the spot as he leaned in to kiss her face. It was like he was trying to heal her with his kiss.

"Come." Suddenly his hands were off her body; his lips were gone from her face. He opened the door to the room, leading her inside.

It was too much to take in at first, but the first thing that struck her was how warm it was. Not the temperature, but the feeling. The windows were open, and a breeze was blowing the sheer white curtains. The room smelled of sea air and fresh paint. The walls were painted the softest shade of blue, a beautiful old wooden mirror hung on the wall. There were two old white nightstands, which someone had lovingly restored. And in the center of the room was a large canopy bed with a seahorse-printed bedspread.

The room was beautiful. She could spend hours looking at the small details, but in that moment she wanted to look at Wylie more.

"I want you to be comfortable while

you're here."

"You remembered," she said, ignoring him. "I told you when I was fourteen years old that I wanted a canopy bed and you remembered."

"I didn't." The tips of his ears grew red and she knew he was lying. "I just thought it would look nice in here." He walked away from her to the closet in the back of the room. "This is your room now, Cass. I moved your things in here."

As soon as she saw it, she knew that he had done this for her, given her this beautiful space. But it didn't dawn on her what that meant until that very moment.

She was going to have to sleep away from him. Be away from him. It was for the best. She knew that deep down inside. She stormed in on his quiet life, disrupting everything, even though she didn't mean to. But she had grown accustomed to sleeping beside his hard body every night. To smelling his smell, to feeling his rough facial hair on her skin every morning. Even when they were together, she never got to sleep with him often, because they had loved in secret.

"This room is beautiful, Wylie. Thank you for doing this for me."

"It was the excuse I needed to start fixing up the house."

"I can help you with that, if you want. I would like to help you out more. While I'm still here."

He stiffened for the briefest of moments before he came over and kissed her forehead. "I would like that." He touched her face. "And I really do like your haircut. Good night, Cass."

Wylie lay in bed that night, feeling exhausted, but sleep wouldn't come to him. He felt like he had lived a week in that day. It was Cassandra's fault. She was like a war zone, throwing little bombs in his way. He wasn't sure if he knew how to dodge the explosions anymore.

And that damn haircut. She blew him to pieces. Over dinner, sitting on the porch, being with her in that room, he had a hard time concentrating. He kept looking at her. He kept wanting to kiss the curve of her neck and those soft shoulders. He wanted to slip his hands beneath her cute little dress and feel her thighs. All day he had been hyperaware of her. All day he had trouble controlling himself. He thought having her sleep away from him, all the way down the hallway, would be better. It would help him restore his sanity, but it only made things worse. He missed the way her body tucked into his. He missed the soft sound of her breathing. He missed her.

He'd been alone for so many years. The Marines took him away a lot of the time, and he was alone because no woman seemed worth more than a few nights. Now that Cass was back in his life, it got him thinking about what he wanted for his future.

Was he happy?

Did he have a good life?

He heard soft footsteps in the hallway. He thought they would stop, that he would hear the bathroom door shut, but he didn't. His bedroom door opened and Cass was there, in a new nightgown, which was tiny in comparison to the old ones he was used to seeing her in. He was already hard, had been for hours. It was why he left her to go to bed so early, but he grew even harder when she walked in.

She tried to creep toward the bed, but then she saw that he was awake and staring at her. She crossed her arms across her chest, taking on a defiant posture. "I don't want to sleep alone. I know you need your —"

"Okay," he said, cutting her off. "Come here."

She slipped in bed beside him and this

time he didn't even go through the pretense of trying to stay away from her. He gathered her close, her head settling on his chest, his hand sliding beneath her nightgown to cup her behind. "I see you got new underwear today too. I like them."

She grinned up at him and it was like she threw another bomb at him, like he stepped in a land mine. He hadn't seen her smile once since she'd arrived. Her happiness was only a memory to him, but there it was in his face and it blew him away.

"Thank you for noticing."

He knew they couldn't go on like this anymore. He had to send her away if he wanted his old life back, the peaceful, quiet one where nothing shook him.

"Thank you, Wylie," she said as she stroked her hand up his arm.

"For what, Cass?"

"For being you."

He looked down at her sleepy face and the way she just fit into his arm and realized he didn't want his old life back. Cass was there for a reason and he needed her to stay.

Cass waited outside Mansi's house a few days later. She was waiting for Teo. At first she didn't want to admit it to herself, but that's why she was sitting on the porch. It was not for fresh air or a change of scenery. She had spent every day after school with him, helping him with his homework, exploring his neighborhood with him. He was even teaching her how to play video games. Somehow, when she wasn't looking, that five-year-old had become her friend. And that made her think about what Wylie had told her, about how he used to spend most of his time with his grandmother while his father worked. Teo was just like him in that way, but he didn't have to be. He was already too grown-up for a little kid

Three P.M. came and went, but the vehicle that pulled up in front of the house was not a school bus. It was Nova's red Jeep. Today it had doors on it and in the passenger side was Teo. The little boy jumped out, flung his book bag on the porch floor and squeezed in next to her in the oversized Adirondack chair, resting his head on her arm.

"Hey, Miss Cass," he said, greeting her.

"Hey, Mr. Teo." She touched the boy's messy curls. "How was work today?"

"I don't got a job, Miss Cass." He frowned at her in confusion. "I went to school."

Cass shrugged. "School is work too. You just don't get paid for it."

"You could give me money every day that I went to school."

"If I gave you money, then you would have to wear a little three-piece suit." She took his face in her hands and tilted his head as she studied him. "I think you would look pretty freaking cute in a suit. Maybe with a red tie. Red ties mean power. Did you know that? If you walked into kindergarten wearing a three-piece suit and red tie, you'd own the place."

"What are you talking about?"

"I don't know. I'm crazy." She looked toward Nova's Jeep to see that she hadn't gotten out yet.

"She's on the phone," he said grumpily. "It rang as soon as we got in the car. She's going to work late again tonight. Or maybe she has a date. She's always gone."

"Oh." Cass didn't know what to say to that. She liked Nova. Cassandra knew Nova loved her son, but they didn't seem to connect. Nova was always dashing off to do her own thing. But none of her family said anything about it. Not Mansi. Not Wylie. They all seemed to think Teo was better off without her. "You never told me how your day was."

"We have a class pet now. A guinea pig. His name is Mr. Peepers. It was my day to feed him. One person gets to take him home every weekend. I asked Mansi if we could keep him next week."

"What did she say?"

"She told me people eat guinea pigs in Peru."

Cass shut her eyes briefly. "I can't believe she told you that."

"It's true. She saw it on TV."

"I'm sure it's true. I just wish she hadn't told you that. Did you ask your mother if you could bring it home?"

"They don't allow pets in the apartment. It says so in our lease."

"How do you know what your lease says?"

"Mommy tells me. She says just in case I start getting funny ideas about asking for a dog."

"You could bring Mr. Peepers to our house — I mean your uncle's house one weekend." She caught her mistake. It was a dangerous one. She was a guest in Wylie's home, a temporary visitor to this place. She had to keep reminding herself of that. Wylie was still the guy who walked out on her. He was still the man who broke her heart. She tried not to think about it. She was here to heal, to feel again, to live again.

She was going to focus on that.

"I don't know. We have to ask Uncle Wylie."

"He'll say yes. Maybe we could have a

sleepover. We could come get you from school."

"You want me to stay with you?"

"Yeah. And while you're with us, you can help me scrub the toilet and kitchen floor."

Teo grinned at her. "You're funny."

"That's what you think." She wrapped her arm around him, bringing him closer. "Things will be cleaned, my friend. You just better hope I don't use your toothbrush."

They both looked up as they heard Nova's door slam. Overlarge sunglasses shielded her eyes. She was dressed in all black. The hairstylist uniform.

"Don't you look fancy today, Ms. Nova."

Nova looked at them for a long moment, her eyes pausing on Teo's face before she spoke. "I've got another wedding to do tonight. In Edgartown," she said distractedly. "A senator's daughter this time, so I've got to be on my best behavior. The tip from this gig alone could pay the rent for the next two months."

"You coming home late?" Teo asked, sounding more like a father than a five-year-old.

"About midnight." She nodded. "Wedding season is slowing down. It's going to be about three more weeks of this."

"I never sleep at home anymore."

She nodded again. "I know," she said softly. "I've been working."

"Miss Cass said I could sleep at Uncle Wylie's next weekend."

"You can, if she says so."

"She's going to let me bring the guinea pig."

"That's nice, baby." Nova looked helpless for a moment. Like she was unsure what to do with or say to her son; Cass felt sorry for her. The tension between Nova and her son was palpable.

"I made you a peanut butter and marshmallow sandwich," Cass told him. "It's sitting on the table."

"I like those," Teo said. "Thank you." He got up, tossing one last look at his mother before going inside.

Nova took a step forward as if she was going to go after him, but she stopped herself. Cass wished Nova hadn't stopped. Cass wished the woman had hugged her boy.

It's what she would have done. Her baby would have been nine months old now if he had lived. She tried not to think about that too; but seeing Teo, being around him, made her wonder what her child would have been like. It made her wish she could go back and change things. It made her wish she could at least have seen what he looked like.

"This is the first time in my life that I've ever been good at something," Nova said, breaking Cass from her thoughts. "I went to school and finished. I've got a good job. I'm finally making enough money to support us. Without his deadbeat, shithead father. He's safe here. I never had that growing up. We were dirt poor. We lived in cars and slept on couches when we couldn't afford a motel. My mother went through men like tissues. My life was shit growing up. I don't want him to have a shitty life. I take that money from my brother and put it in a college fund so he'll have something. I'm doing everything I can."

"You don't have to explain that to me, Nova. I'm not judging you."

"I know," she said, still looking through the door that her son disappeared through. "I'm judging myself."

When Wylie pulled up to Mansi's house that afternoon, the first thing he heard was Cass screaming. The hairs on the back of his neck went up in the air; he was out of his truck before he realized she wasn't screaming out of fear or hurt.

"Teo, quit it! You're shaking like a wet dog."

"Ruff. Ruff!"

Wylie walked around to the back of the house to see Teo running around in his underwear, soap suds covering him from head to toe. Cass was chasing after him with the sprinklers.

"Oh, you're barking now?" Cass laughed. "What kind of dog are you, a poodle?"

"A 'poodle'?" Teo stopped, crossing his arms over his small chest. "I'm a bulldog!"

"Nah, you're too hyper. I'd like to think of you as more like a rat terrier."

"A 'rat terrier'?" He thought about it for a moment. "People are afraid of rats. I'm cool with that."

"Good. Now get over here so I can throw this big bucket of water at you."

Wylie almost didn't want to intrude. Cass was laughing. Her face was lit up, and for once he saw no signs of sadness or traces of despair that had hung with her since she had come back into his life.

And then there was Teo. He had tried to keep his nephew away from Cass at first, but he realized that maybe Teo needed something from her that he couldn't get from anybody else.

"What are you guys doing?" he finally said just as Cass dumped a large bucket of water on Teo's head. They both screamed again as water splashed all over the both of them.

"Uncle Wylie!" Teo shook like a dog again.

"Hey! What the hell are you guys doing?"

"Taking a shower," Teo said as if it were obvious, water dripping down his face.

"In the backyard?"

"Yeah." He nodded. "Lots of people take showers outside. We just don't got an outside shower like them."

"I've got an outside shower at my house."

"You do?" Teo and Cass both asked.

"Yes, it's in the back, and it's got a little stall so no one can see you prancing around the yard half naked. Get in the house and put some clothes on, boy."

"I was going inside anyway." He shook one more time. "I don't want to freeze my raisins off out here."

" 'Raisins'?" Wylie shook his head. He couldn't believe the stuff that came out of the kid's mouth half the time. "Where did you hear that?"

"From Mansi."

"Of course you did. Because all grandmothers talk like that. Get inside. I don't want you freezing any of your fruit off."

He turned to go, but looked back at Cass. "Can you stay for dinner, Miss Cass?"

She nodded. "I told you I would. We're going to use the grill to make the chicken."

"And you're going to talk to Uncle Wylie

about the guinea pig and the sleepover?"

"Yes, sir."

He looked unsure. "You promise?"

"Cross my heart." She nodded. "He'll say yes. Don't worry."

Teo nodded and went inside then, leaving Wylie wondering what the two were up to. "What was that all about?"

He didn't look at Cass closely before, but now that Teo had left them alone, he took the chance to study her. She was soaking wet. The pair of black shorts and pretty cream-colored tank top molded to her body, showing off every sweet, soft curve she had. He could see her bra through her shirt. It was unlike the plain ones he had seen before. This one was blue and leopard printed. His blood pressure rose just from looking at her in it.

"We're taking him next weekend for a sleepover, along with his class pet, Mr. Peepers."

"Oh?" He stepped closer to her.

"Yes." She turned away from him, picking up the abandoned sprinklers.

He followed her. "Are we going to talk about this, like Teo said?"

"Nope. I want to take him and the damn guinea pig, and if you don't like it, you can suck an egg."

" 'Suck an egg'?" He grabbed her elbow. "That was mean. What did I do to deserve that?"

"Nothing." She turned to him, grinning, the flowing sprinkler still in her hand. "I just wanted to do this." She sprayed him, and the icy water soaked his shirt.

She dropped the hose and took off across the yard. He was after her immediately. Her shorter legs were no match for his. Still, she was quicker than he expected, leaping over the myriad toys Teo had left in the yard, but he caught her by the back of her shorts. She turned toward him at the same moment, her feet sliding on the wet grass, causing her to knock both of them off balance. He landed on his back, with her soft, wet body on top of his.

"Are you okay?" She tried to lift herself off him, but he had his hands locked around her waist.

"No, I'm not okay." He rolled them over, so he could be on top of her, so he could look into those pretty brown eyes of hers. "You are mean."

"I am not!" she said, gasping.

"You're mean, and sneaky and bad."

"Three things that are not true." Her eyes grew mischievous. Her grin returned and Wylie's heart pounded in his chest.

"You're also very wet."

"That's because your nephew is a very messy bather."

"Well, I'm going to have to thank him, because I can see right through your shirt. And I like very much what I see."

"And you said you weren't good with words." She surprised him by lifting her mouth to his. There was a split second where he could see uncertainty in her eyes, but that disappeared in an instant and she kissed him, lightly at first. Just her lips brushing his. Since she had been here, he had only kissed her. Kissed her because he couldn't help himself, but now she was the one doing the kissing. And the only way he could describe it was like she was sixteen again and it was her first time kissing him. He didn't want to scare her away by kissing her back. He didn't want her to stop, so he stayed very still and let her do what she wanted.

"Closer," she murmured, and she slid her hands into his hair and pulled him in even more. She deepened the kiss just a little, like she was exploring, taking the time to get to know his lips better. Then her tongue came out, slowing, lightly licking across his mouth. His erection strained against his zipper, begging to be let out. He hurt: his whole body, his arms and legs. His head and gut and heart hurt. He wanted to be with her so badly, needed to be with her. But she seemed oblivious to his pain. Or maybe she was enjoying it, because her legs fell open even more and he found himself between them. Her body grew softer; her kiss grew hotter; her tongue was sweeping all the way into his mouth. His control broke then. He grabbed her hands, pushing them over her head so that he could take control of the kiss. But she wouldn't let him. They were equals in this kiss; both of them giving just as much, both of them taking everything the other had to give. And just as he was about to lose his mind, just as he was about to slide his hands up her body and peel away every ounce of wet clothing she had on, he remembered where they were. They were in Mansi's backyard, in full view of anybody who happened to come by. He broke the kiss, but he couldn't force himself away from her.

"Damn it, Wylie," she said breathlessly. "Damn it."

"I'm sorry."

"I'm not." She looked up at him and there was awe in her eyes. "I felt that all over. I felt that in my toes. I've been numb, but you make me feel."

She took his face in her hands, bringing him close once again to leave a soft kiss on his lips. But he felt her wedding ring on his skin and this time it made him stop cold.

He pulled away from her.

"What's wrong?" She grabbed him, keeping his body on top of hers. "Wait. Not yet."

He touched the cool metal, knowing he shouldn't have, knowing it was wrong to draw attention to it. "It's nothing. The water was cold and your ring feels like ice on my skin."

"My *ring*?" She frowned at him and then realized what he was speaking of. *"Oh."* Guilt flashed in her eyes and he wondered if it mirrored his, if she could see it.

She's Terrance's wife.

As long as she wore that ring, he would have a hard time forgetting that.

"We have to get up anyway, Cass. I don't want Teo to walk out on us like this." He got up, knowing he was walking away. "I'm going to go get some towels. Why don't you lay in the sun and dry off for a little while."

CHAPTER 12

That evening Cassandra stepped into the beautiful room Wylie had made for her. She had cooked dinner for everyone at Mansi's house. She and Wylie had played cards with Teo afterward, but Cassandra's mind wasn't there. The evening passed by in a blur. and when Wylie pulled back into his driveway, she made an excuse to escape him. She told him that she needed to change her slightly damp clothes. In truth, she needed space, time to think away from Wylie. The ring her husband had given her, the ring she never paid attention to anymore, because it had become so a part of her, was burning her hand. It now felt heavy there; and all throughout the evening she kept looking at it, remembering how it felt the day he slipped it on her finger.

It was a symbol of love from a man who was always loyal to her, who loved her tremendously and wasn't ever afraid to tell her. It was a gift from a man who had been gone for . . . She had to think about it, because sometimes it seemed like just yesterday that they were laughing over one of his corny jokes, and sharing a home and sharing a life.

But it had been a long time now. Over a year, and for the life of her she couldn't remember how she had spent those months. All she could remember was that the hole inside her was so big, it threatened to swallow her up.

But now she didn't feel that way, didn't feel so bad. Because instead of the raw, searing pain she felt when she first thought about him, she just felt a dull ache. Like something was missing.

She touched the ring, twisted it around her finger. Wylie said it felt cold, but it only felt hot to her because she couldn't forget the hurt look that crossed Wylie's face when he felt it on his skin.

But why should he be hurt? He walked away from her without looking back. And Terrance was there. Terrance loved her.

And she was kissing Wylie James while she wore Terrance's ring. She was sharing a bed with him, and thinking about him when he wasn't there, and happy to see him when he walked into a room.

It wasn't right to wear Terrance's ring when she was with Wylie. She twisted her ring again and it slid off her finger. She looked at it, her hands trembling slightly. It had never been off her finger since her wedding day. Her hand looked different without it. But as she looked up into the sea glass–decorated mirror that Wylie hung over her dresser, she realized that she was different. She looked different. She felt different. She wasn't the same heartbroken twenty-three-year-old girl who married her best friend for all the wrong reasons.

Her cell phone rang, startling her. She reached for it, letting her abandoned ring slip from her and onto the dresser. She welcomed the distraction of a phone call. She didn't want to think anymore. She thought it might be her mother, but when she answered, she was surprised to find that it wasn't.

"Hello, Cassandra."

Her father's deep voice filled her ears. She hadn't heard from him in a long time, not a phone call, not a visit. They had never been close. He was always busy. Not just a doctor, but an oncologist. Top in his field. He saved people's lives. That's what her mother kept telling her to explain away his absences. But he had retired three years ago and, even then, Terrance had seen more of him than she did. They golfed together. They went out for drinks. They were friends, more than friends really, and when Terrance died, she rarely saw her father. Maybe just a few times and then he could barely look at her. She felt like a disappointment.

"Hello, Dad."

"How are you, sweetheart?"

She didn't know how to answer him. How could she put it into words? There weren't enough of them in the world. "I'm pretty good. You might even be able to stand looking at me now," she said with a laugh, even though she knew it wasn't funny. *Bitterness.* That was what she was feeling in that moment and she was surprised by it.

He was quiet for a long moment. "Damn it, Cassandra. I saw you lay in a coma for over three months. We thought you were going to die, and when you came out of it, it was like you were still dying. I've been a doctor for forty years. I've seen people die before my eyes, but if you think it was easy for me to see my own daughter waste away, you're fooling yourself. It was killing me. I just wanted you to be yourself again."

"He shot my husband right before my eyes. I watched Terrance die. I watched as the police officers put a bullet in the gunman's brain. His blood spattered on my face. I could smell it. I would wake up at night still feeling it. Do you know what that's like? Do you know what it's like to wake up from a coma and find out your baby is dead and your husband is buried and you didn't even have the chance to say good-bye? Maybe there are others who are stronger than I am, strong enough to take it, but I wasn't. My life was gone. My whole life was taken from me and I just didn't know how to handle it. And you wanted me to be myself again? You didn't know me, and I don't think I even knew myself."

"Do you know now?"

The question took her off guard, but she nodded. "Being here helps. I'm living again. Sometimes I even feel happiness."

"You're happy there." Her father cleared his throat uncomfortably. "How's the boy?"

" 'The boy'?" She shook her head, thinking about Teo, but realizing that her father didn't know about him. "You mean Wylie James?"

"Your mother tells me he was a Marine. I see that he was a decorated soldier. A hero."

"Yes," Cass said, but she hadn't known that. She hadn't talked to Wylie much about his service or his life at all. It had just been about her. Selfishly about her.

"I didn't know that your mother was going to call him," he said quietly. "She wouldn't tell me where you had gone at first. I thought she had you . . ."

"You thought she had me committed?"

"We talked about it. When you didn't respond to the therapist we brought to you, we were worried you were going to try to —"

"No," she cut him off. "There were days when I didn't care if I lived or died, but I was never there. I never wanted to end it."

"I'm glad to hear that."

"Wylie has helped me." She looked around the beautiful room that he had made for her, at the details he had put into it, at the time he had taken to make her happy. "Part of him is still that same sweet boy he always was."

"Oh," he said, and then fell quiet for a moment. "Do you think you'll be ready to come home soon? It's been a month."

"Home"? Harmony Falls was the place she had spent her life, but it didn't feel like *home* to her. It would probably never feel like home again. "No, I'm not ready to go back there."

"Your mother and I miss you."

"I miss you too," she said truthfully. Her father had been absent, but he wasn't a bad father. She knew she was loved. "Call me again, okay?"

"Yes, sweetheart. I will."

She disconnected, placing her phone back on her dresser, and she felt dazed. There were too many emotions going through her, too much to process in that moment.

"Cass? You all right?" Wylie was standing just outside the door, worry in his big brown eyes.

"Um, yeah." She turned away from him to sit on the bed. Her knees felt like they might give out on her.

"I heard you yelling." He crossed the room and sat next to her on the bed, his big body giving her no space.

For a moment memories of that afternoon invaded her, when he was on top of her, kissing her, and the sun was beating down on them and she felt warm and safe and beautiful and wanted.

"Tell me what happened?"

"My father called."

"Oh." Wylie's body stiffened slightly, causing her to look up at him. "I'm sure he's worried about you here."

She nodded. "I haven't seen him in months, you know. They live five minutes away from me and I couldn't remember that last time I saw him. He said it was killing him to see me that way. But part of me thinks he didn't want to come over because not having Terrance there was too much for him."

"He loved Terrance, ever since we were kids. He wanted him for you. When Terrance died, all his dreams for your future died with him."

Wylie's words brought back a memory of her wedding day. She had been terrified that day. Unsure. Knowing she was about to enter a marriage with a man she wasn't in love with, but too afraid to back out, too afraid she was going to break his heart and lose the only man who really loved her. She thought she had hid her feelings from the world, but her father came to her a few minutes before he was supposed to walk her down the aisle: *I'm glad you're with the right man. Terrance will love you. He'll take care of you. You'll never regret marrying him, just like I never regretted marrying your mother.*

At first she thought his words were just meant to be encouraging, something that any father would say to his daughter on her wedding day, but now she wondered if those words had a greater meaning.

"He wants me to come home."

He searched her face, his expression unreadable. "Do you want to go home?"

"No," she said without hesitation. "He asked about you."

"Your father does not like me, Cass." Wylie's eyes flashed with something that looked suspiciously like anger. "It's probably killing him that you're living with me."

"He shouldn't care."

"He thinks I'm trash," he said harshly. "I wasn't good enough. He probably thinks I'm still not."

"Good enough for what?"

"For you." He looked down at his rough hands. They were the hands of a workingman, so different from her father's, so different from Terrance's.

"Last time I checked, I was the one deciding who was good enough for me. And I still don't understand why you think that. He's never spoken poorly about you to me. I think he's proud of your service."

" 'Put your life on the line for my country, but stay the hell away from my daughter.' " He laughed without humor. "I knew when I first came to Connecticut. I knew the first time he saw me. I was trash and no doctor wants a Bubba from Alabama to come anywhere near his daughter."

"But my father didn't know about us."

"He did. He'd always known, even before there was *an us*. I couldn't hide it. I couldn't

239

stop looking at you. But in my defense you were a smoking-hot sixteen-year-old." He grinned that boyish grin of his and her heart slammed against her rib cage.

"Did he say something to you?"

"Yeah." He shrugged. "A few times, but that's not important. It's in the past. And you married Terrance. That's all he wanted for you."

She was silent for a moment, with that too-overwhelmed, numb feeling sweeping across her.

"Are you sure you're all right, Miss Cass?" He touched her face lightly.

She ignored the question, because she wasn't all right. "Is my father the reason you left me?"

He hesitated and then shook his head once. "Your father is a good man, Cass."

"And so are you. He told me you're decorated. I didn't know."

Wylie frowned. "He's had me checked out. I shouldn't be surprised."

"Tell me about it."

"Not today." He brushed his lips across her. "I'm going to run you a bath. Your clothes are still damp. You're good with Teo. I know he can be a lot, but he's been better since you've been here."

"Five-year-olds are kind of my specialty.

When he turns six, it's all over for me."

The side of Wylie's mouth curved into a half smile. "Do you think you'll want to go back?"

"To Harmony Falls?"

"To teaching."

"I — I don't know. I don't think I'll see school in the same way."

"I understand that." He nodded and rose from the bed. "You need time. Take as much as you need of it here."

Wylie walked toward the door and a flash of gold caught his eye. It stopped him dead in his tracks. Cassandra's ring was on the dresser, sitting next to her cell phone. She had taken it off — taken it off, even though she never did; even though he thought it was going to be a permanent fixture on her hand. He felt it every time he held her hand and it reminded him that she married a better man than he was.

She had been distracted all evening. She pretended not to be, fooling Teo and Mansi, but not him. He saw how many times she had looked down at it. Saw how many times she had twisted it around her finger and he felt guilty. He shouldn't have said anything. He heard her speaking to her father. She had watched Terrance die, wasn't there when he was buried. She had every right to wear that ring . . . for as long as she wanted, forever if she needed to.

"What's the matter, Wylie James?"

"Nothing," he lied, but when he turned around and saw the worried look in her eyes, he knew he couldn't walk out of the room without telling her the truth. "Your ring? You know it's there?"

"Yes." She nodded, her eyes glued to his face. "I took it off. It was time to come off."

He wanted to tell her that she didn't have to, to forget about that afternoon and what he had said, but he couldn't force himself to say that. "Nova sent over some of those fancy bath salts her salon used to sell. You want me to dump some of those in the water?"

"Yes, please." She gave him a tiny smile. "And bubbles, if you've got them."

"Of course I've got them, girl. Who says Marines don't like a good bubble bath every once in a while?"

He walked away from her then. Maybe hopeful was the wrong thing to feel, but he was feeling it.

CHAPTER 13

A purple streak of lightning lit up the sky behind her parents' house as pretty white flakes of snow floated to the ground. She had never experienced thundersnow before. And even though she was feeling a jumble of things, she couldn't take her eyes off the skies. She was alone in her parents' house rather than being in her own tiny apartment in town. Her parents were away in Antigua for their anniversary and Cassandra was there to keep her mother's little dog company. She looked over to the terrier, who was curled up on her bed fast asleep, unbothered by the turbulent weather going on around her.

Cassandra wished she could say the same, but she hadn't heard from Wylie in two days. That was odd for him. They had spent every free moment they had together. It was the reason she had gotten her own place. So nobody would question why she didn't sleep in her bed every night. But when she went over to his apartment last night, his car was gone and the lights were off. When she went in, she found that his duffel bag was missing.

But she knew he couldn't have left. He wouldn't have. It wasn't like him to leave and not say a word. She knew him too well, had been with him too long for him to do that. But this morning she found a note on her door. It just said, *I'm sorry.* There was no signature, but she knew it was him by his small, neat handwriting.

But he hadn't left. She knew he wanted to go into the Marines. She knew he had been putting it off for her, but he hadn't gone without telling her. Without discussing it.

He couldn't have.

Right?

The doorbell rang, making her jump. She ran toward it, not meaning to, but it might be him. He might be there.

She threw open the door and froze. "What happened to you?"

Terrance was there, with his lips busted, eyes black and nearly swollen shut, nose twice the size it normally was.

She pulled him inside and immediately pulled him into her arms. "Who hurt you?" She was crying. She hadn't realized it till she felt the hot tears splash on her chest. "Who did this to you?"

"You don't know?" he asked into her hair. "He didn't tell you?"

"Who didn't tell me?" She looked up at him. "What happened?"

He looked at her for a long moment and she could tell he was hiding something from her.

"Terrance, you tell me what happened. We'll call the police. You can't let whoever did this get away with it."

"I got into a fight the other night."

"Where? At school? You're supposed to be in Boston. Why are you home?" So many questions were rolling around in her head. "What the hell happened?"

"Bar fight. Patriots are playing the Giants in the Super Bowl. I ran my mouth. Said some things I shouldn't have said and I paid for it."

She didn't believe him. She couldn't believe that something like that could have happened to him. But what other reason was there for it?

"Does Wylie know about this?"

"You haven't spoken to him?"

"No. I haven't seen him in two days."

"Oh." He nodded. "Do you think I could stay here with you, Cassandra? I've been hiding from my mother. I don't want her to see my face like this."

"Of course. Let me get you some ice."

■ ■ ■ ■

Cass opened her eyes, looking up at the ceiling in Wylie's bathroom. The water was cooling off, but she didn't want to get out yet, not while the memory of that night still circulated around in her mind. It was the first time she felt truly torn between the two of them. She couldn't stop thinking about Wylie, but she had been so worried about Terrance. He had needed her that night. He had come to her when Wylie had walked away.

But Wylie . . . he needed so much more: a home, a family. He needed to be loved.

She looked around the bathroom again. She could tell that Wylie had replaced the sink, tub and toilet to make the room functional, but that was all. The room needed to be painted, maybe a soft teal or sage green. A new vanity in white would look nice, with an old-fashioned sink and a vintage mirror. She thought about the living room too, with those beautiful built-in shelves that needed to be refinished.

He had lived in this house for a while now, but he still hadn't made it a home. He deserved a home.

She looked down at her fingers, which

were now wrinkled and pruney from the water, but she didn't care. Her body felt limp, and she was warm and exhausted, but in a good way. Despite everything she felt relaxed, and she hadn't felt this way in a long time. She wasn't normally one to take baths, to sit still and relax, but tonight she did. And it was only because Wylie had run one for her, with bubbles and lavender-scented salts. He even had lit a few candles and produced a book for her to read.

He took care of her so well. She wondered if anybody had ever really taken care of him.

She forced herself out of the tub and wrapped herself in his never-used bathrobe, which hung on the back of the door, ignoring the silky one she had purchased for herself. She wondered who had given it to him. It wasn't something he would buy for himself, let alone use. But still it held his smell — the smell of soap and shampoo and aftershave, the way the bathroom smelled after he got out of the shower.

She walked back to her room, thinking about Wylie, only to find him sitting on the bed. He had a jar of her scented cream in his hand.

"Hey," she said, surprised to see him there. His hair was damp and he was only in his boxers.

"I used the outdoor shower," he said, reading her mind.

"It must have been cold, now that the sun has gone down. I'm sorry I took so long."

"You shouldn't be. I kind of like it out there. The water was hot and it's nice to see the stars when you shower. It almost reminds me of when I was in Afghanistan. We were in the mountains, and the terrain is like nothing I've ever seen before. There were no showers there, just some wipes to keep us clean, but we got to clean ourselves beneath the stars and sleep beneath them and eat beneath them. Being out there makes you think about life in a whole other kind of way. There are kids who never get a shower, never know when and if they are going to get their next meal. And every time I get to thinking about how my life could have been better, I think about those little kids we met who have it a whole hell of a lot worse than I did, and my life seems pretty good, in comparison."

"Oh, Wylie." She felt ridiculously close to tears.

He patted the bed beside him and she sat, wanting to wrap her arms around him. "Lean back on the pillows."

He unscrewed the lid on her jar of cream and scooped some into his hands. Taking one of her feet, he began to rub.

"I've done two tours in Iraq and three in Afghanistan. I've been to Africa too. That's where I met Tanner briefly. I've been shot at more times than I can count, but none of that made me lose sleep at night."

His strong fingers worked every groove in her foot as his deep, soft Southern drawl lulled her. She wanted to keep her eyes open, so she could capture every expression on his face as he spoke, but Wylie was hypnotic.

"My unit was on patrol one day and it was one of those days that just didn't seem right from the moment you woke up. You ever have them days?" His hands drifted up her foot to her ankle and then her calf, where he started to rub in slow, deep circles. Her body went limp, but her nerves seemed to wake up the way they only did when Wylie was touching her. "I knew something bad was going to happen. There was a street kid I used to play soccer with sometimes. His father had been killed by his government and his mother had to take care of his two little sisters, so he fended for himself. I know he used to steal sometimes, just so he could feed himself, and I woke up that morning afraid he had gotten caught. So when I saw him that day, I stopped to talk to him, to see how he was, and that's when it happened. That's when a rocket attack landed on my unit. I didn't get hurt. I was too far away, but I felt it, just like it had hit me. I heard them screaming and smelled the fire and the blood. I watched my commander as half of his body burned in flames and I froze. It was too much. I didn't know what to do."

"Wylie." She sat up. "That's horrible. How could you know —"

"Lay back down now." He gently pushed on her chest. "Don't interrupt a man when he's spilling his guts." He smoothed his hands over her calf again, slowly up and down, and she didn't know if he was soothing her or himself. "I unfroze. My commander, Lieutenant Howard, is one of the biggest sons of a bitch I've ever seen, and he acted like he wasn't hurt at all — though he'd been badly burned. He was helping those men, pulling them toward the medics when they arrived, even though I knew the pain had to be killing him."

"You helped them too," she said, and it was a question.

"Yes, I helped them too. Only three of us survived. Howard was one of them. They gave him a Purple Heart and made him a captain. Hell, they should have made him a damn general. I've never seen a man so brave."

"You were brave too, Wylie James."

He had switched legs, slowly massaging the lavender-scented cream into her foot, his fingers gliding over every single one of her tender toes. His touch was distracting. She wanted to ask him to stop so she could listen to every word he said, but at the same time she didn't want him to stop, because his touch felt so good and she had waited so many years to feel this way again.

"I was scared, Cass. Marines ain't supposed to be scared," he said, his accent deepening. "I would have died for my country that day. In fact, there are some days I wish I had, so this damn guilt wouldn't eat me alive. I was there, right in the middle of it, watching them burn, watching them die, and I realized that I didn't want to die. I wanted to live."

"Where's . . ." She swallowed hard as Wylie's fingers traveled up her thigh. It was the lightest of touches, but she felt it right between her legs in that spot that often throbbed for his relief. "Why be ashamed for wanting to live?"

"It took me a long time to realize that I shouldn't be. But it was a long time after they gave me the Silver Star, a long time after everyone was patting me on the back and thanking me for my service."

"You had PTSD. You said your friend Art helped you get through it. I should have asked you before about your life. I'm sorry I didn't. I've been so self-centered."

"Hush now," he scolded gently. "I'm not going to tell you again." He pulled the tie on the bathrobe, opening it just enough to see her skin. She watched him as he stared at her slightly exposed flesh. "I'm telling you this because I understand how you feel." He slipped one hand between her thighs, touching the supersensitive skin there. A shiver ran through her and her nipples tightened. Her toes curled and she wanted him to do it all over again. "There was a time when the smell of anything burning sent me back to Afghanistan." He opened the robe all the way and dipped his fingers in her cream again. This time he touched her hips, running his hands across them, his thumbs stroking her belly. "If a car backfired, I would hit the damn ground." He moved up her torso, until his hands came to the undersides of her breasts. He lingered there for a minute. When she opened her eyes, she saw that he was kneeling over her, looking down at her with heat in his eyes. The same way he used to look at

252

her when they were younger and she was all that he wanted.

"The thing that brought me to my knees was I couldn't look my commander in the eye. Not because he was burned, but because I knew that I wasn't half the man that he was. I hadn't fought hard enough for the important things. I was a coward in so many ways, during so many points in my life."

"But . . ." His large hand covered her breast, his thumb reaching out to stroke her nipple. Instead of words a moan escaped her lips.

"He's married now. His wife just had another baby. He's got a little girl who thinks he makes the sun rise." He touched her between her legs, one of his fingers running over the seam of her lips. She felt herself grow damper, more ready for him. "He was a mean, scary-looking son of a bitch and now he's happy. He laughs. He puts bows in that little girl's hair. I saw that his life went on despite everything. And it gave me hope."

He stopped speaking then, bending over to kiss the middle of her chest, right where her heart was beating uncontrollably. And then he kissed her again, her collarbone, the tops of her breasts, as his finger nudged inside her, gifting her with one long stroke, which made her tremble.

"Honey," he whispered, pushing one of his long fingers all the way inside her.

The pleasure was so sharp that it almost verged on pain. Her nipples were tight, hard with arousal. She throbbed painfully between her legs and he was barely touching her. It was just his one finger, when she wanted him all over, when she wanted his heavy weight as relief.

"What are you doing to me?"

"I'm going to make love to you, Cass." He bent his lips to take her nipple in his mouth and the gentle sucking nearly undid her. "I need to, and I think you need me to." He switched to her other breast, taking his time tasting her, as his finger slowly worked inside her.

She couldn't speak, couldn't form words if her life depended on it. This was Wylie touching her; Wylie, whom she had thought about too many times over the past ten years; Wylie, who was the only person who could ever make her feel this good, cherished and wanted.

"Tell me no if you want me to stop."

She opened her mouth to say yes, but she didn't get the chance because he took her mouth in a kiss so deep the rest of the world ceased to exist. It was just him and her, and their tongues touching, and their hands stroking, and their bodies coming together.

He broke the kiss, breaking away from her completely to stand up and strip the boxers from his body. He was beautiful when naked. Thick and sacred and perfect. She wanted to reach out to stroke him, to take him in her hand and touch him, to take him between her lips and give him an ounce of the pleasure he had given to her that evening. However, she could do nothing but look at him; her body was too tight with anticipation to make a move.

Wylie didn't make her suffer long. He came back to her, settling his weight on top of her. The simple contact felt so good and she groaned.

He wrapped her leg around his waist, and slid his hard cock against her opening, not entering, just rubbing her, driving her closer to the edge. "Tell me no if you want me to stop."

She couldn't tell him no, even if she wanted. He was slowly nudging his way in, slowly filling her up, when she had been empty for so long.

"Please" was all she said. It was all she could manage.

"God, Cass. I missed you." He stroked all

the way inside her. "I missed you so damn much."

She missed him too. Missed his touches and his smiles and the slow, deep rumble of his voice. She couldn't tell him that because he took her mouth again and kissed it. It seemed like he was making up for all the kisses they had missed for the last ten years.

She wrapped her arms around him, opened her legs wider to him in an effort to get as close to him as possible. It was too much though — his fast, deep rhythm, and his hard, drugging kisses. She was all sensation, all raw nerves and good feelings. And he was too good; her climax was building. She wanted to stop it, slow it down, make this feeling last even longer, but it hit her hard and she cried out, her breath coming from her in sobs.

"Damn it, Cass." Wylie slammed into her, spilling himself inside her. For a long time they just lay there, their breathing hard, but slowing. Their bodies were an entwined mass of damp skin and limp limbs.

"Thank you," he whispered after a while. "Thank you." He separated from her, but just long enough so he could tuck her into his side and kiss her cheek. She fell asleep almost instantly, feeling happier than she could remember in a long time.

■ ■ ■ ■

Tanner Brennan walked up to Nova's salon, kicking himself for coming. He knew he should have stayed away from the big-mouthed little sister of his friend, but he couldn't. He needed a damn haircut, and the last time he went to the little barbershop in town, they royally screwed up his hair. Plus Nova was good.

As he spotted her cleaning up her station, he knew that the hot mess of a woman was good at so many more things than most people gave her credit for.

"Stretch!" She greeted him with that sassy smile of hers. Her full lips were painted red today. The shade could have looked sleazy on her, cheap, but it didn't. It suited her. Combined with all that thick, long, lush hair of hers, and the tight, long skirt she was wearing, she looked like she stepped out of a 1950s pinup magazine.

"Hey, big mouth." He looked around the empty shop, knowing that they always had clients until late on Friday nights. "You stayed open for me."

"I told you to come by." He sat in her chair and she draped a smock over him, studying him closely. "What would you like today?" she asked him in her husky voice.

He looked at her full mouth, and felt his groin tighten painfully. What he would like and what he could have were two very different things. He learned that a long time ago. "You mean you're not going to insult me today? I don't get many thrills in life anymore. Fighting with you is one of my only few."

She smiled softly at him; her lips wobbled a bit and he knew something was wrong. "I don't feel like busting your balls today. Okay? Now shut up and let me work my magic." She ran her fingers through his hair, rubbing his scalp, feeling the shape of his head. "You showered before you came here. Your hair is still damp."

"Well, I work hard. I can't be playing in people's hair all day, like you."

She looked thoughtfully at him, not taking the bait. "I would have thought you would have taken pleasure in stinking me out of the salon, but you smell good."

"A couple of our guys are out with the flu, so Wylie and I had to pull extra weight today. Although Wylie didn't seem to mind. He was so damn relaxed I thought he was going to float."

"It's Cass. He probably slept with her. Wylie's been in my life for two years now and I've never seen him act the way he's acting now."

"What do you mean?" Their locked eyes met in the mirror.

"Like he's alive. Like he has something."

"He's in love with her, Nova."

"Everybody is in love with her. My mother-in-law, my brother, even my own damn son." Her eyes flashed with tears and in a million years Tanner never expected to see prickly Nova melt so easily, especially in front of him.

"Are you jealous of Cassandra?"

"Duh, jackass! She's the only thing my kid talks about now. Cass helped him write his letters, and Cass reads his words with him, and Cass gave him a shower in the sprinklers."

"If it makes you uncomfortable, tell her to back off."

"I can't!" The tears spilled down her face. "I really like her and she's good for my boy. She was raised right and she's smart and she's got good manners. She's not fucked up like I am."

"I think she is, Nova. That's why she's here."

"No." She shook her head. "What happened to her was different than what happened to me. She was sad, but she's not screwed up like I am. She's not broken."

Tanner pulled Nova into his lap and hugged her close, smoothing kisses along her wet face. "You're not broken."

"I am. You don't know what it was like, how bad it was. I'll screw up my kid, just like my mama screwed up me."

"You won't. You are not your mother. Don't cry, baby." He rubbed his hand across her shoulders, feeling the smooth brown skin her tank top left bare. "You're not broken. You're just a little damaged, like me."

"You're damaged?" She looked up at him, her eyes full of tears.

"Like a dented can of peas. But I'm still good on the inside and so are you. Why don't you believe that about yourself?"

"Because I've screwed up so much."

"I bet you I've screwed up more. I've done some horrible shit in my life and some days I can barely look in the mirror, but I do. Because I try to be better than I was, and as long as I keep doing that, I know I'm on the right track."

"You should be a motivational speaker," she said, sniffing, resting her head in the crook of his shoulder, "because that shit was *almost* believable."

She wrapped her arms around his middle,

bringing herself closer, and he hated to admit that she felt comfortable in his lap, in his arms, like she had been sitting there forever. "Such a filthy mouth. You ever going to get some class?"

"Maybe. If you get some first." They looked at each other for a long moment and he couldn't help himself; he pushed his fingers deep into her thick, black hair. It felt like silk between his fingers. He could imagine how it would feel dragging across his chest; he could imagine how it would look spread across his pillow. She was the exact opposite of the type of woman he needed; but right now, as she sat in his lap, looking up at him with those sad, seductive eyes, he knew she was the only type of woman he wanted.

He wasn't sure who closed the distance between their lips, but they were kissing. Not him kissing her, or her kissing him, but they were kissing each other, slowly and deeply. Her kisses were sweet, even though they had a little heat to them, and he knew that there was a whole hell of a lot more to Nova that he wanted to get to know.

"Oh, my God." She broke the kiss and scrambled off his lap. "I can't believe you tricked me into doing that! You're good at it, but we are never, ever doing that again!

And if you come near me, I will zap you with my stun gun, and if you tell anybody, I'll stab you!" She grabbed a pair of scissors and angrily chopped into his hair. "I'm lethal with these things."

She was, and he walked out of there with the best haircut of his life.

CHAPTER 14

The smell of warm bread greeted Wylie as he walked into the house that evening. It was a welcome smell. For so long he had been used to coming home to an empty, quiet house, eating dinner over the kitchen sink and watching TV until he passed out. Since Cass had come, he realized that returning to his house at night felt entirely different.

For a moment he leaned against the doorjamb and watched her work. She was making dinner again, chopping tomatoes for a salad and humming softly as she did. She wore a baby pink shirt and jeans that hugged her increasingly beautiful body, but she was barefoot, with her toes painted a bright shade of red. So different than how he saw them last night when he ran his fingers over them. He couldn't take his eyes off her — not just because she was beautiful, but because part of him still couldn't believe she was with him again.

He had made love to her last night, and all throughout the day he kept thinking about it: the way her legs felt wrapped around him, the way she moaned his name and pushed her sweet body against his. And the smell of her scented cream lingered on his skin even in the morning. He thought about not washing it off so he could take her scent with him wherever he went that day. Every time he thought about her, he hardened, wanting to rush through his work so he could get back to her. Yet, he felt guilty for seducing her. And he had seduced her. He knew as soon as he walked into her room, he was going to make love to her that night.

He wasn't sure if she was ready to take such a big step. Ready to make love to a man who wasn't her husband. That's why he talked to her so much, so she would know it was *him* she was with, so she would equate *his* words with *his* touch.

She said *his* name while he was inside her. She looked *him* in the eye while they were making love. Still, he wondered if she thought about Terrance while she did it. It was an ugly thought after a beautiful moment, but it was there.

"Are you just going to stand there being

creepy, or are you going to come over here?"

"How did you know I was here?" He walked over to her, placing his hand on the small of her back.

"I can feel your eyes on me. Plus the sound of your truck pulling in the driveway is a dead giveaway."

"And here I thought all my special military training helped me be sneaky."

Her lips curled into a smile that simultaneously aroused him and brought him comfort. She was so lost when she first came here. Sometimes he thought she was never going to smile again. "Didn't anybody ever tell you never to sneak up on a woman holding a knife?"

He pulled her into him, her back into his front, her soft behind into his groin. His slid his hand up her arm till it met her wrist that held the knife. Finding her pressure point, he squeezed slightly, causing her fingers to release her grip. "I can still disarm anybody. I'm really good at that. Top of my class in school."

"Were you, macho man?" He let her go, but she didn't move away from him, instead she leaned into him more. "Sometimes I wondered if I knew how to disarm him, would all those people have had to die?"

Her words left him speechless. He was just

playing, being silly, but he of all people knew that anything could trigger a nasty flashback. He wrapped his arms around her, resting his lips on her ear so she would remember where she was, remember that she was here with him and not in some hellish nightmare. "You saved those babies in your class. You did exactly what you were meant to do. There was nothing you could have changed."

"I yelled at Teo today," she said, her voice coming out shaky. "He was pretending his finger was a gun and shooting at imaginary bad guys. He kept saying, 'Die! Die!' and I snapped at him. I asked him if he really knew what it was like to see somebody die and I told him it was horrible and that it haunts you. I yelled at him and he was just being a little boy. He was doing what all little boys do."

"Don't beat yourself up. You couldn't help your feelings. It takes time." He kissed the side of her face. "And Teo needs to be yelled at once in a while. It helps keep him grounded."

She turned in his arms, stood on her tiptoes and gently pressed her mouth to his. "Thank you." She kissed him again, a little longer, a little deeper this time.

"For what?" he asked. He felt breathless

again, excited. She was the only one who ever made him feel that way.

"For accepting my crazy." She went to kiss him again, but he pulled away.

"You're not crazy," he said firmly. "You're normal. You're going through what any person who lived through that hell would go through, and I want you to stop thinking that there is something wrong with you."

She looked at him for a long time, as if processing his words, and then kissed him again. Her tongue swept into his mouth; her hands crept up his shirt to feel his skin. He went rock hard then. It didn't go unnoticed, because she pushed herself into his erection, rubbing against him, wearing at his already-thin control.

"Cass, what the hell are you doing to me?" he asked in between her deep, drugging kisses.

"You're beautiful, Wylie."

"Not as beautiful as you." He kissed her forehead and stepped away from her. "But if you don't stop that, I'm pretty sure we're going to end up with a burned dinner."

She bit her lower lip, looking at him through her lashes. She nodded, then did the sexiest thing he had ever seen her do. She turned off the oven and in the process turned him on more than he had ever been.

He felt a low growl escape from his throat. Her eyes widened, but she didn't step away. She didn't run like she should have. She stepped closer; her hands trembling slightly as she reached for his zipper. He froze; his breath came out ragged; his heart slammed against his rib cage.

She looked into his eyes as she unbuttoned and unzipped him. Her warm hand slid over his swollen member and he shuddered. Her touch was too good. He clenched his teeth, watching her as she licked her lips and took him in her mouth.

He cursed, letting out a long string of foul words, because it felt like she was hurting him. That warm pull from her silky, wet mouth was so damn exquisite that it was painful. She took him all the way into her mouth and he couldn't take it.

He yanked himself away from her and she let out a little yelp as he pulled her to her feet and savagely tore at her pants. He was never going to make it to the bedroom or living room. The kitchen table was even too far, so he leaned her against the wall and pushed inside her. She was wet and tight and hot and welcoming, and he pumped inside her wildly like the ruffian some people accused him of being. She came, squeezing around him, urging him to come to his own climax, but he didn't want to let go yet. The sex was too good, and too raw, and too hot, to be done so soon. So he kept pumping, loving the way their smells mingled, loving the way the bodies sounded as they slapped together, loving the way Cass wasn't quiet, the way she cried out and groaned, and dug her nails into his arms.

Orgasm struck her again and this time the pull of her sweet wetness around him was too much. He let go, spilling himself inside her as he chanted her name. When his breathing slowed, he let her down and she slid to the floor, her jeans around her ankles.

"I think I've gone blind," she said, exhaling, a tiny smile playing at her lips. He got on the floor with her, pulling her pants completely off. The sight of her sitting on the kitchen floor, with her bare bottom, was enough to cause him to go half hard again.

He couldn't help himself; he slid closer to her so he could feel the smooth skin on her legs.

"Was I too rough with you?" he asked, kissing the curve of her neck.

"No. No." She shook her head. "I just think my legs are not good anymore."

"They feel good to me." He ran his hand up to the back of her thigh, his fingers just brushing her body.

"Take off your pants. I shouldn't be the only one with none on."

He did as she asked and she watched him, her eyes never leaving his quickly forming erection. "You see what you do to me?" He sat down next to her again. "You probably should sleep somewhere else tonight, like another state."

She grinned at him, leaning over to set a chaste kiss on his mouth. She reached beneath her shirt, unhooking her bra, and sliding it off without removing her shirt. Her nipples pressed against the thin fabric and she knew he was watching her. She knew she was arousing him even more. She took one of his hands, placing it under her shirt, right on her breast. His thumb immediately went to her erect nipple.

"See what you do to me?" She lay back on the floor, pulling him down with her so that he settled right between her legs. "One more time, please." She kissed his mouth softly as her hand settled on his behind. "One more time and then take me out to dinner. We're going to need to eat after this."

"Where's Miss Cass?" Teo asked Wylie from the passenger seat of his truck.

Wylie smiled at the mention of her name.

Last night . . . he couldn't find the right words to describe it. They had been wild and rough in the kitchen, then tender and slow that night in the bedroom. He didn't know what was going on between them. He didn't want to think about the future or the past. He just wanted to live in the present. But he knew he could only live that way for so long.

"She's at the house, buddy. It's Saturday. I figured I'd let her sleep in today."

"She came with us last Saturday," he said with a little bit of a pout in his voice.

"Yeah, but that was before fall T-ball started. I always take your games. It's man time. I thought you liked it."

"Miss Cass didn't come because she's mad at me." He looked down at his feet. "She don't want to see me no more."

"That's not true. She's tired today, Teo."

"I was bad yesterday, Uncle Wylie. I was playing too much."

"You weren't bad," he said as he pulled into the parking lot of the field. "You just made Miss Cass think of her husband. She got upset, but not at you." He paused for a moment, floundering to find the right words to explain it all to a five-year-old. "She's upset at the bad man who hurt her and her husband."

"He's dead," Teo said bluntly. "She told me."

"Yes, that's right. But she was sad last night when I got back from taking Mansi to the doctor, because she felt bad for yelling at you. She wants you to like her."

"I love her," he said matter-of-factly. "She's good with me, you know."

"I know," he agreed, trying to hold back a grin when his nephew was so somber. "She takes care of me too, and she's not mad. I promise. We stayed up late last night and she was tired. And I don't know why you're so sensitive about her yelling at you. Me and Mansi yell at you all the time. You don't seem to care about that one little bit."

He waved a dismissive hand at Wylie. "Ah, I don't even hear you guys anymore."

That time Wylie did laugh. "You don't hear me anymore, boy?" He ruffled his nephew's hair. "Well, I guess you aren't going to be able to hear me when I invite you out for hot dogs at Jimmy's this afternoon. Or when I order ice cream later. Me and Miss Cass will go without you."

"She's going to come?" Teo looked up at him hopefully. The kid had it as bad as he did. He couldn't blame him.

"Yeah, unless she's still sleeping. I told

you she was tired. We stayed up late last night."

"Were you kissing?"

"What now?"

"Were you kissing Miss Cass last night? I saw you kissing her before. I know you like to."

"She's pretty," he said, not giving an answer.

"Yeah, I think you should marry her," Teo said, nodding. "That way you could be her husband and she won't be sad that she don't have one no more."

He looked at his nephew's innocent face and wished it could all be that simple, but it wasn't. Things between him and Cass never were. "It sounds like you really care about her feelings. You want to marry her?"

Teo looked horrified at that suggestion. "No. She's really too old for me. I want you to marry her so I can live with you and her."

"Live with us? What about Mansi and your mother?"

"Mansi's too old. She's too tired for a little boy."

"Your mother's not too old."

"No, but she's too busy for me. She doesn't want me anymore."

Wylie found Cass in the kitchen when he

came in from T-ball later that day, but this time her head was in the oven and the whole kitchen smelled like lemons. It was also sparkling clean. He felt uneasy about it. He didn't like the idea of her cooking and cleaning for him.

"What are you doing?" He grabbed her by the hips and pulled her into him. She wore yellow rubber gloves and one of his T-shirts. There was a smudge of something on her cheek and he couldn't help but think how cute she looked. Although it never mattered what she wore, because he found her sexy no matter what.

"I'm performing brain surgery. What do you think I'm doing?" She turned in his arms and kissed his cheek. "How was T-ball?"

"Good." He frowned at her. "You were supposed to be lounging around the house today, acting like a well-satisfied woman, or maybe I'm not taking care of you good enough?"

She grinned at him, a full happy grin that lifted his mood just being in the presence of it. "Are you saying my not staying in bed all day is an affront to your manhood?"

"Yes." He nodded.

She laughed and rested her face against his chest. "You take care of me. I feel more taken care of with you than with anybody else. But I spent a year in bed. I wasted a year of my life doing nothing."

"You were mourning!"

"See? You even make excuses for me. I can do stuff around here. I thought we talked about this already."

"But I thought that meant you were just going to cook sometimes. Not scrub my oven."

"Your oven needed to be scrubbed. Have you ever cleaned that thing? It's bad."

"It never occurred to me to clean it."

"You're so different than Terrance. He would knock me out of the way to clean the kitchen. And I like to clean, but I couldn't do it as well as he could, so I just let him do it. I wasn't going to argue with him over who gets to clean."

"He would have done well in the Marines. I've never seen a man make a bed so well."

"No. He wouldn't have. The man couldn't take an order to save his life. He was too outspoken, too intellectual. His mouth would have gotten him in trouble."

He had always been compared to Terrance. It was unfair, but Terrance always came out the winner in the end. "Yeah, and I'm the big, dumb guy who can always take orders. That's a point in my favor."

She smacked the back of his head, her eyes sparking. "What the hell does that mean? Do you think that I think you're dumb? Because if you do think that, then you don't know me at all. I have never —"

He cut her off with a kiss, knowing it was never Cass who made him feel less than. "Hush. I'm jealous of Terrance sometimes."

"Why?" Her forehead scrunched in confusion and suddenly things became much clearer for him.

"Because he ended up with the only thing I've ever really wanted. And sometimes I hate him for it."

Cass was quiet for a long moment, studying his face as if trying to find meaning in his words. "You shouldn't hate a dead man. It's not doing either of you any good. What happened ten years ago, Wylie? You didn't just disappear from my life. You disappeared from his too."

"Nothing happened, Cass." He shook his head, hating to lie to her. It was clear she didn't know the thing that ended their friendship and he wondered why Terrance never told her. Surely, it would have made him look like a hero in Cassandra's eyes. "We were talking about my dirty oven. It's on its last legs. I was thinking I should get a new one. You can pick it out if you want.

You can pick out some other things too. It was past time I started fixing up the house, and you might be better than me at picking out the pretty stuff."

"I wouldn't be." Her expression didn't relax and he knew his effort to distract her wasn't working. "You made our room beautiful all by yourself."

"Our." She said *our* like they had something together. Like whatever it is that they were was lasting. "I had help. Tanner did a lot."

"You're an idiot sometimes," she said, still studying his face. "You don't ever realize how good you are. I want my own car."

"What?"

"I want a way to get around the island without having to depend on you all the time. I want to be able to go to the grocery store and visit Nova and take Teo places sometimes. It doesn't have to be new, just something to get me around."

A car meant that this situation was more than temporary. They should talk about it, about what it meant for them, but he couldn't bring himself to bring it up. Because he didn't want to risk her coming to her senses and going away. "Okay," he agreed. "We'll go today. I came in here to tell you that Teo is waiting outside for you on the porch. I brought him back with me."

"Why didn't you tell me sooner, you dope?" She took off her gloves and he followed her outside to the porch.

His nephew was sitting on the swing, his feet dangling high above the ground. In his lap was the bunch of sunflowers they picked up at a local farm stand.

"Hello, Mr. Teo." Cass sat next to him on the bench, wrapping her arm around him, bringing him close like it was the most natural thing in the world.

She would have been a mother by now. He knew the loss of her unborn baby sent her reeling, but he felt sorry for that baby too, sorry that he would never know a mother like Cass.

"How was T-ball today?"

"It was good. I slid into home plate. Coach said I had good spirit, but said I should save my sliding till I get to Little League."

"Oh, did he?"

"Coach is a lady. Girls can be coaches too, you know."

"How silly of me. Of course they can." She took off his cap and ran her fingers through his curls. "Why do you seem so down today?"

" 'Cause I hurt your feelings yesterday

and I feel bad." He dumped the flowers in her lap. "Uncle Wylie said when he makes a lady feel bad, he gets her flowers and she stops being mad."

"But I'm not mad at you, Teo."

"That's what he said, but I wanted to make sure."

"You can be sure." She took his small face in her hands and kissed him all over. Wylie thought Teo would squirm at the affection, but he didn't. Wylie realized that Teo didn't get that a lot from his own mother. And he needed it. Wylie knew how hard it was to grow up without it. "I'm not going to promise I won't yell at you again, because I probably will. I'm not going to promise to never be mad at you, because let's face it, you're an icky little boy, and icky little boys can be annoying sometimes. But I promise never to stay mad at you, because you are a good boy and I like having you as my friend." She kissed his nose. "And thank you for my flowers. They are very beautiful."

Teo looked close to tears, but he blinked them away. "Uncle Wylie said we were going to get hot dogs and ice cream for lunch. You can come if you want."

"I want." She nodded. "Go inside and get washed up. We are going to look for a car for me today too. You can help me pick it out."

"Okay," he said, getting up. "I think it should be red. You like red. You said it was a power color."

As soon as the screen door closed behind him, two fat tears slipped out of Cassandra's eyes. "What a beautiful, sensitive little boy he is. Now I feel doubly like shit for yelling at him yesterday."

Wylie eased down next to her on the swing, wrapping his arm around her. "I think I want to take him."

"What do you mean?"

"From Nova. I think I should keep him. I think he would be better off without her anyway."

"You're wrong," she said firmly. "You're a thousand percent wrong."

"Why do you think he got so upset when he thought you were mad at him? He thinks you're going to be like Nova and stay away from him. The boy thinks she doesn't want him anymore. He told me so today."

"Nova is not the world's best mother, but she loves that boy. It's in her eyes. It's in the things she does for him, how she washes his clothes, how she makes his lunch. You should see her face when she talks about him. She's proud of him, but something happened to her along the way that has her convinced she's bad for him. And it doesn't help that you and Mansi and everybody else let her continue to think that way."

"How could I convince her otherwise when the only thing I see her do is pawn him off on somebody else?"

"Weren't you listening? She's not spending nights on the town. She's working, taking weddings to put money away for him. And that check you give her to help support him goes directly into his college fund. If you talked to your sister instead of arguing with her, you might know that. She's not a bad person, Wylie, but some bad things have happened to her along the way."

CHAPTER 15

Cassandra was surprised when they pulled up to Tanner's house that afternoon. They were there because Wylie said Tanner knew about cars and he would be the best one to help her pick out a used one while she stayed.

"While you stayed." Those words made her think back to Harmony Falls, to the perfectly good, sensible Volvo she had parked in the garage in the home she had shared with her husband. She hadn't used it in months, hadn't driven herself since that day she had the breakdown in the supermarket. It was just sitting there, as well as her house and her things — and the life she once had there. But she tried not to think about that as Tanner's house came into view. She was taking things one day at a time. And today she wanted a car.

Tanner's house had an ocean view too. Not like Wylie's, which was only visible at a distance, but this house was directly on the beach. The ocean seemed to be his back-yard. It wasn't one of the old, charming, cottagelike houses that populated their neighborhood either, but rather an impressive-looking, modern house with a huge wraparound porch and a two-car garage.

"Being a government contractor pays well, doesn't it?" She looked over to Wylie as he stopped his truck.

"Pretty well, but not this well."

"It must be nice waking up here every morning."

"You thinking about leaving my house, Cass? Tanner might have one-hundred-eighty-degree views from his bedroom, but nobody can fry up bacon like me."

She reached over and slid her hand across Wylie's face. Her thumb brushed his strong jawline and she couldn't help but think how much he needed to be taken care of. There was a lot of hurt inside him, probably even more than she had. He was hiding some-thing from her, maybe he was hiding many things from her. Each day she learned more and more about the past they shared, but she had been too afraid to come out and ask him, too afraid that she wouldn't like what she learned, too afraid to let hurt stomp on the happiness she was just beginning to feel again.

She had always suspected that something went wrong between Terrance and Wylie. Because even if Wylie hadn't wanted to be with her, even if he needed to find his life elsewhere, it didn't explain cutting himself away from the only family he'd had at the time. And Terrance was his family. They were more brotherly than most brothers, and they had never spoken another word to each other. Terrance hadn't ever tried to reach out to him. He never tried to track him down and demand an answer. He never mentioned his absence to her, but she knew it affected him. It had to affect him. She knew that his life was different without his best friend in it.

"You think I would trade delicious bacon for a house with a million-dollar view?" She shook her head. "But if a man comes along who knows how to make little bowls out of bacon, I'm out of there faster than you can blink."

Shaking his head, he smiled at her. "I wouldn't blame you, Cass. Not one little bit." He turned around to Teo in the backseat. "How you holding up, champ? You think you can hold off on lunch for a little while longer?"

"Yeah." He nodded. "Miss Cass gave me half a peanut butter sandwich and some milk. I'm good for almost two hours."

"Almost two hours? We'll hurry then."

"You don't have to. A good car is an important thing to buy."

Cassandra turned around to look at him. "Who told you that?"

"My mother. She said to always have a good car, no matter what, because you never know when you might have to live in it."

Cassandra locked eyes with Wylie. He shook his head slightly; she knew what he was thinking. He wanted to take Teo. She wanted him too, but Nova, deep down, was a good mother, or she would be once she worked her issues out. "Come on, Teo." She got out of the truck and took the boy's hand. "Let's see how nice this house is."

Tanner stepped out on the porch just as they made their way up the stairs. The former ranger was lean and tall, but he was ruggedly handsome, with his crooked smile and wrinkled button-down shirt.

"This is quite a house you have here," Cass said when she walked up to him. "Do you have an elderly sugar mama we don't know about?"

Tanner's eyes widened in surprise, but he laughed at her comment. "I think she would object to 'elderly.' She says eighty is the new thirty."

"I didn't know you were into cougars. Actually, I think eighty might be too old to be called a *cougar.* Maybe *saber-toothed tiger*? They are prehistoric, aren't they?"

He grinned at her and then looked to Wylie, who had come up behind them. "She's gotten sassy with her new haircut and a little mean. I like it."

"Sampson lost all his power when his hair was cut. She gained more with hers."

"I'll say." He picked Teo up and lifted him till he was at eye level, which she had seen him do before. "Hello, sir. How are you today?"

"I went to T-ball this morning. My coach is a girl. I had to tell Miss Cass that it's okay for girls to be coaches too. You can come to T-ball next Saturday if you want. It's man time."

"Teo . . . ," his uncle began, "I don't think —"

"I'll come. I'll bring the beers."

"You can't drink beer there," Teo scolded.

"Oh, all right. I guess I'll still come." Tanner put him down with a ruffle to his hair. "Come inside, guys. I know of some cars I think you'll want to take a look at."

They stepped inside to see the interior of

Tanner's house, which was as lovely as the outside. It was beautifully decorated and elegant, yet it felt warm and homey. It didn't seem like the home of a single man in his thirties "Tanner, I was just joking about the sugar mama, but do you really have one? Or are you rich? This place is truly beautiful."

"*I'm* not rich. I just know someone who is and they are letting me have the place while I work here."

"You've been here for a year, right? Don't the owners ever want to use their house? It's so lovely. I mean it's very nice of them to let you use it, but they must miss it."

Tanner frowned as if he disapproved. "They have others. Trust me. They've only been here a handful of times. Plus I've done plenty for them to earn staying here."

"Oh." It seemed that she had touched a nerve. There was a lot to Tanner she didn't know, but then again there was a lot to the men she loved that she didn't know either. "I wished you would have lied to me and told me you were rich. If you knew how to make bacon bowls, I would have moved right in here with you."

" 'Bacon bowls'?" He frowned again.

"Don't mind her," Wylie said as he kissed her beneath her ear twice. "She's in a weird mood today."

She was. The whole morning she felt punchy and jumpy, like she couldn't settle in her own skin. It was why she'd cleaned the kitchen and scrubbed the oven. She had been left alone too long with her thoughts. And besides the usual ones of Wylie and Terrance, another troubling one kept popping into her head.

What are you going to do with the rest of your life?

She didn't know. She had no idea where life was going to take her next week, and she was okay with that for now, but she wasn't sure if she was going to be okay with that forever.

"Uncle Wylie," Teo called to him as he tugged on his hand. "I have to go to the bathroom."

"It's down the hall, on the right." Tanner motioned with his thumb. "I'm going to show Cass the listings." He brought his laptop over to the couch, inviting her to sit with a motion of his head. "So you and Wylie," he said softly, "I knew he was crazy about you, but it seems like you two are" — he struggled for a word — *"closer."*

He was asking if they were a couple and she didn't have an answer for that. Ten years ago he was so hell-bent at hiding them from the world, and then he walked out on her without an explanation. However, that was ten years ago and so much had changed.

"Thank you for helping Wylie make that beautiful room for me. We enjoy sleeping in it."

"He's happier now," he said, glancing at the hallway that Wylie and Teo had disappeared through. "He's always been a good guy, but he's smiling a lot more recently. He's alive now. I know that the thing that brought you here was horrible and tragic, and that you came here to heal, but you're helping him too. I think you're good for him."

"Thank you." She didn't know what else to say to that. Wylie did need to be loved. He did need to be taken care of. He was human. Needing people was human.

"These are some solid cars," he said, returning his attention to the computer. "This Volvo only has thirteen thousand miles. And here's a Subaru that's really good in bad weather."

"I had a Volvo in Connecticut. I don't want something dependable and reliable. I want something fun and red. Teo said I should get a red car."

"You want a fun red car?" His grin turned devilish. "I think I got something for you right here."

"You do?"

" 'You do' what?" Wylie walked back into the room, with Teo just ahead of him.

"I've got the perfect car for Cass in the garage."

They followed him through the house to the garage, where they found that it wasn't just a garage but a workshop, with every tool imaginable hanging neatly on the walls.

"Whoa," Teo said as he looked around.

"Best part of the house," Tanner agreed as he looked around the space with a smile. "There's your car, Cassandra."

She set her eyes on a vintage Camaro convertible in cherry red. She never had a fancy car or anything in a flashy color. Immediately thoughts of Terrance floated into her mind. Her next car was supposed to be a minivan — the safest one out there, with the best gas mileage, in the color gray.

"I'll take it," she said as she walked over to it, running her hands along the shiny body.

"What? Cass, I thought we were going to a car dealer."

"We don't have to." She looked at Teo. "What do you think?"

"You have to drive it first," he said sensibly. "That's what people do when they buy cars."

"You're right." She looked over at Tanner. "I still want it."

Wylie shot him a look, but he said nothing.

"Don't you want to know more about it? It's a 1969 Camaro convertible. I got it from a guy in Vineyard Haven whose wife was making him get rid of it. It took me almost eight months to fix it up. It's a muscle car, and it's got a lot of power, but it purrs like a kitten."

Cass opened the door and sat in the driver's seat, stroking her hands along the smooth steering wheel, feeling excited about finally choosing what she wanted. "How much do you want for it?"

"Give me a hundred bucks."

"What? No." She shook her head as she looked at all the work he must have put into it. "It's worth way more than that."

"It is, but consider it a rental fee. Use it as long as you want while you're here, and if you still want it at the end of two months, I'll sell it to you."

"Terrance would have never let me have this. He would have said it's foolish and impractical and dangerous. Not for a lady like me." She looked at Wylie, whose expression was unreadable. "Why aren't you saying anything?"

"You're an adult. You can make your own decisions, and if this car is something that you really want, you should have it. But if you want to know my opinion about this car, I would tell you that I would have been on the same page with Terrance and would rather see you in an armored car than a steel trap that will crumble like an aluminum can when it's hit. I would rather see you in a car that's good in the snow and rain. I would rather you drive anything but this. But if it's what you want, then I think you should definitely get it."

She looked at his stern face and felt that familiar pang she felt whenever she looked at him lately. Was it love? It couldn't be. She had loved him since she was thirteen. She was in love with him since she was eighteen years old. This was something else she was feeling.

She left the car and hugged him around his middle. "Where can I get some fuzzy dice around here?"

He cracked a smile. "We'll find you some. Come on. Let's go eat lunch."

"Nova, come out here!"

Wylie watched Cass yell excitedly as she

threw her new car into park. He hated the idea of her driving around in that old muscle car, but when he saw how her face lit up as she was getting into it, he couldn't say anything to dissuade her. Not that he had any right to do so. He wasn't her husband. Getting the car wasn't their decision. It was hers alone.

But she was living with him, sharing his bed. She had become a part of his life, a part of his thoughts and plans and routines. And if she left . . . He didn't want to think about what his life would be like with her gone.

He would go in and meet other people and have good times. But he would feel empty, be empty, like something vital to him was missing.

"Nova!" Cass called again, this time honking the horn and fairly vibrating in her seat. "Come see what I got!"

Wylie pulled his eyes away from Cass and looked over to Tanner, who had driven with him. "See what you did? She's more hyper than Teo."

"What was I supposed to do, man? Did you see her face when she saw the car? It was like forty-five Christmas mornings fell in her lap." He looked out the window at Cass and to Nova, who finally came out of her house. "She was so sad when she came here. I like seeing her happy, and if letting her drive the car around for a few weeks will make her happy . . ." He shrugged his shoulders. "It's not a big thing."

"She hasn't driven in months. She hasn't left the house alone. Before I went to get her, she wouldn't even get out of bed. She's come so far, but I'm scared for her because I know what it's like. I know what it's like to hear a sound that takes you back to that day."

"Or smell a smell that brings up a memory so strong you want to curl up in a ball and cry."

He stared at Tanner's profile as the other man looked out the window. He knew Tanner had nasty scars on his chest, but he never shared what had happened. He just showed up one day and offered his experience. "What happened to you? I don't think we've ever talked about why you got out."

"You want to know my war story?" He shook his head and grinned. "I need to tell that story over a couple of strong drinks." He opened the door and stepped out. "I wouldn't worry about Cass with the car though. She drives like my grandma."

He nodded as he got out of the car. Teo had driven over with Cass, and Wylie knew that she was extra careful as they made the short trip to Nova's place because of Teo.

"Is this why you were making all that damn racket?" Nova said as she ran her hand along the body of the car. "Well, honey, it's beautiful. We're going to have to take it for our girls' night out." She looked over to her son, still sitting in the front seat. "Hi, baby," she said almost shyly. "How was your game today?"

"Good." He kept his answer short, which was odd for him. He seemed to have so many words for everyone except his mother. They were almost like familiar strangers.

"What about your shoes? Were they too tight? You need to tell me if they are so we can get new ones. Okay?"

"They're fine. Uncle Wylie checked them before I played."

"Oh." She looked over to him. "Hey, brother," she said quietly, which was un- usual for her. In fact, everything was quiet about her today. Her hair was loose and long, as it always was, but she wore no makeup, plus an old T-shirt and torn jeans. Nova was usually glamorously beautiful; today she was just plain pretty, and that made him wonder what was up.

"Hey."

"You finally stopped being such a damn

control freak and let this woman get a car." She injected some sass into her voice, but he could tell it was halfhearted. "It's about time. I'm surprised that you don't keep her chained to you."

He walked over to his sister and put her in a gentle headlock. "Why are you so mean to me? Huh?" He ruffled her hair. "Is it because I'm smarter and better-looking and generally a nicer person than you are?"

"Yeah." She leaned into him, wrapping her arms around him. "That's exactly why."

He hugged her back, resting his chin on her forehead. A memory of the last time he hugged her like this came to mind. It was just before his father died, one of the few times his mother came to see him after she left. Nova had been six at the time and their mother . . . She was drunk. The whole entire visit had been colored by her alcohol-infused happiness, her slurred words and clumsy behavior. And yet he hadn't wanted her to leave. She was his mother. She wasn't always supposed to leave. She was supposed to want him. When it was time to say good-bye and Nova wrapped her arms around him so tightly, he had the distinct feeling that Nova hadn't wanted to leave — if Nova could have traded places, she would have been glad to stay. Somehow that image of the sad little six-year-old she was had drifted from his mind.

"What's wrong?" he asked her seriously. "You need something?"

"No." She pulled away from him. "It's PMS." She looked at Tanner, not saying anything, but their eyes locked and held for just a little longer than Wylie was comfortable with. Tanner was a good guy and Nova was a beautiful girl, but Nova was his baby sister.

"Hey, big mouth." His eyes wandered over her, but there was concern there.

"Hey, stretch. Your hair actually looks good today."

"I know. I brushed it two hundred times before I went to bed last night."

She nodded. "A lady should always take care of herself — even one as ugly as yourself."

"We were going to get ice cream, and your kid suggested that we bring you along too."

"He did?" She looked over at Teo, who was in deep conversation with Cass. "I'd better not. I have a sink full of dishes."

"Get your big mouth in the car, Nova." Tanner pushed her toward the convertible. "Your kid wants you there."

"You're lying," she whispered. "You're just using what I said against me."

"I don't care enough to do that. Just get in the damn car." She looked at Wylie. "Is it true? Did he ask for me?"

"Yeah," he said truthfully. "He said that you liked black-cherry ice cream."

"I do." She nodded. "Okay. I'll come. Let me get my wallet."

"Ice cream is on me today," Cass said to them all while she was still focused on Teo. "Get in the back, kid. Mommy is going to ride next to me."

Two nights later she was sitting next to Wylie in bed. He was reading *For Whom the Bell Tolls,* and he looked so engrossed in the story that she didn't want to disturb him. She hadn't seen him read much since she had been there, but there were books all over the house and there was a library card in his wallet. Cass remembered that while growing up, Terrance had been good in every subject, acing every class with ease, but Wylie was good in English. He made it into the honors class his junior year of high school, which must have seemed like such a little accomplishment to the Millers compared to all the ones Terrance had. But it was something to be proud of and she wondered if they ever told Wylie that.

"Is the light bothering you?" He set the

book down on his chest. "I can turn it off if you want to go to sleep."

"No. Don't. You really like to read, don't you?"

"I didn't before. I used to hate it, but my pop couldn't read so good. Neither could my grandmother. I used to read all the mail to him and help him with the taxes. At night he used to make me read the newspaper to him. Reading wasn't something I liked to do. It was something I had to do. It was like a chore. But then Mr. Miller gave me *In Cold Blood* by Truman Capote and I realized that books could have sex and violence and cusswords in them, and that opened up a whole new world for me."

"Give a boy a dirty book and you'll turn him into a lifetime reader. Eric gave you that book, huh? You two had a pretty good relationship, but you never called him anything but Mr. Miller."

"No. I knew my place, and you know how I feel about children calling adults by their first names. We don't do it where I'm from."

"But you're a man now." She leaned over and kissed his cheek. "You're a good one who loves his baby sister. She told me you stopped by the shop today."

"She has her moments, and I can't believe she told you that."

"She can't believe you showed up."

"I think Tanner has a thing for her."

"Of course he does. She's the most beautiful woman on the island and she's sexy. There's a sweetness about her too, which is hard to see sometimes, and when I mistakenly thought you had a kid with her, I wanted to scratch her eyes out."

"You did?" He chuckled. He wrapped his arm around her and rested his lips on her forehead. "I don't have children yet. My grandmamma always said don't have sex with anybody you don't want to be the mother of your babies."

"And did you follow that advice?"

"Not always. It's hard being a sixteen-year-old boy and trying to keep it in your pants. Common sense doesn't often prevail. But the older I got, the more I listened to her advice."

"And you don't have any babies yet." She looked up at him, studying his strong profile and sleepy face. "Are you going to make love to me tonight?"

"Do you want to?"

"Yes. Unless you don't want to. It's okay if you just want to sleep tonight."

"Come here." He sat up straight and patted his lap. She straddled him so that they were face-to-face. He cupped her cheeks in his hands, bringing her closer. He looked deep into her eyes like he could see inside her, and sometimes she was sure he could. Sure that he knew all her thoughts, could see all her feelings. "I always want to make love to you. Always. I always have wanted to make love to you. I don't think there has been a minute or a second since I've met you that I haven't wanted to be with you."

Then why did you leave? She wanted to ask that question so bad that sometimes it burned a hole in her stomach, but she didn't want to have that conversation now, because she wanted to make love more.

She leaned in closer and gave him a soft kiss. He kissed her back just as gently, but his tongue swept deeply into her mouth. His kiss made her feel good and beautiful and special. Like she was important to him. She wondered if every woman Wylie kissed felt this way; and if they did, then every woman should experience kissing him just once.

"Take this off." He touched her night-gown, and his voice was even huskier with arousal. He was hard already. His erection was gently probing between her legs, even though the thin material of his boxers separated them. "I want to see you."

She slipped her nightgown off over her

head, revealing herself to him. He just looked for a while, looking as though seeing her for the first time instead of the hundredth. They had often made love like this when they were younger. Face-to-face. Eyes open. No covers or darkness or barriers. "You are beautiful." He touched her breast, simply sliding his rough palm across it, making her nipple tighten at the sensation. "Sometimes I wonder if you really want this or you are just doing it because you know how much I need you." He cupped her breasts, squeezing them, running his thumbs over her sensitive skin.

"W-what" — she stuttered because his touch felt so good that she couldn't keep her thoughts coherent — "do you mean by that?"

He peppered kisses across her collarbone and then the top of her chest. "You never say no to me. Sometimes I feel greedy for wanting you so much."

"You shouldn't. I want this. I want you."

He pulled her nipple into his mouth, gently sucking on it, laving it with his tongue. "I thought about you all the time, Cass. Even after I knew you were with him. Even though I knew it was wrong," he told her as he kissed her heart. "It was the worst when I was on my first tour in Afghanistan.

I was surrounded by other men, but at night sometimes I thought I could smell your soap."

Why was he saying these things to her? Why did he have to be so sweet and so beautiful? He had left her. And by doing so, he had changed her life. He had changed all her plans.

He captured her mouth just as that thought settled in her brain. It was like his kiss had powers, because soon she couldn't think straight anymore. His hands were stroking down her body, arousing her, soothing her, loving her. His mouth was on top of hers, pulling her out of her thoughts, making her want him more.

"Are you ready, honey?" He touched her between her legs, only to groan when he found her slick. "I don't think I can wait anymore." He leaned back against the headboard, looking at her. "I want you to be in charge tonight. Do what you want tonight."

She hesitated at first. She liked the often-reckless feel to their sex, the way her mind shut off when he touched her. But tonight he was asking for the opposite. She ran her hands across his shoulder and then used her lips, kissing the little white scar that was there. She moved her lips up to kiss his throat, flicking her tongue across his Adam's apple. He swallowed hard. His erection twitched between her legs. He still wore his boxers, but she wanted to feel his skin. She released him, rubbing him against her wetness, sliding his head along her engorged nub. He inhaled sharply, dug his fingers into her hips, and she knew that he was on the edge. But she didn't care because he felt too good there, and his thick fingers biting into her skin felt even better. She placed him at her opening, sliding down just a bit so she could feel his girth, but not enough to let him enter.

He cursed violently as she retreated and rubbed him along the length of her. She eased herself down into his lap, continuing the slow grind, bringing herself closer and closer to orgasm, not caring how bad he was hurting. The pleasure was too intense.

"Ride me, Cass. Please. I need to be inside you. I need you. I need you." Hearing those words brought on her climax. She cried out his name, collapsing against him, but Wylie was impatient, lifting her up and settling himself inside her while she caught her breath.

"Move on me," he whispered. "I won't be able to control myself much longer if you don't."

She looked up at him, at the hunger in his eyes, and did as he asked. Her movements were slow and deep at first. She hadn't made love like this in years, not since she was with him. She was unsure of herself. But his hands were there to guide her, and he spoke soft words of encouragement with each stroke.

"You're the only one who can make me this crazy. You're the only one for me." Her movements grew faster as his words and the pleasure caught up to her. "I need you."

"I need you."

They were words every woman wanted to hear, that she should want to hear, but they were clogging up her pleasure with emotions and memories. Memories of one of the hardest times in her life.

But she kept riding him, faster and faster, trying to drown them out, trying to focus on how this felt and how close she was to the edge again.

He brought her face closer, giving her hot, wet, openmouthed kisses as he guided her down on him. He seemed to take note of her urgency and moved himself so that he slid even deeper, made her feel even more of him. And then it came again, her orgasm. It struck her so hard that she screamed. His body jerked, and his cry mingled with her own.

It was intense and in that moment she felt closer to him than ever before, but she was also angry with him and she couldn't stop the tears that had formed in her eyes.

He disconnected them, but he did not move her away from him. Instead he held her, cupping the back of her head in his hand. "Why are you crying, my sweet girl?"

"It's better with you." She struggled to get the words out. "I loved my husband, but I feel better with you, closer to you, and I hate myself for that . . . because you walked out of my life." She looked up at him. "Why did you?"

Sadness took over Wylie's normally expressionless face. "He never told you, did he?"

"Who? Terrance? Told me what?"

"Why I left?" He wiped his hand over his face. "I almost killed him, Cass. He didn't tell you? He didn't show you?"

She knew what he was talking about. She remembered Terrance's face: how he could barely see out of his eyes, how his jaw was so swollen he could hardly talk. "He said he got into a bar fight."

"He didn't. I did that to him." He fell silent and she waited for him to go on to tell her the story, to give her the reason, but he didn't. But she knew there was a reason. There had to be, because they loved each other.

"No more hiding!" She punched his shoulder. "No more! Not from me."

"He found out about us."

"He knew?" She shook her head. She had never told him and he had never said anything to her about it. She had gone their entire marriage holding that secret inside. But it wasn't a secret. He knew the whole time.

And the thought of that left her breathless.

"I don't know who told him. It might have been his father or yours. They came to see me to tell me that somebody saw us together and it would be best if we ended things. They said that I wasn't right for you and there was no use in breaking up two friendships for something that was never going to last. I told them to fuck off. It was the first time I'd ever been disrespectful to the man who took me in, but I was sick of the whole damn world telling me I wasn't good enough, that I couldn't measure up to Terrance. What the hell made him so much better than me? He was lucky, lucky that his pop could read and his family had money.

But I loved him, Cass. I loved him, but I was mad at him. And then he showed up two nights later and he was pissing mad. He called me 'trash,' Cassandra. *Trash.* Said I better not have forgotten where I came from, and the only reason I wasn't in foster care or with my drunk of a mother was because his family saved me. He said I stole you, that I knew he loved you and I took you from him anyway. And I told him that — that I couldn't take something that was never his and that you never wanted him in the first place. That's when he punched me." He shut his eyes and she felt his body go rigid beneath her. "I tried to control myself, but I was so damn angry. When he hit me, it was like I broke. I hit him back and I just kept hitting him and hitting him." He dragged in a ragged breath. "I heard his nose break and felt his blood splatter on my face, but I couldn't stop myself, because he was my brother and his words hurt. He wasn't supposed to think I was trash. He was supposed to love me like I loved him."

She shut her eyes, trying to take it all in, to absorb what she was hearing about her husband and her father. These were the men she was supposed to be able to trust the most, but they both had lied to her. "Tell me more."

"I couldn't stop myself until I saw his eyes roll back in his head, and then I realized that he was on the floor and that I was on top of him. I was beating a man who was no longer fighting back. I hated myself and I knew that everyone else would hate me when they found out what happened. I knew my time in Harmony Falls had come to an end."

"So you left without a word?"

"I knew you loved him too and I thought you would think I was a monster for what I had done. And he was right. He loved you first. He always loved you, and I knew that, but I couldn't stay away from you."

"But you could leave me? What Terrance did to you was wrong. And I don't like what you did to him, but I would have been on your side because I loved you that much. I'm always on your side. Don't you know that?"

"I hated myself then and I wanted to show them. I wanted to come back and show every one that I could make something of myself. I had to leave to do that."

"I was holding you back."

"I didn't want to leave you. And if the fight hadn't happened, I would have stayed there forever, but I knew you deserved better than a guy who worked two jobs just to feed himself. In my mind I always told myself that I was going to come back for you, but then I heard about your engagement to Terrance. It wasn't even a year after I left. I thought you two had really fallen in love, and in the end I knew he loved you and would treat you like you deserved to be treated."

"I wasn't in love with him," she said aloud for the first time, and she felt like she was betraying Terrance. "I only married him because you broke my heart."

CHAPTER 16

Wylie went to Mansi's house the next afternoon, only to find Cassandra's car gone. He didn't know why he was nervous to find her gone. She didn't have to tell him where she was going. She was an adult. She was responsible, but she had been quiet since the other night when he told her the real reason he had walked away from her and the only family he had at the time. She said she was on his side. She said she didn't hate him, and she didn't act like she did. But how could she not, when sometimes he still hated himself. Hated that he never made things right before he lost Terrance. He meant to make things right. He told himself he would, even if they could never be friends again. He just never thought Terrance would die; and now that he had, Wylie felt guiltier than ever.

If he couldn't make things right with him, he could at least take care of Cass. He could make it up to his friend by making sure the woman they both had loved was happy and wanted for nothing. He knew Terrance would have wanted it that way.

He walked up to the door, only to find it locked. Mansi's door was never locked. Never. The uneasiness he felt rose a few notches. He pulled out his cell phone, calling Cass. It rang so many times he was sure she wasn't going to pick up, but she finally did, after the sixth ring.

"Hey, Wylie James."

She sounded fine. Happy even. He exhaled. "Hey, I'm at Mansi's house. The door is locked. Are you all okay?"

"Yes, we're at the cultural center."

"The cultural center? Why?"

"Because Mansi needs to get out of the house. I don't think she should be watching TV all day. Plus I was sick of getting my butt kicked in card games. She's now playing poker with some of the elders. I think she's up fifty bucks."

"I think she cheats."

"Probably does. But she's having a good time. Teo's here too. He had an early release. Come down. I've ordered pizza for everyone. We're going to have lunch."

"You've ordered pizza for everybody?"

"Yes. It should be here soon. Hurry up."

She hung up on him and he shook his head at the phone. She seemed to be back to the person she was before the shooting. Seemed to be. He knew from experience that you could never go completely back to who you were. Things like that changed a person. But Cass was fully alive again and she was getting bored with the routine. He had seen her in action as a teacher; she was so full of energy and life. He wondered if the little island had enough for her.

He got in his truck and drove to the cultural center. There was a little museum there for tourists, and a gift shop that sold handmade crafts, but it mostly served as a sort of senior citizens center, a place where the older folks sat, drank coffee and gossiped.

He walked in the front door. The building was big, with a gymnasium/auditorium that was used for events like proms and weddings. But he found his family in the community room. Teo was sitting with Mansi and a group of pizza-eating seniors. Cass and Nova were in the kitchen area, dishing out plates of salad to the line of people.

"Nova, you're here too?" he asked as he walked up.

She looked at Cass, who was chatting with a pair of elderly men, both of them World

War II vets. Her face was lit up. She was smiling. "I come here once a week to give haircuts, but your girl over there tricked me into staying the afternoon."

"You do?"

"My boss used to do it, but she can't stand on her feet much anymore, so I took over some stuff for her."

He hadn't known that about his sister. He didn't know much about her at all. "Cass said you're doing real good at your job." When he first got here, she was just sweeping up hair. But it seemed Nova had worked her way up from shopgirl pretty fast. "I'm glad to hear that."

"Yeah." She shrugged. "That woman right there is like an old-man magnet. You better watch out, brother. They might steal her from you."

Cass walked over to them then, sliding her arms around Wylie and resting her head on his chest. "You came."

He kissed her forehead, hugging her back. "You ordered me to."

"She's like a happy little drill sergeant. She's been ordering people around all day, and you know what? They listen to her! She's got me serving food to the elderly. It's like I'm doing community service for a crime I didn't commit."

Cass grinned. "You love it here, you big, complaining pain in the butt. And the men love you! I heard Mr. Castle say he hopes you wear your red tank top next week. He thinks you have very nice décolletage."

"That man is ninety-two!" Nova half shouted, but a small smile curled on her lips.

Cass hugged Wylie tighter and closed her eyes as she rested against him. "I'm glad you came. I can't lean on anybody else like this without them getting the wrong idea."

He smoothed his hand down her back, liking the way her warm, curvy body felt against his. "I've got the wrong idea. How could I not, with you hugging on me like this?"

"No, honey, you've got the right idea."

"Is this your boyfriend, Cassandra?" a small elderly woman, whom Wylie didn't know, asked her.

"Isn't he cute?" She opened her eyes and smiled at the woman, but she didn't let him go. "This is Wylie James. I've known him since I was twelve."

"And you haven't married her yet?" The woman frowned at him. "What's the matter with you, boy?"

He kissed Cassandra's forehead. "I'm a stupid, stupid man."

"Now that Cassandra is going to be working here, you'll have to watch out. These fellas around here may be in their golden years, but they've got more charm in their pinky fingers than most young men have in their entire bodies. Don't think she's safe from them."

"I'll make sure no one gets her, ma'am. Thanks for the warning."

"Why don't you get some food, Mrs. Haber? I've got dessert coming in a few minutes."

The woman walked to Nova and started chatting with her, leaving Wylie alone with Cassandra. "You're working here?"

"The director offered me a job. Their last person quit over a year ago when she moved off island for a higher-paying job. Did you know they don't even have an after-school program for the kids here? We're going to start one. We've got all of these people here who have so much knowledge. We can use some of them to help the little ones. There are four former teachers in this room alone. I think this is a great place to have a buddy reading program."

"You're right. It is."

She looked up at him. "Is that all you're going to say? You don't have a dozen questions. You're not going to ask about the hours or the pay, or try to talk me out of it?"

"You want to do this, right?"

"Yes." She nodded. "I feel like I need to do something more."

He knew that. She was alive again. She had to live life. He just wanted her to live it with him. "Then I'm good with it. I'm more concerned with how you're feeling. You've been quiet since we talked about Terrance. I think we need to talk about it more."

She shook her head. "I don't want to talk about that. I told you I wasn't mad at you."

"But you have to be feeling something, Cass."

"I've been tired the past couple of days. Like rundown. I think I'm getting a little cold." She sounded convincing, but Wylie knew there had to be more to it than that. Terrance might not be in Harmony Falls anymore, but she still had a life there, a family, unfinished business. She couldn't leave everything unsettled for much longer. It was going to catch up to her soon.

"Come eat." She pulled away from him and grabbed his hand. "I've got a sausage pizza in the back. Nova, you've dished out enough salad. Come eat too."

It was a little before nine when Cassandra

climbed into bed that next night. She was exhausted, but in a good way. She hadn't worked in over a year. She hadn't done anything meaningful. She had simply just existed, but she was done with that now.

"When I was young, staying up all night was cool, but now getting into bed at nine is like damn near heaven," Wylie said as he walked into the room. He eased beneath the covers next to her and took her hand. "You all right?" He stroked his thumb over the backs of her fingers.

"Yes." She turned on her side to look at him. "I'm fine. I'm good, actually. How are you?"

He looked at her for a long moment. She thought he wanted to say something to her, but the words never came.

"What is it?"

"I want to know . . . ," he started, but then he stopped himself.

"Tell me."

"I want to know if things get too much for you, okay?"

"I didn't do much today. I just talked to the director about some ideas that he had. He's a good guy. He's been applying for grants for a year and he just landed a big one that's going to bring some more programs to the center. Exercise and nutrition help for seniors, as well as the after-school program. He's even looking to start adult-education classes there. It's a lot, and right now they are just ideas, but I'm excited to help him with some of them. I need to feel useful."

"I know, baby," he said softly. "But making yourself busy doesn't make the pain go away completely, it just masks it for a while."

"What are you talking about?"

"It's okay to still miss him. It's okay to still feel sad or hurt or whatever it is you want to feel. It's only been two months since you've left Harmony Falls. Maybe things are happening too soon."

"They aren't. I'm happy."

He nodded, but he didn't look convinced. "I just don't want you to run yourself ragged, trying to escape —"

Her cell phone rang then, stopping the rest of his words. She glanced at it, ready to ignore it, but she saw that it was her mother calling. She had to pick up. She hadn't spoken to her in over a week.

"Hi, Mom."

"Hello, sweetheart. I hope it's not too late to call you."

"Wylie and I were just lying here, talking."

"Oh." Her mother fell silent for a moment. "You don't have to answer this, if you don't want to, Cassandra, but are you and Wylie sharing a room?"

She looked at Wylie, who was lying next to her, his eyes closed. "Yes. I like being here."

"I know your father had some strong feelings about him, but I've always liked him and I'm glad you're happy there."

"I got a job, Mom. At the cultural center. It's only part-time right now, but I like it."

"Oh, you got a job. That's wonderful, honey, but are you sure you're up for it?"

"You sound like Wylie."

"Worried? I am, and he's smart to be. I thought that going away from here might be good for you, but do you think you'll know when you are ready to come back?"

"No." She didn't want to think about Harmony Falls or Terrance or her own father, who told the man she loved that he wasn't good enough for her. Her life had been built on lies there. Her marriage had been too, but she didn't want to think about that. She didn't want to go back there, because she knew being there would remind her of all the things she wanted to forget. "I'm not ready."

"Okay. But you have things waiting for you here. Your house is sitting empty. Your car is here. Your things are here. People who love you are still here. They are asking about you."

"Tell them I'm okay, Mom. I am okay. Really."

"I need to see you. I have this image in my head of how you were, and I can't erase it until I see you again."

"I've got to fix up the house before she comes," Wylie said, taking her hand again. "Give me a few weeks."

She squeezed his hand. "Okay, Mom. You can come next month and stay for Thanksgiving."

"I would like that. Your father wants to see you too."

"He's good enough for me. You tell him that before he comes. He was *always* good enough for me."

"I know, sweetheart. I'll call you next week."

"Good night, Mom."

"Good night, Cassandra."

Wylie rolled over, burying his face in her neck as soon as she settled back in bed. "You're staying for Thanksgiving, huh?"

"Yeah."

"I don't recall inviting you." She felt him smile into her neck. "Now I've got to change my plans."

"It'll be good," she told him and herself even as the uneasiness settled into her stomach. "Things will be good."

"I'm glad I don't work Fridays," Cass said to him as they drove toward Teo's school. It was their weekend to take him and his class pet for a sleepover, and Cassandra had spent all morning making sure things were ready for him. "Four days a week is just enough for me. I have time to do all the things I need to do." He glanced over at her, noticing the slightly higher pitch to her voice. Her face was turned away from him, staring out the window, but he could see her hands. They were clenched into tight little fists in her lap. "What color were you thinking about painting the bathroom? I hope not white. White walls seem so sterile."

"We can paint it whatever color you want." He reached over and grabbed her hand. He ran his thumb over the backs of her knuckles, causing her to loosen her hand. His slid his fingers through hers, only to find her palm hot and clammy. "What's the matter, baby?"

"He's never slept over at your house before," she went on. "He told me yesterday. He's excited. He wants to build a bonfire on the beach and make s'mores. He said he saw it on TV." She swallowed so hard that he heard it.

"He's going to have fun, Cass. He's five. It really doesn't take much to entertain him."

"Maybe we should invite Nova and Tanner over for the bonfire. Nova said she was happy to send him away for the weekend, but I think she's lying. She seemed sad this morning when I went over there to get his bag. She's been giving him a choice, you know."

"A choice for what?" he asked softly, feeling her nervousness spike as they drove on.

"If he wants to stay at Mansi's or sleep at home. The past few nights he said he wanted to stay with Mansi. She lets him, but she calls him every night. They talk on the phone for a long time. Teo tells me she's good to talk to on the phone. He says it's better to talk to her on the phone than in person, because she pays attention to him more. I taught kids his age my whole career. He's too bright." She swallowed again, squeezing his hand. "Part of him is still a baby, but most of him is an old soul. He's really special."

"I know." He pulled into the parking lot, slipping his hand from hers so he could park. They were a little early. Some classes were still on the playground for afternoon recess, but there were other parents waiting in their cars to pick up their kids. Wylie and she were going to have to go inside, though, to get the pet and talk to the teacher about how to take care of it. He turned to look at her just as the warning bell rang.

She had pressed herself to the back of her seat, her fingers digging so hard into her legs they were shaking. Her forehead was shiny with sweat and her eyes were closed tightly, but there were tears streaming out of them.

"Cass . . ." He felt choked, helpless. "Tell me."

"I — I . . . ," she wheezed out in a breath. "I can't go in there. Go get him. Please go get him."

"No." He threw the car into drive. "I'll call Nova."

"No!" She grabbed his hand. She was crying almost uncontrollably now, her chest heaving. Her face was covered in sweat and tears. "If you pull away from here, I'll never forgive you. I promised him. I just can't go in. Please, please, please just go inside and get him."

"I can't let him see you like this, baby."

"I'll stop." She tried to drag in a slower breath. "I'll be fine when you come back. I promise, Wylie James. I've never broken a promise to you."

He put his truck back in park, not at all sure he was doing the right thing. He didn't want to leave her — he was afraid to leave her — but he knew it was important to her that he did. "Okay." He leaned over to kiss her wet face and she grabbed him, wrapping her arms around him in a tight, crushing grip.

"Come back soon."

"I'm coming back."

She had woken up in the morning, feeling off. She had been feeling off for the past few days, but she ignored the feeling, because she *was feeling.* After having felt nothing but despair or numbness for so long, she was grateful to feel anything other than that. She thought maybe she was getting sick, or that she was worried about her parents coming up for a visit. That was probably it. She was anxious after not seeing them for so long because she knew they wanted her to go back to Harmony Falls.

They told her she had a life waiting for her in Harmony Falls.

Neither one of them seemed to realize that being there would kill her: going back to that house, seeing his things, seeing signs of the marriage that probably never should have happened, seeing those people and that goddamn GOD BLESS FARNSWORTH. GOD BLESS HARMONY FALLS sign.

They couldn't make her go back there. And as long as she got to stay here with Wylie and the ocean and the soothing balm that was Martha's Vineyard, she would be okay.

She thought she would be okay. But as the time got closer to three o'clock, and the knowledge that she was actually going to a school to get him hit her, the uneasiness spike, the nausea, rolled in her belly. Her heart raced.

It's a school, she told herself. *A different school. Not your school.*

But she hadn't set foot in a school since the day of the shooting. She had avoided driving past the ones in her town when she was still driving after she got out of the hospital.

But as they got closer, the rational thoughts disappeared and Terrance's face kept flashing in her mind. The way his arm hung limply where he had been shot, a crazy contrast to the sweet surroundings of an elementary school, with all of its positive signs and brightly colored bulletin boards. That was supposed to be a safe place.

Their safe place.

She tried to push the invasive, nasty memories from her head, but she kept hearing the gunman's crazed, desperate voice. She kept seeing Terrance's eyes. She kept seeing that he was scared for her, that there was love for her in his eyes.

She kept thinking about how it was her fault. It was her fault that man killed the secretary, her principal, her very best friend. It was her fault that the town and its people had irrevocably changed.

But Teo's school is not your school. She kept telling herself that, over and over, as they approached, as she chattered on to Wylie about other things.

But when they pulled up, she saw the kids in the playground and heard the sounds of their laughter. She saw the happiness of the building, and that place became her school. It became Farnsworth Elementary all over again. That day was real to her once again.

But she wasn't there. She was near the ocean and with Wylie and a little boy who was counting on her to give him a fun weekend.

And she had to pull it together. She was mad at herself for falling apart in the first place. So she kept breathing, kept reminding herself where she was and what she had to do. She was sick of being weak. She was sick of being scared and sad and pathetic. She couldn't stay in the past. She had to move on. She couldn't leave like she wanted to, like Wylie wanted her to, but she had to stay here to prove to herself that she could, if nothing else.

The door opened and the cool October air hit her face. She forced her eyes open to see Wylie staring down at her. Wylie who looked like he was in so much pain that he wanted to cry.

"I'm better." She took a deep breath, noticing he was blocking Teo from seeing her. "I am."

He nodded and then stepped aside. Teo was standing there, holding Mr. Peepers in his traveling case.

"What's wrong with you, Miss Cass?" His face was full of worry. "Why was you crying?"

She stepped out of the car and scooped him into her arms, kissing his small face a dozen times, taking comfort in his little-boy smell. "I had a headache, but I just took some medicine."

He was her medicine. She used to have a hard time being around him because he reminded her so much of the kids she used to teach, but now she couldn't imagine her days without him.

Wylie smoothed his hands over his arms, feeling chilly despite the fire they had going. They had a warmer than usual early autumn, but as they got closer to November, things had started to cool. He looked over to Cass, who was sitting huddled with Nova on the other side of the fire. She wore a pink cardigan and jeans, but her feet were bare in the cool sand.

She had been chatty since their guests arrived, and for Teo she had been amazing. She made brownies last night, and they chased each other around the yard for an hour today. Teo saw no problem with her, but Wylie did. At moments she had been quiet, and the run-down look never left her. She was occasionally distracted, listless. When they came back from T-ball, he found her curled up in bed. He worried that the depression would come back, that PTSD would overcome her.

"Uncle Wylie," Teo called to him. "Come make a s'more!" He was standing with Tanner; Tanner's hand was on his shoulder, making sure Teo kept his distance from the fire.

He was surprised when he saw Tanner show up at Teo's game today and so was

Nova. She had arrived unexpectedly too, and stood off to the side, trying not to be seen. It was an impossible task for his sister. She didn't look like the other moms. She didn't blend in, especially in her stilettos, red lipstick and tight jeans. And she got looks for it.

"I don't want Teo to see me," she said when Wylie walked over to her. He was just about to ask her why, when Tanner walked up to them. Her mouth dropped open, her shock clear. Tanner just nodded to her; it was the first time they hadn't traded nasty barbs.

"What are you doing here?" she asked.

"I told him I would come, so I came. He's a good kid."

And he was here again tonight, taking Cass up on her offer for dinner as soon as she called. It was a Saturday night. Tanner was a good-looking guy. He could have spent his time with some willing woman, but he was roasting marshmallows with a little boy. Wylie suspected he was lonely. He had never heard his friend speak of his parents or any siblings since they had met. Wylie realized that he didn't know Tanner very well at all.

"Dude, the kid called you. Get over here."

"Sorry." He left his spot. "Find me a good

330

marshmallow, Teo."

As his nephew went digging in the bag, Tanner stepped closer to him. "What's going on with you? You've had your head up your butt all evening."

"I'm just thinking about things."

"Cass?"

"Yeah, she's one of them."

"What's going on between you two? I know you're together, but . . ."

"But for how long?"

"No." He shook his head. "I don't know what I mean. I think you'd be an asshole if you let her go twice in your life."

"I don't know what she wants. She lost her husband. She's still a mess from the shooting. How can I make plans for the future when she's just living day to day?"

"How do you know she's not making plans too? Have you talked to her?"

"No," Wylie admitted. He tried the other day, but Cora called, asking her when she might return home, and he got scared she would leave. "Her parents are coming for Thanksgiving. They want her to go back."

"So? She's a thirty-one-year-old woman. They don't control her. Ask her what she wants."

Chapter 17

"Tilt your head back, girl," Nova told Cassandra that next day. "I want to be able to see up your nose." They were sitting at the kitchen table at Wylie's house. Nova's new makeup kit was spread across it, all over the place. She had called that morning and asked if she could come over to practice her makeup application skills on Cass. Cass was surprised to get the call, since Nova had been there so late last night. However, she was glad Nova had come. Cass had friends in Harmony Falls, mostly the wives of Terrance's friends. They had lunch together sometimes, saw plays, went to wine tastings. They were nice women. She enjoyed their company, but Nova was a different kind of friend. Nova was the kind of girlfriend she always wished she had when she was growing up.

"Do you have fake lashes in there? Can you put them on me?" Cass asked her. "I've always wanted really thick, long lashes."

"You don't need fake ones. All you need is a better brand of mascara, but I'll put them on, because I need to practice evening makeup too."

"I know you do a lot of bridal parties, but do you really get to do a lot of evening looks here on the island?"

"Not really. Lots of fancy people come up here in the summer. Politicians, actresses, just plain, old rich folks. If word gets around that I'm as good with the makeup as I'm getting with the hair, then maybe they'll start hiring me. And maybe I can move to Boston and work on the big shots there, before next summer."

Cassandra's head snapped up. "You want to move to Boston."

"Tilt your head back. I'm trying to contour your cheekbones, and yes. Eventually I would like to head to Boston. Maybe New York. My mama moved us out to L.A. when I was a kid for a little while." She shook her head and Cassandra thought she saw her shudder a bit. "I hated it there. That's one place I would never want to live again, but if the money is good, I'll make the exception."

"Wylie moved here because of you."

"He didn't. The government got him that

cushy job here and his friend gave him this house. His decision to stay here has little to do with me."

"He's out with your boy right now. He takes him to T-ball and your grandmother to the doctor. He puts air in your tires and calls to make sure you got home safe when you work late at night. Why do you think he does that, Nova? You can pretend that he's only out for himself all you want, but you know that Wylie James is all love."

"You're just sticking up for him because you're his girlfriend."

"He won't like it if you move away and he'll be hurt if you take his only nephew away from him."

"I was going to leave him behind for a little while." Nova said it so softly it was almost a whisper. "You're going to stick around, right? I was thinking he could stay with you guys until I make a go of things. He'd rather be with you anyway."

"You want to . . ." She heard the kitchen door open behind her and little footsteps hit the hardwood floor.

"Mommy, you're here?"

"Yeah, I'm practicing putting makeup on Cass. I've got to get good at it."

He came around and stood close to Nova, hesitating for a moment before he rested his head against her thigh. Nova stiffened for a moment, but then she relaxed and rested her hand on his cheek, stroking his skin with her thumb. She looked down at him with a mixture of love and pain in her eyes; it was hard for Cass to be a witness to that moment.

Nova was a liar. She didn't want to leave him. She wouldn't be able to leave him.

"Are you going to take me home with you?" he asked. "Or are you going to drop me off at Mansi's?"

She took a moment to answer. "With me," she finally said.

"Okay." He looked up at Cass, but he didn't move away from his mother. "You don't look the same."

"It's the makeup. I told your mother I wanted to look like Dorothy Dandridge."

"Who's that?" he asked as she heard Wylie's heavy footsteps on the floor.

"A very beautiful actress from a long time ago. I want to be beautiful like her."

Wylie kissed her cheek. "You're already beautiful like her." He looked at his sister. "She doesn't need any of that junk."

"You would love her if I shaved her bald and made her wear a shredded bedsheet."

He nodded. "I would." He grabbed her ponytail and gave it a playful tug. "Since you're here all the time this weekend, why don't you make yourself useful and make that hummingbird cake Mama used to make for us."

Her eyes went wide. "You got all the ingredients?"

He searched her face for a moment, then nodded. "They're in the car."

"Why did you get that stuff?" Her eyes watered, but she blinked back the tears.

Wylie stepped toward her and kissed her forehead. "I didn't forget her birthday," he whispered. "I'm glad you came over today." He scooped up Teo and flung him over his shoulder. "Let's get the groceries out of the car. Then it's back to the hardware store."

"See?" Nova said to her after they had left. "That's why I hate him sometimes. He gets in my damn head."

That evening Wylie walked into the bedroom that he shared with Cassandra to find her lying on the bed, her hand resting on her forehead. She looked wiped out, which wasn't unusual for her lately, but he couldn't help but think how pretty she was, still in her almost-prim little white cardigan and jeans. But he found himself worrying about her despite that. She was disconnected today. Every time he looked at her, she seemed lost in thought, even though Nova and Teo had been there most of the day to keep her busy. She had gone to lie down just after they left, claiming that she had a slight headache. That was nearly two hours ago. He knew she was tired. Their weekend had been busy, but he also knew that there was more to it than that.

She had taken to bed for a year after Terrance had died. She was doing too much too soon. And after Friday, after seeing how she reacted just by being in front of Teo's school, it confirmed to him that she was not as healed as she would like to think she was. Healing took time. It took years.

"Don't stare at me," she said, her voice sounding sleepy. "Come here."

She opened her arms and he climbed into bed with her, pulling her close, wrapping his arms around her, almost wanting to ignore the nagging thoughts in the back of his head and just stay like this. He had gone ten years without her — ten years thinking he might never see her again, but they were together again. At times it seemed surreal, unreal. He spent that time away from her trying his best to be a good man, a good Marine, a good brother, uncle and friend. He had been trying to redeem himself for what he had done to Terrance, to Cas-

337

sandra. He still felt guilty for it — not for beating Terrance unconscious, but for betraying him by keeping his relationship with Cass a secret.

Time had cleared his vision. He should have just told him, told the world. Terrance would have been mad for a while — maybe he would have been mad forever — but he wronged Cass when he asked her to keep them a secret. He made their love seem like it was wrong, or dirty, and she should hate him for it.

"How are you?" he asked.

"Fine," she said into his shoulder. "Good."

"Are you sure?" He pulled away from her slightly so that he could see into her eyes. There was nothing in them that stood out. No sadness. No worry, but he knew her better than to trust that.

"Yeah. Why?"

"You seem a little off this afternoon, and don't tell me it's because you're tired. I know there's something else."

"I am tired, but it's not just that. I've been thinking about Nova and Teo." She touched his face. "And you too."

"Oh?" It wasn't what he was expecting to hear from her.

"I thought there was another reason Nova came over today. At first I thought it was just because she missed Teo."

He nodded. "She's been weird these past couple of weeks. She came to his game yesterday. She never does that, and then I thought about it. About the date. It's Mama's birthday today."

"Will you tell me about her?"

"There's not much to tell." He thought back to his mother, about the pretty woman she once was, about the shell of a woman she turned into. "She was a drunk, or an alcoholic I was told to call her. But drunk is how I remember her mostly. She left when I was six." He shook his head. "Or my father put her out. I don't know for sure. Nobody ever told me and I never asked. I saw her once every few years. She never called. She never wrote. She would just show up one day around her birthday with kisses and presents and I-love-you's. And it would be fun for a while, like Christmas morning and my birthday rolled into one. She would fry her famous chicken and make hummingbird cake every time. And when Nova was old enough, she let us help her. But then something would happen, like the sun would set, or she ran a yellow light, or she dropped something on the floor, and it would give her an excuse to drink. And my father would throw her out again. They got into a big fight when I was twelve, right before he died. She drove drunk in the car with us and got into an accident. Luckily, we just ran into a ditch, but my father told her not to come back again, because she was too dangerous."

"And she listened?" Cass asked quietly.

"Yeah. I never saw her again until I was much older. I never saw Nova again either. That was the worst part. I was too young to understand it then, because I only experienced Mama's manic craziness when she visited every other year. But Nova lived with it. Every day. I had my pop, who was stable, and then I had the Millers. Nova just had her, and they loved each other, and I know she misses her, because my mama wasn't all bad. But she was bad for Nova. I knew my pop didn't want to let her go, but what could he have done?"

"She wasn't his daughter."

"He was too sick anyway." He shook his head. "I'm not sure what happened to Nova in all those years. They moved around a lot. I know Mama had more boyfriends than I could count on my fingers and toes, and Nova's life was crazy until she came here. Until Mansi got a hold of her. I know that's why Nova is hard. She's hard to get close to. She's hard to love, because she doesn't know how to be loved. But you were right about her. There's more to her than I give her credit for sometimes, and I try to ignore that because it helps me forget how guilty I feel when it comes to her."

"Why do you feel guilt? You did nothing wrong."

"I didn't have it easy, but I had it a hell of a lot better than her. Sometimes I think I shouldn't have. I think I could have handled being with Mama better than Nova."

Cass was quiet for a long moment; her forehead was scrunched like she was struggling with something. "She's stronger than you think. She's stronger than she thinks. She told me she wants to move to Boston next year, and she wants to leave Teo with us."

"Next year . . . With us." Those words stuck in his mind, but he couldn't pay too much attention to them yet. He was more concerned about Nova.

He heard her claim that she wanted to get out of this small town, this isolated part of the island, where everybody knew too much about everyone, but this was news to him. She named a place. She had a time line. "Damn her."

"She told me she wants to take her career to the next level and she has to leave here to do that."

"She's just trying to escape. It's going to follow her. Doesn't she know that? It's going to follow her everywhere she goes."

"What's going to follow her?"

"Her past. It's something we can overcome, but it's not something we can ever forget."

She smiled softly at him. "I don't think truer words have ever been spoken."

Wylie pulled away from her completely and sat up, needing some space from her to say what he had to say next.

"I get the feeling, Cass, that you are trying to forget about Terrance."

She shook her head, her expression changing to annoyance. "How could I forget him? I knew him my entire life."

"I keep thinking about Friday. You can't pretend like nothing happened. You couldn't be near that school."

"I'm sorry. I shouldn't have broken down like that. I should have been stronger."

He shook his head. "That's just it. You don't have to be so strong, so fast."

"It's been over a year! I've mourned enough. I've been sad enough. I need to move on. I'm ready to move on."

"It hasn't been a year. It's been two months since you came here. You couldn't get out of bed. You weren't talking. You weren't eating. You were existing."

She moved away from him completely; her eyes were filling with water, his words hurting her. "But I'm getting up. I'm feeling. I'm living! It's what you wanted. It's what everybody wanted. Why are you bringing this up?"

"Because I have to. Because there will be another school. Or somewhere they'll be another shooting. Or one day you'll see a man who looks or sounds like Terrance and you'll have to learn to really get through this. I'm here for you, but I think you need more than me."

"What are you saying?"

"I think you should see somebody — a counselor or a therapist — somebody you can talk to."

She shook her head. "I talk to you. I'm better. You see that."

"You need to talk about Terrance to somebody who is not me, to someone who didn't share a past with him."

"I'm sick and tired of talking and thinking about Terrance all the time!" she yelled at him. "I'm tired of talking about him. He's dead. I've spent a year in bed mourning him. I devoted my life to him. I was a good wife! I gave up —"

"What? What did you give up?"

"Everything," she whispered. "I went along with what he wanted. *All the time.* I lived where he wanted, and watched what he watched, and ate what he liked, because I wanted him to be happy."

"Why did you do that?" he asked her softly, already knowing the answer and feeling the guilt for it. "That's not what he expected from you. He loved you just the way you were. He would have been happy anyway. He wanted you any way that he could get you."

"Yeah, he loved me so much he lied to me our entire marriage. The whole thing was a lie and he knew it."

"What did he know?"

"He knew that if I found out the truth about why you left, I would have never married him."

"You say that, but I'm not sure I believe it. You're mad at him, but I saw how you two were growing up. You got each other the way nobody else did. You loved him, and he was good to you. He loved you. I wasn't inside your marriage, but I know he wasn't a bad husband."

"I loved him like a sister, not like a wife, and that's why I felt guilty. That's why I couldn't get out of bed for a whole goddamn year. He died never having a wife who was in love with him. I tried. I tried to fall in love with him. I should have been in love with him. He was good to me, and he was smart and funny, but I couldn't. I beat myself up for not being able to, and that's why I bent over backward to try to be a good wife. But he knew about us all along. He knew that I was in love with you and he pretended like he knew nothing. He acted like you were the bad one for leaving. I put him on a pedestal and he let me. I can't believe he just went along with it."

"Why did you marry him if you didn't want to?"

"Because when you left me, I felt unlovable. Like there was something wrong with me. I thought that if I didn't marry Terrance, if I threw that good guy away, that I would never find another one."

"Why aren't you mad at me?"

"What?" She looked at him, bewilderment crossing her face.

"You're blaming Terrance for what? For fighting for you? For doing what I should have done? You should be mad at me, not at him. I walked out on you. I made you hide our relationship from everybody. You should hate me. But you don't. You don't blame me for anything, and sometimes I wish you did."

"Why?"

"Because I'm afraid that one day you'll realize how much you really do hate me and disappear from my life again."

She locked eyes with him, and her lost look was gone in that moment. "I did hate you. For years. Every time I thought of you, my heart hurt. Do you know what it was like after you left? At first I didn't know what to think. I thought you were hurt or dead, and I was so worried that I couldn't sleep at night. But when I realized that you just didn't want to be with me anymore, it killed me. Because I thought I spent all that time loving you for nothing. And the worst thing about it was I couldn't stop thinking about you. I couldn't make love to my husband without comparing him to you, without thinking about you! I spent the entire first year of my marriage wondering about you, dreaming about you, wishing he were you. You made me disloyal in my heart." She touched her chest. "You made me feel like a fool and I hated you for that."

"I'm sorry for that. I haven't said it, but I'm sorry for hurting you. I'm sorry I had to walk away. There are times I can't forgive myself for what happened between us. I'm not sure how you ever could."

"I was so mad at you, Wylie — don't think that I wasn't. Even now I look at you sometimes and get angry with you. But hating you doesn't do me any good. Not then. Not now. Hating you didn't help me to love my husband more. It didn't help me be a better wife. It just made me miserable. I'm done with being miserable." She shut her eyes. "I'm done with feeling guilt. I feel happy here. I laugh here. I'm making friends here." She opened her eyes and looked directly at him. "Why are you questioning that?"

"Because you left a whole entire life behind. Because you're avoiding your parents and the house you lived in and the town we grew up in. You may not want to look back right now, but at some point you're going to have to."

"Why? I don't have a life there anymore! How many times do I have to say that?"

"Maybe that's not where you want your life to be, but you did have a life there, and friends and family and a community, and even if you never want to live there again, you have to have some closure. Especially with Terrance. You haven't been to his grave, Cass. You never even said good-bye."

"You should talk. You never said good-bye

either. You never made your peace with him."

"I'll make my peace in my own way. I lost Terrance before you, but this is not about me. This is about you. My life is here now. This is where I want to be. This is my home and my future. I don't get to walk away, but you do. You need to decide what your future is, what you want in life."

Her eyes widened in shock. "You think I'm going to walk away?"

He shook his head. He hoped she wanted to make her life here. He prayed that she would, but in the end she could decide that this life wasn't for her at all. "I don't know what to think."

She opened her mouth to speak, but no words came out and it confirmed what he already knew.

"You need to think about what you want out of life, Cassandra."

"What about you? What do you want?"

"For you to be truly happy. I don't ask for much, but today I am. I want you to talk to somebody. I want you to get counseling."

CHAPTER 18

"Thank you for coming to get me," Cass said two weeks later as she took the bags out of Nova's Jeep and put them in the back of her car. "I didn't want to go off island alone."

"You know I'm always up for a trip off island. The shopping is much better there." Nova dug through her own packages, searching for the things she had brought for Mansi that day. "I really like those boots you got."

"You could have gotten them," she said as she eased herself onto one of the old chairs in front of Mansi's house. Fall had finally arrived in full force. The heat left the air much sooner in the day and the sky was already growing dark, but Cassandra was coming to love this time of day. The cool air, combined with the smell of the ocean in the distance, made her feel at peace, even though peaceful was the last thing she should be feeling.

"You know I don't wear anything with less than a four-inch heel." Nova sat next to Cass. She could feel Nova's eyes searching her face. She didn't have to look at her to know that she was curious about why Cass had needed her company that day. "Why did you need to go off island to go to the doctor anyway? There are a few good ones here."

"I did go to one here earlier in the week. I've been feeling a little run-down lately. The doctor thought it was a virus, but wanted me to go off island to get some more extensive blood work done. It's no big deal, but since I spent so long in the hospital after the shooting, they wanted to be extra careful."

"Tanner told me that Wylie told him he has been worried about you. Wylie always is worried, but does he have a good reason to be?"

"You've been talking to Tanner?" Cass raised her brows and grinned at Nova. "He's awful cute, girl. You sure you haven't been dating him?"

Nova rolled her eyes. "Please. That tall, arrogant pain in my ass is the last person I would want to date."

"You could just sleep with him. That

would be nice too."

"Cassandra Miller!" Nova's eyes went wide with horror. "What has gotten into you?"

She giggled, the laughter bubbling out of her. "I don't know. Your brother thinks I'm depressed."

"Well, are you?"

"No. Not like I used to be. I didn't care if I lived or died. But I do care now. I feel happiness now. Being here has helped me so much. But he doesn't believe me. He's making me see a therapist."

"*Making you?* I know my brother can be controlling, but I didn't think he could *make you* do anything you didn't want to do."

"He asked me to go and I want to make him happy, so I'm going. He's not controlling at all, Nova. He just wants the best for all of us, so stop picking on him. He loves you."

"I know." She sighed. "I can't help it. It doesn't feel right to be nice to him. Makes my damn skin just crawl. Is seeing the therapist helping?"

Cass nodded. "More than I thought it would. He says the real reason I stayed in bed for a year wasn't just because of the shooting, but because it opened up a bunch of issues between my husband and me that we never dealt with in our marriage. These were issues that might have caused our marriage to collapse in the long run."

"How does he know that? He didn't know you or your husband. How could he make such a crazy statement?"

"He's right," she admitted. "I knew Terrance was unhappy before he died and so was I. But we never said anything about it. We were best friends growing up and we used to talk all the time, but we found ourselves seven years into our marriage not talking at all. He tried to be closer to me, taking a job at my school and seeing some of his counseling clients from his home office so we could be together more. By that point in our marriage, though, we were essentially roommates. We put on a good show to the world. Hell, I put on a good show for myself. I pretended I was happy. I had a good guy. We had nice things, a nice life. I should have been happy, but I wasn't. I got pregnant because I thought it would fix things between us, give us something to bond over. And for a while it did, but it would have never changed the fact that I was married to a man I wasn't in love with."

"Wow." Nova went silent for a moment, her eyes thoughtful. "You learned all that about yourself in one session? Maybe I should go to him too."

"Two sessions." She smiled. "Maybe you should go. There's no shame in talking to someone else."

"Nah. Most of my shit needs to stay buried in the deep, dark hole I put it in."

"Hey!" Teo bounded out the front door. "I didn't know you was here. I thought you wasn't coming today."

"Sorry, Teo. I had to go to the doctor after I left the cultural center today, but I brought your mama back with me."

"Hi, Mommy," he said softly as he turned around to look at her. "I had a good day at school. I got a hundred on my sight word test. Miss Cass helped me learn to write the words."

"That's real good, baby," she said quietly. There was heaviness in her voice, almost like she was sad. "I'm glad to hear that."

Cass stopped herself from shaking her head. Teo was clearly proud of himself. Reading and spelling didn't come easy for him, but he worked so hard at it. If Nova spent just a little more time with him, she would know that.

"A hundred!" Cass grabbed his shoulders and playfully shook him. "You are such a hard worker. I'm so proud. Go get that paper so I can see it!"

Teo's face bloomed into a smile as he scurried off to get his paper.

"I think you might want to start reading to him at night, Nova," she told her gently. "He wants to show you how good he's doing."

"I work late a lot," she said, making an excuse.

"Bullshit. Read with your kid."

Nova's eyes went wide as she opened her mouth to respond, but Teo came flying out the door, his test in hand, and he didn't stop at Cass. He was heading toward his mother when he tripped and fell, landing hard on his hands and knees. Again he looked to his mother as his eyes filled with tears, but Nova sat there, almost like she was paralyzed, like she couldn't comfort him. Like she couldn't act like his mother.

"Oh, Teo." Cassandra left her seat and pulled Teo into her arms. "You fell really hard that time."

He looked back to his mother before he turned to Cass. "I — I hurt my hand real bad." He held out his bright red palm to her.

"We'll fix it." She kissed his hand. "We'll put some ice on it and then I'm going to take you to get some ice cream because you worked so hard on your test."

She took him inside and placed him in Mansi's care for a moment while she went back outside.

"What the hell is wrong with you?"

"What?" Nova looked up at her, wide-eyed. "He's all right, isn't he?"

"He'll be fine, but that's beside the point. He wanted you, Nova."

"He's got you. You're just as good."

"I'm not as good! I'm not his mother! I don't know what your problem is, or why you can't stop getting in your own way and just love him. But you're hurting him every time you send him away, every time you push him off on somebody else, every time you ignore him. Don't you know how lucky you are to have him? He's beautiful and sensitive and smart, and he thinks you don't want him. And the funny thing is, he still adores you. He loves you and wants to be around you, but you're screwing up things. One day he's going to look up and hate you. What are you going to do then? I lost my baby. Some maniac shot me in the stomach and took my baby away, but you've got one here and you are throwing him away. And if you can't woman up and be the mother he deserves, I'm going to take him from you. I may not be what he wants, but I'm a hell of a lot better than someone who can't be bothered to love him like he deserves."

Nova's red Jeep was parked in front of his house when Wylie pulled up that evening. He wasn't surprised to see it there. Nova had been there a lot in the last couple of weeks. Not to see him, but to see Cass. Nova's relationship with Cassandra was growing closer by the day. The last thing he expected when he brought Cassandra here was that she would become best friends with his sister. He had thought she was too delicate for his sister's strong personality, but he should have known better. Cass wasn't as weak as he first thought she was, and Nova wasn't as tough as he expected. Still, he wondered how the women would fare when they went their separate ways. Nova said she was moving away, and Cass . . . He still didn't know what her plans were or if she had any. She had gone to counseling twice, and both times she had come home red-eyed and blotchy-faced.

She told him it was helpful, that she would keep going, but he wondered if that was true. He wondered how long it would take before he would come home and find her gone.

He got out of his truck, with the pie she had asked him to get for dessert in his hand.

Thanksgiving was coming soon. Her parents would be here soon. He studied his house as he walked up to it, searching for faults, for things Cassandra's father would judge. But there wasn't much. The porch was freshly painted. Cass had placed pumpkins and gourds on the steps. There was a planter full of mums by the door. For the first time since he moved there, he took pride in his house, which was slowly morphing into a home.

"Wylie James."

He turned to see his sister, still in her Jeep, teary-eyed.

"Nova? What's the matter?"

She stepped out of her car and rushed over to him, but she wouldn't look him in the eye. "Your girlfriend took my kid."

"What? Without your permission?"

She shook her head. "I knew she was going to take him. She told me she was, but —"

"But what?"

"I don't think she's going to give him back."

"You want to explain to me what happened?"

"She blew up at me. She thinks I'm a bad mother. Maybe I am. Maybe I don't know what I'm doing. Maybe I'm afraid to screw him up like Mama screwed me up, but I love him and I don't want her to keep him," she said in one breath.

"Well, then go in there and get him."

She shook her head. "I want to. I should have, but sometimes I think he might be better off with you guys."

"Damn it, Nova. Stop it. You're not her. You're not a drunk. You're not a screwup. You love your kid."

"But I'm fucked up, Wylie. You don't know what it was like. You don't know some of the things that happened to me."

"No." He shook his head. He didn't know what Nova's life was like after she left the last time. And part of him didn't want to know. He hated to think how unhappy she might have been. "You could tell me. You could talk to me. I'm not so bad, you know."

"I — I know. I don't want to tell you. I wish I didn't even know about it myself."

"I don't want you to go, Nova," he told her. "Cass told me you wanted to move away from the island, that you wanted to leave Teo with us. You know I'll keep him, raise him like he was my own, but if you leave him here, don't think you can just traipse in and out of his life whenever you want. Don't think you can be gone for a few years and then just pop up and act like nothing happened. It'll hurt him, and I won't let you hurt him. So go if you want to, but know running away from here won't solve anything. And leaving him behind won't do Teo any good. Your boy needs you and I want you to stay. You're my family."

She nodded. "Sometimes I hate you, Wylie, but I love you too." She wrapped her arms around him. "You're good to me. Thank you. I think I'm broken sometimes, but I'm going to try harder with him. With you too. I don't think I can stand losing either one of you."

"I'm your brother. I'm not going anywhere. I promise. Now let's go get your boy."

"Can you get him for me?" She pulled away from him and swiped at the tears running down her face. "I don't want him to see me a mess."

He walked inside, and the scent of garlic and tomato sauce immediately made his stomach growl as a thousand thoughts churned in his head.

"Hi, Uncle Wylie." Teo was snuggled with Cass in the new, oversized armchair they had just picked out last week. "We're reading. Miss Cass bought me two books and some ice cream because I did real good reading my sight words at school."

"He got a hundred, Wylie," Cass said, running her fingers through the boy's curls. "I'm so proud."

"I am too. He's smart, just like his uncle." Cass looked so natural curled up with Teo in that chair. If she stayed, she would be good to Teo, good for him. She would love him as much as she would love a child that came from her body, but Teo wasn't theirs. Teo had a mama who loved him, who was waiting right outside. It took him a while to understand it, but Nova was the one Teo should be with. "Your mama is here for you," he told him.

"No," Cass said, kissing his forehead. "He's mine. I'm keeping him."

"I'll stay with you, Miss Cass." He looked at Wylie. "She'll be sad without me."

"I'll take care of her," he said, trying to suppress a smile. "You don't have to worry. Go home with your mama."

"Nah. I'm good here." He snuggled farther into Cass.

"Teo," he warned.

"But I wanted to eat dinner here. It's in the oven. It's almost ready."

"Your mama is waiting for you outside. I'm not going to tell you again to get moving."

He sighed as he eased out of the chair.

"Yes, sir. Good-bye, Miss Cass. I'll see you again."

"Yes, Teo." She grinned. "You will."

Wylie walked him out and put the pie he was still holding in the kitchen before he returned to Cass. She was still sitting in the chair, wrapped in a throw blanket, looking so at home there that it made his chest swell painfully. It made him afraid too, afraid of how empty his life would be again if she left him. He knelt before her, wrapping his arms around her waist, placing his head on her belly.

"What was that all about?"

"I don't know." She sighed. "I got mad at Nova and stole her kid."

"Why?"

"Because I'm hormonal and I wanted her to realize how lucky she is to be a mother. I lost my chance once to be one. I still think about the baby, who they could have been, what they would have looked like."

"You could have another baby one day, Cass. You know that, don't you?"

"I didn't until today, when I went to the doctor. I'm pregnant, Wylie. That's why I've been so tired lately. I'm not sad. I'm going to give you a baby."

"What?" His head snapped up and he looked her in the eyes for a sign. Searching

361

for a sign that she was joking, a sign that what she was saying wasn't real. But it had to be real, because if it wasn't, it would be too cruel, too unbearable.

"You're not happy," she whispered. "I know it wasn't planned. I know this is bad timing, but I want this."

"Hush," he ordered as he smashed his mouth to hers, kissing her so deeply that his mind went blank. All he could do was feel. *A baby.* A family of his own. The thing he always wanted with the woman he always loved. "That car is going back to Tanner."

"What?" She shook her head. "Are you happy about this, Wylie?"

"Happy?" He threw back his head and laughed. "Damn it, Cassandra. I love you. I'm crazy in love with you. I want you as my wife, my partner, my family. My forever. Don't you know that?"

"It would be nice if you told me that more often."

"I will. I wanted to, but I didn't know how you would take it. I wasn't sure if you were ready to hear it."

"You never told me that when we were together before. You never said, 'I love you.' "

"But you knew. You had to know. You had to feel it."

"I did." She nodded. "I do. I know you love me."

"So much it hurts." He studied her a moment longer, trying to read her face and seeing a little sadness in it. "I know you want this baby, but what about me? What about this life? Is this the life that you want?"

She leaned forward, cupping his face in her hands and gently kissing his mouth. "I'm happy here. Why would I want to leave that?"

She didn't answer his question and uneasiness rolled around in his gut. "It's okay if you're unsure about this. I know this isn't the life you had planned."

"But it's the life that I was given and I'm happy to have it." She kissed him again, softly, slowly. Her tongue swept into his mouth, arousing him with her gentleness. "Dinner can wait. Turn off the oven and take me to bed."

CHAPTER 19

Cassandra looked into the pot that was on the stove. The smell of the brown rice she was cooking made her stomach queasy. She didn't know why. The brown rice, steamed broccoli and grilled chicken breast was a meal she made and ate often. There was nothing spicy, nothing flavorful about it, but it was healthy. Terrance liked for them to stay healthy. He had requested salmon and kale salad for tomorrow. Maybe she would sneak in a baked potato with sour cream and butter. He wouldn't like it, but she was craving it: the butter, the salt, the fat, the fluffiness of the potato. She couldn't wait until Friday when he took her out for dinner. Terrance enjoyed fine dining. He loved to savor his food, and discuss the flavors, and so did she. But sometimes she just wanted a cheeseburger, with bacon and ketchup and pickles. And to eat on paper plates instead of china.

Sometimes she just wanted to say the hell

with her quiet, scheduled, tidy life and do something different. And she hated herself for it.

"Hello, Cassandra." Terrance came up from behind her and kissed her cheek as he always did, but he lingered today, instead of asking her how her day was as he usually did when he finished his work for the day.

She turned around to face him, placing her hands on his chest as she reached up to kiss his mouth. *Really* kiss him. Not those gentle pecks they usually shared, but with her tongue and open mouth. She used to feel so close to him when they were kids, but somehow they had lost that in marriage. She had married her best friend, but they weren't friends anymore. She missed that, and by kissing him she was trying to recapture that closeness. He returned her kiss, wrapped his arms around her, held her tightly, a little too tightly, as if he were trying to hold on to something that was slipping away. But she didn't get that feeling she was seeking, and she wasn't sure what else she could do to recapture it.

She pulled away from him, looking up into his eyes and seeing pain there. "What's wrong?" She touched his face. She loved him. She did. She hated to see his pain.

"I would like to make love to you tonight, if that's okay with you."

She nodded, feeling a little disappointed. She wished he didn't have to ask, that he would just take her upstairs, peel her clothes off and do what he wanted. But he never did. He always asked, always held himself away.

"You don't have to ask, Terrance. You know I will. You know I never say no to you."

"I know, but sometimes I think you don't want to. You're always asleep when I come to bed."

She held her breath for a moment, knowing that was true, knowing that sometimes she pretended she wasn't awake because while their lovemaking was nice, while he always took his time to try to bring her pleasure, it somehow never felt quite right. "I'm pregnant, Terrance," she blurted out, not meaning to, but she needed a way out of the conversation she didn't want to have. "I'm pregnant."

She didn't need the doctor to tell her how far along she was. She was exactly eight weeks. She had gotten pregnant the last time they had made love.

"Excuse me?"

"I'm going to have a baby. I know we didn't discuss it, but you told me you would like to be a father a few months ago, so I stopped taking my pills."

"You're two months pregnant?"

"Yes." She nodded. He knew how far along

she was. He knew the last time they made love.

"You did this for me?"

"It's what you wanted, isn't it? I think you will be a great father. I want you to be the father of my child."

Terrance looked at her for a long moment and then he did something that surprised her. He pulled her into a hug and started to cry.

"You look so damn pretty in the morning, Cass." She awoke to Wylie's lips brushing across her neck.

"You think so? I feel like a sack of potatoes."

"A beautiful sack of potatoes. In fact, I would like to cook you up and pour some gravy on you, just so I can eat you up."

"There's some gravy downstairs. I bought some, just in case I mess up my mother's recipe tomorrow. You can go get it and I can try really hard not to screw up tomorrow."

He lifted his head and looked down at her, the heat in his eyes sending tingles throughout her body. "Don't tempt me, woman." He settled himself on top of her and she welcomed his heavy weight as he kissed her along her throat. "I can barely look at you now without getting all hot and bothered.

367

How do you think I'll survive Thanksgiving dinner with your parents if the vision of your naked body covered in warm brown gravy keeps popping in my head?"

"Warm gravy? You're going to heat it up first?"

"Well, yeah. No self-respecting Southerner eats cold gravy."

She laughed, pulling him closer so that her lips could meet his. His kiss was deep and sensual. His kiss was fun and happy. He was happy, lighter. The news of the baby caused a shift in him she couldn't describe. How could things be so easy with him when their relationship was so damn complicated?

Why did she have to dream about Terrance last night? About the last time she had seen him happy? About her last-ditch effort to save their marriage just before their life together ended so tragically. Lately she wondered how life would have been if that day had never happened, if they had never been shot. She wondered how life would have been if they had a chance to raise their baby together. Would it have fixed the slow bleed that was killing their marriage? Would it have served as a Band-Aid, a temporary solution to a problem that could have never been healed? They would have thrown themselves into being parents. They would have done everything for their child, their *children*, because Cassandra knew just one wouldn't have been enough to distract them from each other.

"Stop thinking about whatever you are thinking about." Wylie said. His hands had already slid up her nightgown. His palms were smoothing over her thighs.

"My parents are going to be here at noon."

"Are you nervous about seeing them?" He rolled over, taking her with him so that they were both on their sides. "We haven't talked about them coming. We've just been so busy getting the house ready."

"You've been busy getting the house ready. You wouldn't let me do anything but pick out the decor."

"I don't want you to overexert yourself. You're tired enough as it is."

"I could have at least helped you paint, Wylie."

"No, you couldn't have. The fumes are bad for the baby." He rested his hand on her belly, and a small smile immediately came to his face. "Are we going to tell them about the baby?"

"Do you think we should?"

"I'm having a hard time not shouting it from the rooftops! I've been so damn happy. But what do you want to do?"

"I asked you first, Wylie James. It's not just my decision. We're partners."

"I know." He nodded, his eyes going soft. "I think I should first tell them that I want you to become my wife. I'm going to ask your father for your hand."

"You don't have to. It doesn't matter anyway. It's my choice." It's what Terrance had done. He had asked her father before he had even discussed it with her. He had planned out this elaborate proposal and asked her in front of both of their families. It had been incredibly sweet and she would have been incredibly touched if she had been prepared. If she really had wanted to become his wife.

And here was Wylie prepared to ask her father, prepared to spend the rest of his life with her. She didn't feel the same now as she did then, but she did feel guilt. She should have felt strong enough to say no and save Terrance, save herself from years of unhappiness.

"Do you think he'll say no?" he asked her.

"I don't care if he does." It was the truth. She had never cared what her father thought, what Harmony Falls thought about the man she loved.

"Where I come from, we ask the woman's father. It's just what we do."

"Please, Wylie. I don't want you to. It's what Terrance did. He asked my father and there was a big, huge ring and an enormous wedding, and I didn't want any of that."

"What do you want? Do you even want to marry me, Cass? I didn't ask you. Like an ass, I just assumed you would." He rolled out of bed and went to his dresser on the far side of the room. "I got this a long time ago, before I knew about the baby, but I wasn't sure what you wanted. Or if I should give it to you. But you should know that this is what I want. This is all I've ever wanted."

He handed her the little black box. His face was so full of fear and hope that her heart shifted painfully. The ring was simple — a pretty square-cut diamond on a silver band. Unlike her last engagement ring, with the huge diamonds and extravagant setting, this ring was her.

"It's perfect. It's beautiful."

"I love you. I have since the moment I shook your hand when I was thirteen years old. I walked away before, because I thought you deserved better. You still deserve better than me, but I'm selfish and I can't imagine spending the rest of my life without you."

"What if I say no?" She kissed his lips. "What if I don't want this?" She kissed him twice more. "What would you do?"

"I would lock you in the basement until you came around." He winked at her. "Hopefully, that Stockholm syndrome would work in my favor."

She grinned. She couldn't help it. "You did kidnap me from Harmony Falls, if I remember correctly. I think it's already worked in your favor. I'm stuck on you."

He kissed her forehead. "I don't want you to answer me now. I don't want you to feel pressured. But just remember you got my baby in there, so you're going to be stuck with me for the rest of your life anyway."

"I know." She pulled him down on top of her. "I'm looking forward to it."

"Do you think the Trellis Inn is the right place to go for dinner?" Cass asked Wylie as she wiped down the kitchen table for the third time.

"Yeah. It's a nice place. It's got good reviews."

"But is it *too nice*?" She scrubbed an invisible speck of dirt. "Too fancy?"

"What's the matter with fancy? You afraid I won't know which fork to use?"

"Stop that!" She slammed the dishcloth on the table. "I hate when you do that. I hate when you act like I'm embarrassed of you. I've never been embarrassed of you."

"I know," he said softly, regretting his offhanded comment. "I didn't mean it, but maybe I'm a little on edge. Your father is coming, and the last time I saw him, he was telling me to stay away from you because I wasn't good enough. I want to show him that I am good enough for you, that I can take care of you. And if that means I've got to take him to a restaurant that is fifty damn dollars a plate to prove it, I will."

"You are good enough for me." She left the table and wrapped her arms around his neck. "I'm the only one who gets to decide if you are. You don't need to impress him. I just want you to be you. I want him to see my life now, the life that I have here with you."

"You're sweet, Cass." He tried to ignore the tension that was rolling around him as the hour grew closer, but it was there and real — and part of him still felt like that kid from rural Alabama who was never going to be good enough for the doctor's daughter. He pushed those thoughts away, tipping her chin up so that he could kiss her. "But I still want to go to that restaurant. I look too damn good in a suit to pass up the opportunity."

"I like you the best in blue jeans." She

grinned at him, putting him at ease. "In fact, I like you the best in no jeans at all."

"This is why you have got to marry me." He took her mouth in a quick, hot kiss. "I need a girl who's not afraid to talk dirty to me in the kitchen."

"Or make love to you in the kitchen."

"And the living room, bathroom and on the beach."

"You make me sound easy." She smiled shyly at him, a flush coming over her face.

"You make me feel crazy." He took her mouth again, allowing his hands to wander over her body, even though he knew he couldn't make love to her right now. "And if I hadn't just heard a car door slam, you would be in trouble."

"You *heard* a car door *slam*?" She froze, her eyes going wide. He had known she was nervous to see her parents again. He had been nervous to see them too, and not because he knew Cassandra's father didn't care for him. Rather it was because he was worried that once Cass saw them again, she would miss her old life, her old town, and want to go back to it.

She was having his baby, but sometimes he wondered if he was just a placeholder in her life, a distraction to make her forget how much she loved and missed her husband.

"Let's go greet them."

She nodded, but she didn't move. "Hold my hand."

"No, you hold mine." He locked his fingers in hers and led her out the front door. Cassandra's parents were still by their car, in a conversation so deep that they didn't even notice that Wylie and Cassandra were standing on the porch.

Cora looked exactly the same as she had when he went to get Cassandra a few months ago, the same as he remembered her from when he was a kid. Beautiful and elegant, full of class and grace. It was Dr. Smith who had changed. His hair was white. His face had aged more than it should have. He was still handsome, still stood proudly, but he didn't seem as large as he used to be. And even from the porch Wylie could see the exhaustion in his face. Not tired from a lack of sleep, but weary, bone-tired, from having your only child, your pride and joy, slip away from you.

"Mom? Dad?"

They both turned to look at her, neither one of them moving for a moment, just staring. She looked so different from that skinny, pale, nearly lifeless woman she was when she came here. She wore a cranberry-colored dress, which fit snuggly against her now-curvy body, her skin was glowing due to the pregnancy, and her short curls were shiny and healthy. She was a new woman.

"My good Lord," Miss Cora said breathily. She unfroze in that moment, rushing to the porch, grabbing Cassandra up in the tightest of hugs, but Cass never let go of his hand, her grip getting tighter as her mother hugged her. "You're beautiful, baby girl." She ran her hands over her cheeks. "And you've cut your hair! I love it. You look like a whole new person."

"I missed you, Mom," she said as the tears streamed down her face.

"I missed you too." She wiped away Cassandra's tears as her own started to fall. "None of that now. This is a happy time. Oh, Wylie James, look at you. More handsome than the Devil." She hugged him tightly. "Thank you," she whispered. "Thank you, thank you, thank you."

"I should thank you. I think I needed her more than she needed me."

Dr. Smith was walking toward them now, his steps slow, his eyes never leaving his daughter's face. "Cassandra," he said when he finally reached her. "You're lovely." He hugged her, not the fierce hug his wife had given her, but it was more affection than Wylie had ever seen father and daughter exchange.

"I'm happy here," she told him when she pulled away. "I'm happy here with Wylie."

Cassandra wrapped her arms around him then, resting her head on his chest, making it clear that they were together. He wished he could have been this brave before. He wished he could have not cared what Harmony Falls thought of them before. It would have saved a hell of a lot of heartbreak.

"How are you, sir?" He extended his hand.

"You've done well for yourself, son." He looked at the house, and his eyes did not miss a single detail. "It seems you've done well for my daughter too."

"I love her." He locked eyes with Dr. Smith. "But you already knew that."

He nodded. "I did."

Another car pulled into the driveway, one that Wylie didn't recognize. At first he ignored it, thinking that it was somebody just turning around in his driveway. But the car came to a stop and the doors opened.

He heard Cassandra gasp, her grip tightening on him. He froze too, his blood rushing through his head, his thoughts slowing down.

It was Terrance who got out of that car. Only it couldn't be him. He knew that, but he felt as if he were staring at a ghost.

Chapter 20

Her knees buckled, and the air whooshed right out of her lungs. Terrance was there, standing fifty feet in front of her, looking the way he did on the day he died. But as he walked closer, as the man's features became clearer and her eyes cleared of tears, she saw that it wasn't her husband, but her father-in-law.

"Do you need to sit down, honey?" Wylie whispered. His lips were on her ear; his hand was on her back; his arm was wrapped around her. He was the reason she was still standing. Somehow he became her backbone.

"No, no, I . . ." She couldn't take her eyes off Eric. Terrance definitely looked like his father — same walk, same chocolate-colored skin, same long, straight nose — but Eric looked like a distinguished man in his sixties. The sides of his hair had gone completely gray since the last time she had seen him. He wore khakis and a suit coat over his expensive button-down shirt, and Cassandra knew that if her husband had lived, he would have looked like this one day.

Would have.

If he had lived.

"I know this must be a shock to you," Eric said when he finally reached them. "But Thanksgiving has been hard. Holidays . . . everything has been hard without him, without you. It's empty. And even though he is gone, you are still our family and we love you. I know we are intruding, but we wanted to see you. Patricia is in the car." He glanced behind him. "She won't come out unless it's okay with you. We'll go if you want us to, but we had to see you. We had to know that you're okay."

She couldn't see again. Her throat burned and her eyes were clouded with tears. She tried to hold them back, to blink them away, but it was impossible.

"Of course you can stay," Wylie said, his slow, Southern-accented voice grounding her once again. "If Cass could talk, she would tell you that."

"Is that right, Cassandra?" Eric Miller looked to her for confirmation. He looked to her with hope in his eyes.

She nodded; it was all she could do in that

379

moment.

"Is it all right if I hug you?"

She couldn't even make herself nod that time. She just let go of Wylie and let herself collapse into her father-in-law's arms as a sob tore from her throat. Eric looked like Terrance, but he wasn't. He was quieter, a more gentle spirit, more stoic. She had always loved him. She had tried not to think about him during her grief. It was too much: his only son, his prize, the person he was most proud of.

"You'll make yourself sick, Cassandra. Hush now." He smoothed a hand over her back. "And I was just getting ready to tell you how pretty you are. You don't want to ruin that with a blotchy face, now do you?"

"I'm so sorry," she managed to choke out.

"For what?"

For surviving. It was an ugly thought, a nasty thought. One that ran through her mind a thousand times a day when she was in her deepest mourning. It wasn't true. She looked back at Wylie, remembered the baby she had growing inside her. She was glad to be alive. Finally. She had reasons to live, to be happy. She loved again, when before the only thing she had ever thought she would feel again was pain.

"For getting you all wet."

"Don't worry about that." He smiled gently at her before he turned his gaze to Wylie. "How are you, son?"

"I'm very well, sir. Thank you." Wylie held himself stiffly. He stood back a little ways away from them. It was like they were kids again, and he was just on the edges of the family. But they weren't kids anymore. And they were all at his house and Wylie was now her family.

"Won't you call me Eric? If you don't, I'll have to go around calling you Master Sergeant Everett, and I think that's a little formal."

"You know my rank, sir?"

"I know your rank. I know you're decorated. I know that you were awarded for bravery twice — once in Iraq and once in Afghanistan. I know that you have risked your life more times for this country than anyone can ask. And I know that I am extremely proud of you."

Cassandra watched as the emotion swelled in Wylie's eyes, but he held it back. "I appreciate that, sir. I mean, Mr. Miller. I mean, Eric."

"You're a good man." He touched Wylie's cheek, just like a father would touch his son. "I wish I could take more credit for it."

A car door slamming distracted them from

the moment. Patricia Miller had gotten out of the car. She was much thinner than the last time Cassandra had seen her. She was birdlike, her face was pinched like there was an unpleasant odor in the air. She had aged twenty years in the last twelve months. The grief was clearly still with her, and Cassandra knew it was the kind of grief that would never let her out of its grip.

"Hello, Cassandra," she said when she came to stand beside her husband. "I see you are doing well."

"I'm much better, thank you."

Her eyes went to Wylie, and the distaste was clear, and for a moment Cassandra was sure she wasn't going to acknowledge him. "Hello, Mrs. Miller." He leaned over to kiss her cheek, causing the woman to stiffen. "I'm so glad you are here to see my home."

She looked around her, her eyes critically taking everything in. "Yes, it's nice. In a quaint little way."

Cassandra's hands curled into fists. She and her mother-in-law had never been close, because she hated the way she treated Wylie when they were kids, as if he were their servant. And even after he was gone and they were adults, she wasn't warm or even kind. She wondered how such a woman could raise a man like Terrance, who loved deeply in his own way. And now here she was disrespecting Wylie's home, their home. And for what? Because it didn't belong to her son.

"We'll be staying in town so we don't disturb whatever it is you have going on here. I didn't want to intrude."

"You're not intruding," Wylie said, still being the bigger man. "Please come inside. I know you've had a long trip and I would love to take you out to lunch."

"Oh, that would be great!" Eric clapped Wylie on the back as he gave his wife a pointed look. "We passed a little seafood shack on the way. Do you think they are still open?"

"Yes," Cassandra's father-in-law agreed. "I would love some fried clams."

Wylie hadn't known what to expect when Cassandra's parents had arrived. He thought that it would be awkward, that today would be tense. And it was, but not in the way he had expected.

Cassandra's parents had been extremely kind to him, Cora praising all the work he had done on the house. Dr. Smith asked to see his medals. Even Thanksgiving dinner had gone well. Tanner had come over with one of the guys on their crew. Nova brought

Mansi and Teo over to celebrate. The food had been excellent. Cass and Nova had handled most of the cooking. Everyone seemed to be relaxed, except for Patricia. She picked over her food, sitting quietly beside her husband with her head held high, as if she were too good for the food and the company. He tried to ignore her, but he knew it was getting to Cass, who tensed at every picky comment the woman made. She had never been easy to live with, but there was definitely a change in her since Terrance had died. He could see the thought on her face every time he looked at her: *Why did you have to live when he had to die?*

He had asked himself that same question. He could have died. He almost died, but he hadn't.

And as he looked at Teo in deep conversation with Cassandra's mother, and his sister laughing with Cass as they did the dishes, and Mansi playing cards with Dr. Smith and Mr. Miller, he knew that he had a lot of reasons to live. He had a lot of things to be proud of.

"That's it, woman!" Mr. Miller — Eric, he was still having a hard time thinking of him that way — threw down his cards and sat back in his chair. "You are going to bankrupt me. How did you learn to play poker like that?"

"Oh, sweet cheeks," she said, playfully pinching his face, "I wish I could tell you. But if you don't want to play for cash anymore, we can play for clothes."

"Old woman," Wylie warned.

"She's just having fun, son." Eric got up from his spot at the dining-room table and walked over to him.

It was weird to hear him call him "son." It was weird for him to be there. Growing up, Wylie had felt close to the man. It was his advice he sought when he was troubled. It was Eric who treated him kindly and took him in when his wife didn't want that. It was also Eric who told him to stay away from Cassandra, who wounded him when he told him he wasn't right for her. The seeds of his self-doubt were staring him in the face.

"Are you enjoying yourself here?" Wylie asked him.

"Yes, it's beautiful." He smiled gently at him. "And so are your little sister and her family. I'm so glad you found them again."

"They're the only family I've got. So I've got to keep them close, no matter what."

The smile melted from his face. "We never put you out. You separated yourself from us."

"What was I supposed to do when you told me that I wasn't right for Cassandra, that she needed Terrance in her life to be truly happy?" He lowered his voice so his other guests wouldn't hear. "You said that I couldn't live up to Terrance. And after we got into that fight and I had come to you, you said that I betrayed you and your son. How the hell was I supposed to interpret that?"

"I — I . . ."

"If you'll excuse me, I'm going to help Cass out in the kitchen."

He walked away from him and into the kitchen, his head throbbing and his chest hurting. He had put all of that out of his head. He had tried to, at least. He had spent ten years of his life loving the Millers, just to have them turn on him. He almost didn't blame them. Blood was thicker than water after all. But it still hurt.

"What's the matter, Wylie James?" Cass dropped the dishcloth that she was holding and hugged him close. "Is it that mean woman? You want me to throw her out?"

"You can't throw her out." He kissed her lips. "It's Thanksgiving. Besides, she doesn't bother me."

"She should." She reached up to run her fingers through his hair and he shut his eyes, enjoying the way her nails felt on his scalp. "You should be proud of all of this. I hope you are. This place is beautiful. You're not that same kid with no place to go."

"If I hadn't had 'no place to go,' I wouldn't have met you."

"Ugh." Nova shut off the sink and threw down her sponge. "Do you two have to be so in love all the time? It makes my damn stomach churn."

"You want some love too, little sis? Come here." He extended an arm to her.

"I'd rather jump into an icy lake than get between you-all's love fest."

"Forget you then." He turned his attention back to Cass. "You feeling okay?" He rubbed her belly. She wasn't showing through her clothes yet, but he could see the roundness forming when she was nude. He made her stay that way for a long time this morning. He couldn't stop staring at her, at the life she was carrying. He was going to be a father, the love he felt for someone who wasn't even fully formed yet was overwhelming.

"I'm fine. I just ate too much."

"You've been on your feet all day. Why don't you go sit down and I'll finish cleaning up?"

"I'm fine." She placed her hand over his

as he rubbed. "I told my mother we would have a bonfire on the beach in a little while."

He nodded and kissed the side of her face. "Let me know if you get too tired."

"I will."

"Cassandra!" Nova called to her. "You're pregnant!"

"Hush!" Wylie hissed at her. "Nobody knows yet, and how the hell did you guess?"

"You're rubbing her belly and treating her like she is going to break. Not to mention that mushy *you-are-my-everything* look you've been giving her all day. That's not the way to go if you want to hide a pregnancy."

"You're right." Cass looked up at Wylie and then back to Nova. "That's why I snapped at you and stole your kid that day. I had just found out I was pregnant after I thought it might never happen again. I'm really sorry for what I said, Nova. I was going through some stuff."

"You've apologized to me already, Cass," she said softly. "And I understand how it is to find out you're pregnant when you least expect it. You don't need to say any more than that."

She nodded. "I do. I love you. You should know that. You're my best friend."

"Oh, shut up now." Nova shut her eyes,

hiding the tears that had formed. "I'm not going to blubber like a baby today because of you. Let's talk about something else."

"Okay. Your brother wants to marry me too." She rested her face against Wylie's chest and grinned. "You think I should?"

"It depends. How big is the ring?"

Every star was visible in the sky that night. The air was cold, but the fire was warm. As the waves crashed against the shore, Cass found the entire evening soothing. It helped that Wylie was behind her, with a blanket wrapped around both of them. His hands were on her belly again, but they were hidden from their guests this time.

He was going to be a good father. There was no doubt in her mind about that. She was happy to be pregnant the last time she found out, but she was truthfully more hopeful than happy. Hopeful that the baby could bring some closeness between her and her husband. It was foolish to put that much pressure on an unborn child. She had gone into the marriage for the wrong reasons. She knew that now; and as much as she wanted to blame Terrance for not telling her what really happened, she couldn't. It was her fault too. She was just sad that Terrance hadn't had the happiness he deserved.

She felt different this time, with this baby. She had a lot of hopes pinned on this child too, but different ones. Hopes that it would be happy and healthy, hopes that it would grow up to be strong and loving, like his or her father was. They were unselfish hopes this time.

"Are you cold?" Wylie asked with a kiss to her hair.

"Not as long as you stay here."

"I'm not going anywhere. I promise."

She looked up and caught the Millers staring at them — Mr. Miller with gentle wonder, Mrs. Miller with disdain. It made her feel uneasy, guilty. Was it wrong to be enjoying herself when Terrance couldn't? Was it wrong to openly love another man in front of them?

Part of her, a big part of her, felt like it was. But she couldn't help herself. She couldn't hide her love anymore. It would be unfair to Wylie, who felt so insecure about himself back then that he didn't want anyone to know. She used to hate him for that, but now she understood why. Now she understood that no matter how much they loved each other back then, they would have never lasted. Wylie had to find his own way, become his own man. And she had to go on her own journey.

"Cassandra." Eric smiled at her from across the fire. "Your mother tells me you're working at a cultural center."

"It's just part-time right now. I'm the activities director. I'm teaching health and nutrition to senior citizens four days a week. We even do a cooking class on Thursday. Next fall we're going to roll out a reading-based after-school program for the local kids. I'm really excited about it."

"Next fall? So you see yourself settling here. You must really like it."

"Of course she sees herself settling here," Patricia said. "She's pregnant. She's going to have his bastard baby."

Tanner cursed. Her mother gasped. Heavy silence fell around the fire. "Patricia!" her husband scolded. His face was stormier than Cassandra had ever seen.

"Why should I be quiet when I find this whole thing disgusting? She got to live!" she spat. "She gets to go on being happy, while my son is cold and dead in the ground."

"You shut up, Patricia!" Cora left her seat, lunging at the other woman, but her husband caught her. Tanner grabbed Teo and Nova by the hand and led them back toward the house. "Where do you get off suggesting that my daughter should have died and your son should have lived? What happened to them was a tragedy. How can you blame Cassandra for that?"

"He loved her so much. Too much! He took that job in the school to be near her. He did everything for her, and she was in love with *him* the whole time." She looked from Wylie to Cassandra as she said that. "You didn't love Terrance like he deserved. And now it's your fault he's dead."

Tears filled Cassandra's eyes. Patricia was right. She didn't love Terrance like he deserved, but hearing it out loud from somebody else was painful.

"It's not her fault," her mother defended her. "Terrance took that job because he wanted to. Nobody made him. And, yes, Terrance loved her, but not like he should. He loved her in a sick way — in a controlling way — because he knew all along that Wylie loved her. He was jealous and he only married her to prove that he could, and that he was the better man. But he wasn't better, was he? He was bitter that she chose someone else over him."

"Then she shouldn't have married him! But she did, and she should have loved him."

"She did!"

"Then why is she throwing him in our face?" Patricia motioned to Wylie. "She should still be mourning Terrance. Not disrespecting us like this."

"Nobody invited you here," Wylie said calmly. "If you don't like what I'm doing in my home, then you can leave."

"You were probably screwing her while he was still alive. Terrance loved you like a brother, when he should have treated you like the trash you are."

Cora broke away from her husband; her hand slashing across Patricia's face in a loud slap. "You shut your mouth!" she screamed. "Wylie is a good man, and the only thing he ever did wrong was being born poor, but he couldn't help that. And I know they weren't sleeping together when Terrance was alive. I know that Wylie would never do that to him and I know Cassandra loved your boy. She mourned him. She couldn't get out of bed for a year — she missed him so much. I know you're hurt, but don't begrudge Cassandra her happiness because your son is gone. She's suffered enough."

"You've been here three months and you're pregnant. You were married to him for over seven years and you couldn't give him a baby. You couldn't have given him the one thing he wanted the most. You couldn't have left us with a little piece of him."

"I — I tried." Cassandra spoke, but her words barely came out as more than a whisper.

"Well, you couldn't even do that right. You should be ashamed of yourself. You betrayed him. You were the only woman he loved, and you couldn't even love him back."

"Patricia, enough!" her husband barked. He looked at Cassandra and Wylie. "Is it true? Are you two going to be parents?"

"Yes," Cassandra answered. "I'm eight weeks."

He nodded. "Then I want to be the first to congratulate you." He came over to her and kissed her cheek. "I'm happy for you. Truly and honestly, and I would like it if I could be a part of this child's life."

She could take Patricia's hatred, the accusations, the anger, but she couldn't take his kindness. It was too much and she didn't feel like she deserved it.

"I have to go." She got up and ran away from them. Ignoring Wylie as he shouted her name.

CHAPTER 21

Wylie was on his feet, ready to go after Cassandra, when Eric Miller placed a firm hand on his shoulder.

"Give her time, son."

"Stop calling me 'son'!" He shrugged his hand off. "I'm not your *son*. You made that very clear to me, sir."

"Damn it, Wylie. I want to talk to you right now!"

"Well, that's the great thing about being an adult. I don't have to listen to you anymore." He walked away from him, heading back toward the house, but Eric was on his heels. The older man was keeping up with his fast pace.

"I'm not going to leave you alone until you speak to me."

"What? What do you want? You come up here, uninvited, bringing your nasty wife to ruin my first holiday with my family."

"I apologize for Patricia. She's in a lot of pain."

"We're *all* in a lot of pain! I loved him too. Everybody seems to forget that. Everybody acted like I was his enemy, but I loved him. He was my best friend and I didn't want Cass to get between us, but it was inevitable because I loved her as soon as I laid eyes on her."

"And he loved her too."

"But she loved me back, and that was the difference. You spoiled him. You told him he could be whatever he wanted, have whatever he wanted — the cost be damned."

"He didn't steal Cassandra from you. *You* walked away from her."

"What choice did I have? We went through this already." He threw up his arms. "I wasn't good enough. You told me I wasn't good enough. But I am now. I may not have gone to an Ivy League school. I may not be as smart as he was, but I worked hard every damn day of my life for everything I got. I fought for my country. I take care of my family. I would be a son that any man would be proud of."

"I know."

"Then why the hell weren't you proud of me?"

"I am. I was."

Wylie shook his head. "I didn't expect you to treat me like him. He was your flesh and blood, but you let her treat me like shit. You all went out of your way to make me feel like I didn't belong, and that was fucked up. I just lost my dad. My mother was a drunk. I was grateful to have a home, but I needed a *family*. I needed more than just your financial support."

"I know. Cora was right. Terrance had a lot of good qualities, but my son was insecure. We did everything to make him feel special. We gave him all of our love and attention, but when you came along, he saw you as a threat."

"A threat to what? He was smarter than me, more popular, better than me at everything."

"That's not true, Wylie. In some ways he was smarter than you, and in some ways you were smarter than him. Your intelligence is not comparable. He thought himself weak compared to you, less of a man. Girls liked you more and he hated that. He hated that Cass liked you when she only saw him as a brother, and that hurt him. Maybe I should have said, 'Too bad, suck it up,' but I couldn't. You'll see that when your baby comes. You'll see how hard it is to let your child be hurt. I had to keep building him up. Can you blame me for that?"

"No. I don't get the point of this conversation." He shook his head. "I'm grateful you took me in, sir. Don't think that I'm not, but I think this relationship is over. There's no point in seeing me again."

"But there is! You were a huge part of our lives for ten years and then you were gone. I needed to stand by my son, but I missed you. I loved you. I *love* you. You brought something to my life. You brought back your father. He was my best friend, and every time I think about how I let you just go, how I missed your college graduation, and your military honors, it kills me, because I know he would have wanted me there."

"You don't have to feel guilty. You don't owe a dead man anything."

Wylie turned to walk away, his head spinning. There were too many thoughts going through his mind.

"It feels like I've lost two sons!" Eric called after him. "I'll never see Terrance again and that is something I can't change, but I can't bear the thought of not seeing you again. My heart won't take it."

That caused Wylie to pause. "I'm not a replacement for him."

"No. You're not. You could never be, but

that doesn't mean I don't need you in my life."

"What do you want me to say?" Wylie felt weak in the moment, so sick of feeling hurt by a past he couldn't change, so confused about the future he was trying to move toward.

"Just say that you'll try. You'll let me stop by at Christmas. You'll let me see your firstborn child. We may never be close again, but we don't have to be strangers."

He didn't want to relent. His head told him not to, screamed at him not to, but his heart ached. He had spent years feeling angry, feeling slighted and bruised. He was exhausted by it, tired of holding on to so much past hurt when forgiveness seemed like the easier choice. The choice that would make him happier. He let out a breath, feeling lighter as he did, feeling some of the pain ease out of him. "Okay, Eric. Okay."

"*Okay?* You're going to let me be a part of your life again?"

"I think I have to. I didn't get to see Terrance before he died. I wanted to. I wanted to make things right with him. I'm never going to get that chance, but I can make things right with you."

"I'm the one who needs to make things right with you. It's what Terrance would have wanted."

He nodded, sure that there was so much more to say, but he just didn't have the words. "I need to see to Cass now."

"Go on. I'm taking Patricia away from here."

Wylie took off once again toward the house. When he got there, he saw Tanner with his arms around his sister. Nova was in tears; even from behind, Wylie could tell she was crying.

"What happened?" The hair on the back of his neck stood up, and that cold feeling of dread trickled along his backside.

"She's gone, Wylie," Nova cried. "She's packed a bag and left."

On the outside Harmony Falls hadn't changed much. It was still that picturesque little town with the beautiful, ancient oak trees lining the streets. Her childhood home looked the same; her high school looked the same. However, the town was fundamentally different. It was quieter. The GOD BLESS FARNSWORTH signs still hung in store windows, and a large banner hung on the fence where the school used to be.

Used to be. It had been knocked down. She hadn't known. Nobody had told her. She didn't know what made her drive past there. To prove she could. To prove she wouldn't fall apart seeing a place that held so many happy and painful memories for her. This place had been a huge part of her life, one she never thought she would leave until she retired, but life was funny that way.

She drove on through town, down Main Street, past the post office and the church where she and Terrance had been married. She didn't know where she was going. She hadn't planned on going anywhere when she woke up that morning; but when she had ended up at the cemetery, she wasn't surprised. She had moved on. She had fallen in love again. She was going to have a baby, but she had never said good-bye to her old life, to her good friend who made her life better in many ways.

It was cold that day, but she still sat on the ground when she found his headstone. She wanted to be closer to him. Just for a moment she wanted to recapture that feeling they shared when they were kids and best friends, and nothing had stood in the way of that.

"I really loved you, Terrance. You should know that. I want you to know that. I need you to know that. You made me laugh and you made me think, and I am a better person for having had you in my life. We were good friends, but we weren't good married. I want to blame you for that, but it was my fault too. I just didn't understand how I could love you so much and not be *in love* with you. I'm in love with Wylie, Terrance. I should have told you that ten years ago, but I was afraid to tell you. I thought I was going to lose you. I'm sorry that I didn't tell you. I'm sorry that you didn't end up with a woman who was in love with you like you deserved. But I want you to know that you were the best friend I'll ever have, and there's a hole in my heart without you. I miss you. I still love you."

She put her hand on the cold grass, not caring that the dampness of the earth was sinking through her clothes. "I've come to tell you good-bye, and I hope that you're with our baby." She choked on her words as the tears clogged her throat. "I hope the baby looks like you. I hope that wherever you are, you see the baby grow up into the son or daughter you always wanted. I'm going to think about our child while I carry this new baby inside me. And I am going to be happy too, because I know that is what you want for me." She stroked her fingers over the damp grass, as if she were touching him for the last time. "Good-bye, Terrance."

She got up and walked away from his

grave, feeling weary but much lighter. She didn't care what Patricia said. Terrance was placed in her life for a reason. He brought her joy, but it was time for her to move on.

"Mrs. Miller?" A woman ran up to her. She recognized her immediately. It was Kayla's mother. The woman whose husband had murdered hers. "I'm — I'm so sorry to intrude. I know you must hate me, and I'm the last person you want to see while you visit your husband's grave, but I needed to say thank you. You almost lost your life that day to save my child's."

"Please don't thank me."

"I have to." She grabbed her hand. "She's not scared anymore. She doesn't flinch when I touch her. She doesn't dread six P.M., because that's when her father came home. She's a different kid and she's happy. And I have you to thank for that. If you hadn't stepped in, he would have killed us all."

"Mrs. Hammond . . . I don't know what to say."

"Campbell. Ms. Campbell. I don't go by that man's name anymore. Call me Suzie and please don't say anything. Kayla has been writing to you. I've kept all her letters, because I didn't know if you wanted to hear from her. But I would like to send them to you, if that's okay. She's writing so well now, and she's reading up a storm."

"I'm happy to hear that." Kayla had struggled. Cassandra had seen that beaten, bruised child and wondered if things were ever going to get better for her.

"You made an impact on our lives, you know. I pray for you. I pray that you find some sort of happiness again, even though it might seem impossible."

"It's possible." She touched her belly. "I've learned that anything is possible."

When she drove back that afternoon to the house she had shared with Terrance, she saw a familiar truck sitting in the driveway. Her heart lifted as she saw Wylie sitting on the porch steps, his face tight with worry. He stood as she stepped out of her car, saying nothing, just staring at her face.

"Hi, honey. What took you so long?"

"Cassandra." He jumped down the steps and yanked her close, pulling her into a hug so tight she couldn't breathe for a moment. But it was a good hug. A safe hug. A warm hug. "Two days. Two entire days. I've been out of my goddamn mind."

"I'm sorry, Wylie."

"I don't want to hear you're sorry. I want to hear that you love me and you want to

404

marry me and raise a family. I spent my life thinking I wasn't good enough, running away from the thing I wanted most. But I'm done running. I want you, because you make me smile, and think and feel. I deserve that. I deserve the chance to prove I can make you happy. And I want to hear you say that you are going to give it to me."

"I was saying good-bye to Terrance. I was settling things here. All the stuff I was putting off, all the stuff that was hanging in the air. The house is going on the market. I'm having our things donated. I'm closing this part of my life. I had to do that before I could marry you."

"You're going to marry me?"

"I'm in love with you, Wylie James. I don't think there is any other choice."

He smiled at her, tears filling his eyes. "Thank you."

"Don't thank me. I thank you for loving me exactly how I needed to be loved."

He cupped her face in his hands and kissed her. His warm lips slid over her cold ones; his body enveloped hers. She felt at home in his kiss and in his hold, and, for the very first time in her life, there were no doubts, because he was exactly where she wanted to be.

The employees of Thorndike Press hope you have enjoyed this Large Print book. All our Thorndike, Wheeler, and Kennebec Large Print titles are designed for easy reading, and all our books are made to last. Other Thorndike Press Large Print books are available at your library, through selected bookstores, or directly from us.

For information about titles, please call:
(800) 223-1244

or visit our website at:
gale.com/thorndike

To share your comments, please write:
Publisher
Thorndike Press
10 Water St., Suite 310
Waterville, ME 04901

18

19